Unforgettable Novels of the West by Jack Ballas . . .

IRON HORSE WARRIOR

JACK BALLAS

BERKLEY BOOKS, NEW YORK

IRON HORSE WARRIOR

A Berkley Book / published by arrangement with
the author

PRINTING HISTORY
Berkley edition / July 1996

The Putnam Berkley World Wide Web site address is
http://www.berkley.com

ISBN: 0-425-15434-3

BERKLEY®
Berkley Books are published by The Berkley Publishing Group,
200 Madison Avenue, New York, New York 10016.
BERKLEY and the "B" design
are trademarks belonging to Berkley Publishing Corporation.

PRINTED IN THE UNITED STATES OF AMERICA

10 9 8 7 6 5 4

My great grandson, Garrett Austin Turney

chapter

one

I SQUATTED IN the shade of a big freight wagon and watched the street teeming with track layers, gamblers, whores, and gunmen. I needed a job and I would find it here with the railroad. Julesburg, Colorado Territory, 1868, roared like a bad dream: hot, mean, dirty, and booming.

The saloons, stores, and livery barns bordering the street could only be called by those names in this town. They were thrown together from scrap sheet iron, wooden boxes, and canvas.

Dust hung heavy in the air, settling into my hair, clothing, and nostrils. It coated everything it touched a dirty gray. I could stand the dust, but the smell was a rougher bronc to ride. It stank of things rotten, tainted with human waste, refuse, dead bodies, and God knows what else thrown into the street for the wind to carry away or rot where it lay.

The crowd milled past, looking for someone to milk their money from them, money they'd worked long, backbreaking days for, hauling crossties, swinging sixteen-pound sledges, and carrying steel rails. It would take only a few hours for the town to get it all.

I grimaced. What they did with their money was not my business. But I watched each passerby. I glanced at their belt buckles and the guns hanging in their holsters. Those were the only clues I had that might help me find the man

1

who shot my brother in the back, and thin clues they were.

I fingered the few coins in my pocket and thought again; I needed a job.

The doors of the general store across the street swung open and a man walked out, the biggest, blackest, and somehow most gentle-looking man I had ever seen. Puzzled, I stared at him. It seemed I should know him.

Arms loaded with packages, he edged through the crowd. Every time a person bumped into him, he nodded and apologized.

I stood and fell in behind, thinking that if I watched a little longer, it would come to me where I had known him.

Where the crowd had been shoulder to shoulder, an opening appeared in front of the Negro. I heard a shot while still only a step or two behind. Dust kicked up at his feet. He'd not been hit; the bullet struck the ground in front of him and ricocheted over the heads of those behind. They drew farther away.

He stopped. His head raised to look at those surrounding him. He held himself proudly, showing no fear. Those closest drew farther back, leaving only six hardcases blocking his path. I stayed where I was, only a step behind.

"Where you goin' with all them packages, nigger? You b'long in the back alley." The man speaking was tall, though I judged he was a mite shy of my six-foot-three inches, and where I was a solid two hundred ten pounds, he was lean, almost skinny, his face narrow, eyes too close together, ferret-faced and mean-looking.

His five friends egged him on.

"Why, suh, I'm going to my horse, pack my possibles bag, and head west." The Negro's voice was quiet, and his pronunciation was clear and concise, although with the softness of the South in it.

Another shot. It, too, hit the ground in front of the darky's feet, but he still didn't give ground nor did he advance. He just stood there looking at those who challenged. I saw he wore no gun and wondered if I would have the guts to do what he did without a way of defending myself.

"You ain't goin' to yore hoss, and you ain't leavin'. We gonna make a good nigger outta you."

I stepped up beside the big black man, feeling a cold, hard knot in the pit of my stomach.

"How you figure to make a good nigger out of him?" I spoke quietly, making my voice sort of conversational.

As one, they gave me their attention.

The lean, mean one, still holding the six-shooter, pointed it at me. I'd looked down the barrel of a .44 more than once, and I'd never seen the bore of any gun that looked bigger than this one did right then, but a devil rode my shoulders. I wasn't one to hold with kicking a man just because he couldn't defend himself.

"What the hell business is this of yours, Yankee?" the skinny one asked, making the name *Yankee* sound like a curse. He lowered the barrel of his gun a bit.

With the war only a couple years behind us, many were still trying to fight it, mostly the ones who had not fought for either side.

I walked closer to him, right into the mouth of that .44. My gut tightened. Sweat streamed between my shoulder blades, and when I stopped, I was no more than a foot or so from him.

Now, Chance Tenery had done a lot of dumb things but, I thought wryly, this would fall right in at the head of that list.

I did not intend to try for my gun. No man, regardless how fast, could draw and shoot before a man who already had his gun in hand. The only thing that could get me out of this was surprise.

"Now, you just back off and leave this nigger to us, we ain't botherin' you."

I nodded, smiled, and turned as though to leave. My smile surprised him enough that his gun dropped a little farther. This was the edge I needed.

I turned only enough to put my weight on my right foot and brought my right fist up from my waist, every ounce of bone and muscle behind it. It caught him on the point of his chin. My left followed through, hitting on the side of his now slack jaw. I felt it give and skew off to the side. He went down. Out cold.

Taking advantage of his stunned friends who seemed paralyzed by the quick turn of events, I palmed my own .44 and pointed it at them.

"Who's your friend? I want to know his name in case I have to kill him someday."

"Mister, you ain't never gonna kill *him*. He's Snake Thompson, from down Texas way, and when he wakes up, you better be long gone. He's fast."

"Drop your gun belts, pick up your garbage, and get."

I watched their gun belts drop into the inch-deep dust of the street. Eyes pinning me with hate, they reached for their friend. If those looks could kill, I'd be in right smart pain, maybe beyond pain.

"That there gun cost me eight dollars, an' that dust ain't gonna do it no good," one of them growled.

"You keep standing there and it won't matter. Get moving!"

Then I changed my mind. If I didn't want to be looking over my shoulder the next day or two, I thought I'd better get them out of circulation awhile.

"Hold on there." I looked at one of the onlookers. "This town have any law?"

He nodded. "Yeah. Town marshal, but he gets pretty scarce when there's trouble, and I'd say *you* are trouble."

His words drained the anger from me. Perhaps someday I would learn to walk around a fight but, I shrugged mentally, that day was somewhere in the future.

"Find him. Tell him the trouble's over, and I have six pieces of white trash here I want him to lock up."

Even if the marshal went along with my request, I didn't think he'd keep them locked up long, but it would give me a chance to put some miles between us.

Judging the way most buildings in town were built, I'd say the jail was of the same careless junk. A hard shoulder against the wall would likely knock it down.

I shrugged and looked at the Negro and again was certain

I'd known him somewhere. He stared at me. A puzzled frown marked his face.

"Thank you, suh. I wasn't bothering anyone. It's not my nature to do so, but thanks anyway."

His words surprised me as I had thought him a Northerner. His words were those of a man with some education. The drawl marked him a Southerner.

I nodded, accepting his thanks. "You'd better get to your horse and leave before any more trouble starts. Besides," I allowed a faint smile to break the corners of my mouth, "I might not be around if another bunch tries to jump you, and you'll end up on the dirty end of the stick."

Another glance at his waist reaffirmed he wasn't wearing a gun. "Don't you have a gun?"

"Yes, suh. It's in my possibles bag on my horse."

"Start wearing it."

"Well, suh, I seem to invite even more trouble when I wear it."

"Nevertheless, wear it, and use it if you have to. Don't try bluffing with it. That'll get you killed." I nodded, indicating the conversation and help were at an end.

A man wearing a badge walked up.

"Hear tell you wanted to see me."

I nodded.

"What you want?"

I pointed a finger at the five who were bunched a few feet from me, holding up their friend. "I want them locked up. They seem to think it's funny to take advantage of an unarmed citizen."

The marshal pushed his hat to the back of his head and frowned. "Who they been botherin'?"

"This Negro man here. I watched him as he came out of that store over there. He did nothing to them."

"Them boys wuz jest havin' a little fun. Why not let them go?"

I shrugged. "Jail 'em or bury 'em; I don't give a damn." I walked off, leaving them standing there. The black man melted back into the crowd.

The livery barn was on the edge of town, only three

buildings away. My horse was there, and even though I'd paid for his keep, I thought I'd better head for end-of-track. I had no idea where end-of-track was. Depending upon the terrain, a good crew could lay as much as seven or eight miles of rail a day.

The first night out of Julesburg, I rode through Lodgepole and stopped in the saloon for a beer and information. The beer was lukewarm and the information scarce. The most I found out was that Sydney, a larger town, lay to the west, so I headed for it.

I followed the rails, and about ten miles west of Lodgepole, I stopped and made dry camp in a buffalo wallow.

There was a lot of fuel to build a fire, but this was Cheyenne country. Even though buffalo chips didn't make a flaring fire, an Indian could spot its red glow from a good distance, so my camp was not only dry, it was cold.

I gnawed on a strip of jerky, hoping all the while that General Grenville Dodge was at end-of-track. *He* would give me a job.

My thoughts shifted to the tough jerky. Hell, this clean air out here was worth missing a hot meal for.

Using my saddle for a pillow, I lay looking at the stars. It seemed that I might reach out and touch them, the air was so pure, and the scent, ahhh, the scent. The grass, cured on the stem to a light brown, threw out its own perfume, and the brown sea of it was endless, with only the swells of the rolling plains to break its flow. The wind sighed softly through the dry blades and sang a melody of its own. I turned on my side and went to sleep.

The next morning, I rolled from my blankets to a slight chill. It was early summer, but the ground gave up its heat quickly at sunset.

Each roll in the land afforded me shelter from searching eyes. I traveled many more miles than I would cover by simply following the rails. This had long been Indian country, and the man who rode careless didn't ride long.

As much as possible, I kept my head below the crest of each hill, wending my way slowly westward. A job waiting at rail's end would do me no good if I lay in some buffalo wallow without my hair.

The day heated up; the sun beat relentlessly against my shoulders. I crossed a small streambed, followed it, and found a hole that held enough water for my horse and me. Our thirst slaked, we climbed the creek bank to level ground.

The world was no longer mine alone. There were tracks of unshod ponies. I ground-tied my horse, squatted beside them, and ran a finger around the inside of each, gauging how long ago they'd been made. Maybe three hours old, the broken turf was still damp around the edges. The tracks showed twelve horses.

I smiled grimly. Had I not spent many of the war years here in the West, and most of them since, I'd not be able to read sign so well. Men said Chance Tenery was nigh as good as an Indian, but I didn't believe it. An Indian grew up learning things I'd been late in starting.

I mounted and rode on, using much more care than before. I rode closer to the rails now, thinking it would be a shorter although more dangerous route. My gaze constantly swept the skyline. If there was any surprising done, I wanted to be the one to do it.

A glance at the sun told me it was getting close to time for nooning, but putting my empty stomach in the back of my mind, I thought my hair more important. Sydney should not be too distant.

After another half hour, I topped out on a swell and saw the unpainted, weathered buildings I guessed to be Sydney, about three miles distant. It took me forty-five minutes to ride that far. The street I rode down was bordered by a few buildings and empty lots strewn with trash. Not too far in the past, these lots had held buildings.

As was the habit at end-of-track, when the tracks moved on, the shanties were knocked down and stuffed on freight cars until the next rail's end, where they were knocked together and again in business by nightfall. They bled the rail workers without missing a day's business. These were commonly called *hell-on-wheels towns*.

This village, like many others, might spring up again when settlers began filling the territory. The businesses that remained were run by those hardy souls determined to wait for them.

I hitched my horse in front of a building with a sign naming it both a saloon and general store. My guess was that it had taken on the function of a saloon when the rest of the businesses moved.

The store's coolness was welcome, and its aroma caused me to breathe deeply. The mingled scent of newly tanned leather, freshly ground coffee, tobacco, and many other items that contributed to its inviting atmosphere brought memories of my boyhood.

A glance at the shelves showed a keg on one of them, and unless it was empty, it held beer. I asked for a glass of it.

The proprietor grabbed a mug and turned the bung wide open, letting a head build so it filled over half the glass with foam. "Not very cool, but it's the best we got."

"The amount of beer in that mug won't be enough so I give a damn. Anyway, long's it's wet, I'll drink it," I said, and tipped my hat back. "Saw pony tracks 'bout fifteen miles east."

"Many?"

"About twelve."

He nodded and shrugged. "We can handle that many. If a big war party ever takes it in their heads to hit us, reckon we're done for."

"Well, let's hope it doesn't happen." I was making conversation, just passing time. There was always the chance in this country that the Sioux or Cheyenne would attack in strength. I finished my beer. "Anyplace to eat around here? Haven't eaten since yesterday morning."

"Well, there's a head o' cheese over yonder. The cracker barrel's full. If you like sardines, I got a few tins on yonder shelf. He'p yoreself."

I shook my head. "Much obliged, but thanks, anyway. A good hot meal would go down better."

"Well, in that case, yeah, there's a place." He smiled.

"Don't know about tomorrow, but today Ma Sundstrom's still in business. Right across the street and west a bit."

Paying for the beer, I thanked him for the information.

I saw the café sign from the store's doorway and angled across the street toward it.

A buxom, motherly looking woman sat at one of only three tables. She and I were the only ones in the room.

"Howdy," she greeted.

"Howdy, ma'am."

"Got coffee, buffalo roast, potatoes, and biscuit. You want somethin' else, ride on."

I grinned. "Ma'am, if you've enough of it to fill me, I reckon I'll eat right here."

I saw her eyes move up and down, taking in my tall frame. "Well, you're might nigh as handsome as you are big. Always did like a black-haired, blue-eyed man. Set. Reckon I can fill you up."

"If the proprietor of the general store hadn't told me your name's Sundstrom, I'd figure you for Irish with all that blarney you just handed me."

The hard shell behind which she apparently took refuge melted. "Ah, go on with you. Yeah, I'm Irish. My old man was Swede. Died last year of blood poisoning from a Lakota arrow."

She stood, poured a cup of coffee, put it in front of me, and hurried to the kitchen. When she came back, the plate she carried needed sideboards to hold the food piled on it.

I eyed the plate when she put it in front of me. "My Gggg-uh, goodness, ma'am! I'm a pretty good-sized man, but this is more food than I've eaten in a month."

Her sharp, blue eyes twinkled. "I'll lay you two to one odds you eat it all." She sat and leaned primly against the back of her chair. "I'm a good cook."

I took my time. Ma sat there watching. When the plate neared empty, she stood. "Get you some more. You ain't leavin' my place hungry."

Still chewing, I shook my head, swallowed, and looked up at her. "Ma'am, if you do that, I might stay here and marry you, and it'd take a heap o' buffalo to feed me."

She laughed. "If you think you're scaring me, mister, think again. I could feed you till it took two o' these tables fer you to set at, and I'd enjoy doin' it."

"And you wouldn't feel ashamed for having made me fat?"

"Aw, go on with you." She filled my cup again.

While eating, I wondered if she'd seen the big Negro come through. The coffee was ungodly hot, so I sipped it and slanted her a questioning look.

"Ma'am, you see a great big Negro come through here the last day or so?"

Her eyes met mine, her gaze unflinching. "You after 'im?" I shook my head. "No, ma'am. That's not my way. I intend him no harm. I just keep thinking I should know him, that maybe he's someone I'd like to know again."

She was through studying me. Her face serious, she nodded. "Yeah, he came through here about sundown last night. I fed him. He paid me, although I tried to talk him outta it. I figured he might be a mite shy o' cash."

Ma brushed imaginary crumbs from her side of the table. "When I made the offer of a free meal, he just smiled a big, gentle smile and said as how he thanked me, but he had money and would pay his way long's he could."

She cocked her head quizzically. "Cain't remember where ye knowed him, eh?"

"No, ma'am. He sounds like he has some schooling. That Southern accent tells me he's from the South, but I don't remember any Negroes from down home that fit."

"You a Southerner?"

I nodded. "Yes, ma'am."

"You holdin' a grudge agin the North?"

"No, just figure to get on with my life. I'll leave people alone as long as they don't push me."

She laughed, breaking the serious vein of the conversation. "I cain't imagine any in their right mind pushin' a man the likes o' you."

Grimacing, I replied, "There are those who try it, ma'am."

She cocked her head to the side, listening. "Seems I hear another supply train in the distance." She looked at me, grinned like an impish young girl, and stood. "Let's go watch it come through."

I got my feet under me. "Yes'm, heard it awhile ago." I held out my arm for her to take.

She looked at it a moment, apparently surprised at the gesture, then laid her rough, work-hardened hand in its crook.

The engine neared. I heard the whistle blowing like the engineer enjoyed its sound. Some engineers bought their own whistles, insisting they have a unique sound. Station agents could tell who was driving an approaching train by its whistle.

The great steam monster came tearing by, loaded with everything a construction crew would need to build a railroad. There were rails, ties, fishplates, spikes, rods, and switch stands. This train even had four cattle cars loaded with cattle and three flat cars carrying potatoes. It seemed General Dodge fed his crews well.

We stood there until the train disappeared in the distance.

It had been my plan to stay the night in Sydney, but seeing that train gave me the hurry-ups, so after paying Ma and taking the bag of sandwiches she packed for me, I headed out of town.

chapter

two

KNOWING I'D NOT get far before sundown, I left Sydney behind and had gone only seven or eight miles before looking for a place to bed down, a place I could defend if need be. Another couple of miles brought me to a likely looking site on a small stream. My big red stallion turned toward it and had lowered his head to drink when a distant sound broke the silence.

My hearing, honed to a razor's sharpness, strained to identify the sound. I cocked my head, listening, separating sounds into harmful and natural categories. There it was again. The sharp crack of distant rifle fire interrupted the prairie's wind song.

I dismounted and led the stallion, walking slowly toward where I judged the shooting to be. I dared not ground-hitch the horse. He'd stay where I left him unless he was led away. In Indian country I'd not take that chance.

Shy of topping out on a knoll, I eased up so only my head showed and peered in the direction of the shots. At first, only the grass waved in the wind before me. Then something moved on the near side of the next ridge.

My gaze locked on the spot and in a moment I spotted a warrior, prone, blending with the dried grass, firing away from me. There was more than one rifle talking out there.

My eyes carefully swept the skyline and picked out two

more Indians. Listening carefully, I tried to judge how many weapons I'd have to face.

There were only four rifles that I could identify. I guessed the fourth came from whomever it was the Cheyenne had pinned down. Figuring them as Cheyenne was not a bad gamble, this being their territory.

A glance at the sun showed only half of the big red ball above the horizon. To make a difference in this fight, I'd better do something soon. After dark, the three would slip up on the lone fighter and he, or at least his hair, along with his horse and gear, would be the guest of honor at some Cheyenne camp. Unlike Apache, who didn't like to fight at night, the Cheyenne fought when they took the notion.

Inching a little higher on the knoll, I sighted directly between the first Indian's shoulder blades and squeezed the trigger of my Henry, then jacked another shell in the chamber. I watched to see what the other two did. I knew from this range exactly where my slug nailed the one I'd fired at. The other two disappeared.

No longer visible, I didn't think for one second they had left. Now, I used the care of an Indian. They knew I had joined the party and about where I lay. There was no way to hide when these old black-powder shells fired. They sent up a cloud of smoke that told the world where the shot came from, so I moved out of there fast.

Moving in a circle and getting no farther from the man being attacked than I'd been before, I tried to move away from the position held by the warriors.

My hand dropped to my Bowie knife to make sure it was handy. I might have to use it. To round a shoulder of hill and come face-to-face with one or both of the warriors was possible. Close combat seemed always to bring out the desire in an Indian for knife fighting. It gave him an opportunity to count coup. Then he'd kill, but only after counting coup. This made him a big warrior.

Their rifles ceased fire, in keeping with what I thought they would do. They wouldn't fire again until they knew where I was, and then *I'd* be their target.

Someday, not minding my own business would get me killed.

Dropping to my belly, I snaked to the top of the swale, peered over, and found myself eyeball-to-eyeball with one of the braves. He jumped to his feet and reached for his knife. Mine came smoothly to hand.

We faced off. He took a practice swing, testing me. I easily stepped out of his reach, then quickly toward him, weaving, feinting, trying to make him commit himself. He stepped in and brought his knife up in a swing that would have gutted me if he'd connected. I swung across my body at his arm and felt my blade bite in. Careful to keep my balance, I stepped back.

The sound of a rifle shot ripped the air, but I dared not look. The brave I faced was bleeding badly from a gash in his side. My swing at his arm must have missed and caught him along the ribs. I stepped toward him, feinted, and brought him toward me. He swung again. I didn't get lucky on that slice. He caught my shoulder with the tip of his blade. The sickening faintness that comes with a deep cut, steel against bone, didn't materialize.

He stepped back out of reach of my next swing. I missed but danced back and avoided another of his slices.

He moved in quickly, his knife held waist high, then stabbed at me. I'd been waiting for such a move.

The big, heavy blade of the Bowie came down with all my strength across his knife arm, severing it at the wrist. His hand and knife fell to the ground at my feet.

I stepped in, knife poised, ready to push it into his gut.

His chin came up, his eyes locked with mine. He showed no fear, no emotion. Proudly he stood, ready for my death stroke. I stopped, stared at him a moment, stepped closer to him, touched his shoulder, and nodded. He would know that I intended the gesture as a symbol for counting coup upon him. He would consider it the ultimate disgrace. Not giving a damn what he thought, I knew I might live to regret making an enemy of him.

He removed his headband, wrapped his bleeding stump, and bent to pick up his knife. He stared into my eyes for a full two seconds, with more hate than I could imagine, and walked away. Only then did I remember the shot I'd heard and dived to pick up my rifle. I had dropped it during the fight. I rolled to my side and glanced around the swale I lay in.

Not forty feet away stood the big Negro, standing over the other warrior.

He stepped away and turned his head. He retched, then vomited.

I stood and walked to him. He shook his head, his face twisted into a mask of agony.

"Mistuh, I never killed a man before. Didn't know it'd do this to me."

My gaze locked with his. "Don't feel shame, boy. The first time affects all of us in some way. The second time will be easier."

He glanced at the Indian's hand lying on the ground behind me.

He retched again, controlled himself, then said, "There's not ever gonna be a second time."

I didn't argue the point because self-preservation is a mighty strong drive in all of us. He'd kill again if he had to. I knew also that the Indian's severed hand had a little something to do with his upset stomach.

"Where's your gear? We'd better get it and get the hell out of here. There's likely to be more than these three."

Silently, he led me to his campsite. He'd picked a good spot but had built a fire. I walked to it, picked up his coffeepot, and poured its contents over the coals, thinking I'd have to teach this man something about survival in Indian country.

"Pack your horse. I want to be one hell of a long way from here before we stop again."

His bedroll strapped behind his saddle, we rode from there slowly, keeping a sharp watch about us. I didn't think we'd have more trouble because deep dusk had set in. The lavender of sunset had shaded into deep purple, and most Indians liked to see what they were attacking. Regardless, I wanted to be a long time gone when sunrise came, because they'd be looking for us and would have no trouble reading our sign.

One Hand would not let it rest. I didn't think for a minute, even though he'd lost a hand, he'd give in to the pain. A white man might, but not a Cheyenne warrior.

We rode silently for perhaps an hour. Then the Negro said, "Reckon I owe you my thanks again, and I do thank you, but why have you helped me?"

I turned my head toward his voice. It was black dark now, and I could only see his outline against the stars. "First off, out here men help each other. If they're white men, uh, what I mean is, if they are decent men, they help others who are decent."

"I don't take offense at your choice of words, mistuh. My name is Adam, Adam Creighton, and I thank you again for what you did. Back there in town, too."

We kept our voices low. Sound carries far on the plains. Only the creak of saddle leather and the low monotone of our voices broke the stillness; our horses' hooves made only a swishing through the tall grass.

"I'm Chance Tenery."

A slight chuckle from Adam told me he'd placed me as soon as I had him.

"You're Mr. Zachary Creighton's houseboy. I knew I'd seen you somewhere before but couldn't place you."

"Yes, suh, I kept wondering, too. How's your pa, Mistuh Chance?"

"Dead. He died before I got home from the war. Pneumonia."

"Ah, I'm sorry, suh. I surely did like your father. He treated his people right."

I nodded, knowing he couldn't see it. Yes, Pa had treated all men right. "How's Mr. Creighton?"

"Dead. Reckon when his life crumbled around him, with the war and all, he just gave up. Before the end, though, he gave me all the money he had, gave me my freeman's papers, and told me to go west, that I could make a life for myself out here. Those papers he gave me were dated ten years ago. Reckon he intended all along that I be free."

"Yes, it sure sounds like it." I chuckled. "As for making a life out here for yourself, you won't, unless you learn a hell of a lot about staying alive." I shifted in my saddle a little. "That fire you built back there almost got you killed. Reckon I'm gonna have to teach you a few things." I grinned into the night. "Thanks for getting that redskin when you did. I was a mite busy at the time."

Silence settled around us again. We were still riding west when I estimated the time at about midnight. Off in the distance, I heard the lonesome wail of a train whistle and thought the engineer might be blowing for a town or perhaps to get buffalo off the track. If he stayed out here long enough, he'd learn that buffalo moved only when they got ready. Whistles, shouts, gunfire, nothing caused a buffalo to move until it was his idea.

I reined toward the sound, thinking there might be a trestle we could spread our blankets under until daylight. We had put about twenty miles behind us, so any friends of the Indians who had attacked us would not find us in the darkness unless they were lucky.

"What you doing out here?" Adam asked.

"When Pa died, I set out to find my brother, Vance. He'd been gone only a couple of weeks, heading west, so I figured I might catch up with him."

"How long you been lookin'?"

"I stopped looking only fifty miles from home. I found he'd been shot in the back, robbed, and left to die. The townspeople told me." I cleared my throat in order to get rid of the huskiness that would betray my emotions. "Now I'm hunting those who killed him. I've been doing that three years now."

"From what I've seen, you know a lot about the Indians and the West."

I nodded. "Yeah. During the war I put in some duty west of Albuquerque. Learned a good bit about the Apache down there."

I saw the gleam of rails not far to my left and reined toward them. Adam followed.

Another quarter mile and we found a trestle, not a long

one, but long enough to afford some shelter under it from the wind and the vigilant gaze of an Indian.

We pitched camp. I took first watch. There was no point in taking a chance.

Adam breathed deeply soon after pulling his blanket over him.

I thought back to our boyhood. When Mr. Creighton came to visit Pa, he always brought Adam, whom he'd reared and educated like a son.

The Creighton plantation had been in South Carolina and ours was in the Piedmont section of Virginia. Adam, Vance, and I had been playmates until Vance and I left home to attend the military academy at West Point. I'd not seen Adam since. But I remembered he'd always been a gentle person. He'd never go hunting with me because he didn't like to kill anything.

I let him sleep until I saw the sky lighten in the east. When I wakened him, I cautioned him that he let me sleep no more than an hour. He started to protest, but I told him we had to be gone by good sunup.

We made a smokeless fire of buffalo chips; had a breakfast of coffee, hardtack, and bacon; put the fire out; and were on the trail when the sun edged above the horizon.

Keeping a distance from the rails, we spotted and passed three settlements by late afternoon. From my knowledge of the territory and talk I'd heard, the towns were Potter, Antelope, and Pine Bluffs. From the looks of them, they weren't worth wasting a visit on. So we rode.

The afternoon of the third day we were riding along the right-of-way, close to the tracks, when the distant sound of a train whistle interrupted my thoughts. I looked back to see the train still a good distance away and slowing because of the long grade.

"That train'll be going at a crawl by the time it reaches us," I told Adam. "I think we'll be able to ride right alongside of it and look it over good."

"Yes, suh, figure you may be right."

When the engine came abreast, it was going little faster than Adam and I rode.

We reined our horses in and studied the loud, smoke-spewing red, black, and green monster.

There were twenty-one cars trailing behind the engine, all loaded with track material; I counted them, even though I'd heard somewhere that it was bad luck to count railcars. The last car was a private passenger car, elegant, the kind that top officials used. They lived in them if the towns had nothing better to offer.

I nudged the stallion on, riding abreast of the luxurious car. Three or four faces were framed in the windows, looking at us. Then I saw her for the first time. Long, black hair framed her face, and her eyes, green as emeralds, stared back at me. Her beauty caused my breath to catch in my throat.

I reached to my hat and tipped it, nodding as I did so.

Most women caught looking at a man acted like they'd been caught with their hand in the cookie jar, but not this girl. When I nodded, she returned my greeting and smiled, all the while looking me right in my eyes. I knew that whatever I had to do, I was going to meet her. I'd heard that a man knows when he's seen the woman for him. Well, I'd seen my woman. She might not agree at first, but I'd take care of that.

The engine topped out on the grade, picked up speed, and moved ahead.

I looked at Adam and found him smiling at me.

We'd not ridden but another hour when the train came back, minus all the freight cars, but the private car was still attached. So I figured that wherever it was going, it'd be back someday, and I hoped the girl would be on it.

chapter

three

SEVERAL DAYS LATER, in late afternoon, a town rose out of the tawny grass sea. At first, only the roofs were visible, but slowly, as we rode nearer, the rest of the buildings emerged from the prairie. A seafaring man would say they had been hull down when first seen.

"I believe that's Cheyenne." I bent my head toward it. "The rails won't be there for a long time yet. By the looks of it, it'll be quite a city by the time they get here. That's Crow Creek down yonder. General Dodge picked the spot to start building." I laughed.

Adam looked puzzled. "What's funny?"

"You want to hear the story about how Dodge picked that spot?"

He smiled. "From the looks o' you, you're gonna tell me anyway, so go ahead."

"Well, the general had been sent out to survey a site to be named Cheyenne. They'd been riding for days without finding a suitable spot. So, hot, dirty, and tired, Dodge and his crew had been riding all day, and it was coming on to sundown.

"Reining in close to the creek, Dodge swung down from his horse and, exhausted and irritable, took a hatchet from behind his saddle, bent over, and ploughed the head of that hatchet into the ground. He turned to his crew, dusted his hands, and said, 'By God! Cheyenne will be right here.'"

Adam laughed. "Can't anyone say he didn't use the very latest scientific knowledge in deciding where to put it." He chuckled again, removed his hat, and wiped his brow. "You s'pose Cheyenne's been there long enough to have a keg of beer cooled?"

I cast him my most innocent look. "Why? You figuring to drink a whole keg?"

"Ah, Mistuh Chance, you know I wouldn't . . ." he started to protest, then realized I was joking. "Well, on second thought, I feel like I could sure do my part toward getting rid of it."

"C'mon, let's go see what kind of town we've come upon."

Only a week old, Cheyenne boasted saloons, eating places, and the beginnings of a hotel. Tents made up most of the town, but there were wooden buildings going up, too. Even the most cursory glance told me that this would be no Julesburg. It was here to stay.

We found the beer we hankered for, and to my amazement, it was cold. "Where'd you get ice out here?" I asked the bartender.

"Our first citizen, Mr. Jim Whitehead, brung it from them mountains down Denver way. He come with several big freight wagons all loaded down with logs for building, this here ice, tools, damned nigh anything a man might need to build with. He parked them wagons over yonder by the creek bank and just waited till folks started showing up. Hear tell he pitched camp here July eighth, only a couple weeks back, and he's already a rich man."

I shook my head and looked at Adam. "That's the kind of foresight it takes to get rich. People come out here lookin' for gold and ride right over where the big money is.

"Is this Colorado Territory?" I asked the bartender.

"Nope. This here's Dakota Territory. Capital's nigh five hundred miles from here, at Yankton, an' you can shore tell, 'cause there ain't no law here a'tall." He drew a couple more beers and came back to stand in front of me. "Reckon we gonna have to do somethin' 'bout gettin' some law. Hear tell General Dodge is fixin' to do somethin'."

"What's he got to do with it?" I tossed a couple of coins on the bar to pay for the beers.

The bartender scooped up the coins, deposited them in a wooden box on the back counter, and turned to me. "Most times he don't mess with the way these towns get run, but lately, too many of his men are gettin' killed, robbed, beat up, you name it. Hear tell him an' the Casement brothers are jest plumb fed up with falling behind on their schedule."

"Are they in town now?"

"Ain't heard about it, if they are. Heard, oh, maybe a couple weeks ago Dodge wuz back yonder at New York, but he'll be back soon. He don't stay away long at a time, an' his surveying crew is out yonder, 'bout three hundred miles west o' here. Yeah, he'll be back soon."

The bartender cast me a questioning look. "You know the general?"

"Nope, can't say as I do, but we got slightly acquainted during the war."

"You a Yank?"

I shook my head. "Nope, a Southerner."

I swallowed the rest of my beer, looked at Adam, and walked toward the flap that passed for a door, leaving the bartender wearing a puzzled frown.

Adam and I pushed our way through the human stream, heading for a store to replenish our scant provisions. We'd left our horses with a liveryman who'd set up in business by building a rope corral. He promised to feed and guard our horses. He mentioned that he had a mite of help in guarding them, and chuckling, showed me a ten-gauge shotgun. I told him I thought that might be enough.

I stopped a man and asked where I would find a store that had the kinds of things I needed, such as ammunition, bacon, flour, and coffee.

"Well," he said, looking narrow-lidded at me, "reckon you can find them things in either o' the two stores." He turned and spat a stream of tobacco juice. "Unless you done had a rich uncle die and don't care about the cost, them things gonna cause you to reach right down to the bottom of yore poke."

I grimaced. "That bad, huh?"

"Worse. My advice, get yoreself a job cuttin' ties or layin' 'em, and let the railroad feed you." He glanced at the Colt tied down against my right thigh. "Course, if you ain't afraid to use that there pistol, Dan or Jack Casement might hire you to sort of keep the peace around here."

I glanced at Adam, then back to the brawny man I'd asked for information. "My partner . . . well, we sort of figured on something without guns." I tipped my hat and thanked him for the information. Walking away from the man, Adam looked at me strangely.

"What's bothering you?" I asked.

"Mistuh Chance, you just told that man we're partners."

I looked at him, allowing a slight smile. "Well, we've ridden a good distance together, fought Indians together, sat by the same fires at night, so, reckon until you tell me different, we're partners."

Adam pushed his hat to the back of his head, looked at the ground a moment, shuffled his feet, then looked at me, head-on, right in my eyes. His were suspiciously moist. "Mistuh Chance, I suppose it took me by surprise. Never thought much that a white man would take a darky on as his partner."

"What the hell's that got to do with us being partners? We've a lot more in common than most. Color of skin be damned."

"Well, yes suh, reckon we have." He smiled that great big smile of his, and we walked on.

I looked at him across my shoulder. "Adam, if we're to be partners, I reckon you'd best stop calling me mister and sirring me."

"I'll try, but somehow it don't seem right."

"It's right, so do it."

"Yes, suh."

I shook my head, grinning.

I looked down the street and saw the crowd thinning. Then I noticed people pushing at others to get to the side of the street. In the middle of the yelling, pushing throng, two men stood facing each other.

I grabbed Adam's arm and pulled him to the side. "Gonna be gunplay," I said. "Now, get the hell in among these people. No point in getting hit by a stray bullet."

With my height, I could look over the heads of the crowd. I watched a scene that was old to the West long before I got here. The gunman facing my direction wore a black broadcloth suit, white shirt, and black string tie. He had the mark of a gambler or professional gunslinger.

The man facing him wore big overalls, a red flannel shirt, and an old, outdated pistol shoved into his side pocket.

"Now, damn you," the gunman said, "you accused one of my girls of rolling you, accused her of taking all your money. Now say it to me."

"Mister, ain't got no fight with you. Don't even know much about usin' a gun, so if'n you're gonna kill me, get on with it. I cain't stop you."

Why I did it, I'll never know. Although some would call me smart, I often do dumb things, and this was one of those times. A few quick steps took me to the center of the street. "I can stop him," I said.

"You drawing a hand in this game?" the gunman purred.

The smile I forced felt frozen. I nodded. "Don't know why, but here I am. If you're itching to kill someone, here's your chance."

There must have been something about me that made him cautious. He pulled back a step, turned so his right hand was hidden from my view, and drew.

His gun cleared leather. Without thinking, I palmed my .44. A spot of red stained his shirt where a button had been only a moment before. Only then did the smoking gun in my hand tell me what had happened.

He was still trying to bring his gun up for a shot. I'd seen many men, hit four or five times, any one of which would have been fatal, still fire and kill their adversary.

I fired again, then again, watching his body jerk with the impact of each heavy slug. He sank slowly at first, then as a tree falls, he toppled to the ground. I stood alone in the middle of the street, shucked the cartridges from my gun, and reloaded.

The crowd rushed back around us, yelling, some pounding me on the back, others staring at the prone body of the gunman, his face buried in the dust.

Disgustedly, I turned from them, my gaze searching the crowd for Adam, and wondered who, if anybody, would see to getting the gunman buried. I shrugged, just plain not giving a damn.

A look at the gunman's pistol told me he wasn't the one who'd killed my brother, although he was of the type.

"Mister?"

I turned. It was the man in the overalls.

"Thanks. He would've killed me. I ain't no hand with a gun." He frowned, then said, "If you're lookin' for a job, see Dan or Jack Casement of the Union Pacific. They're hirin' men to fight Indians and help keep the workers from gettin' killed in these towns."

I acknowledged hearing his words and turned from him. I didn't want any job that would require using a gun. Then I saw Adam. He was staring at me like he'd not seen me before.

"What's the problem Adam?"

"You just made up your mind all of a sudden to help that man. Why? You didn't know him, nor did you know what caused the fight."

"No, I didn't know him, but I know the kind of man the gunman was, and I know the hardworking kind the man in overalls was. The way I saw it, if either of the two deserved to live, it was the one I took up for. The other one, I know from experience, was a parasite and bully. I don't take kindly to that kind. This fight today would have been murder if I'd let it go."

"What you just did, is that the kind of thing Mistuh Casement is hiring men for?"

"I don't know, Adam. If it is, it's a job that needs doing." I took him by the arm. "C'mon, let's see if there's anyplace to eat. Must be a café in a town of this size."

The place we chose had one item for dinner, buffalo stew. You ate it or did without. We ate it.

Over dinner, Adam still cast me puzzled looks, and I noticed others in the café glance in my direction and sit at tables as far away as the small café would allow. I hated the idea, but I knew they'd tagged me for a gunfighter.

"All right, what's gnawing at your gizzards?"

Adam glanced at me, then down at his plate. "Don't know, Mistuh Chance, just don't know how a man gets so he can kill like you did and not be bothered by it."

I reached over and laid my hand on his arm. "Adam, don't ever think I'm not bothered by it, but out here, and in war, too, a man does whatever is required of him. There is no law here. Oh, yes, Fort Russell is out of town a ways, but the Army is not commissioned to keep order in these towns. They're here to keep down Indian trouble. Most times, I think they make more trouble than they stop." I pulled my hand back from Adam's arm. "Until we get law, courts, and a set of rules to live by, about the only recourse a man has is strapped to his leg."

Adam shook his head sadly. "Maybe the West is not for me. I just don't take to killin'."

"Even the men who do kill, most of them that is, don't take to killing, but they do it because they have to in order to survive. And most will help those who can't help themselves."

After leaving the café, we got our horses and bedded down outside of town as most did who wanted a good night's sleep. The noise of the drinking, hell-raising men in town could wake the dead.

I lay in my blankets, staring at the clouds that hung heavy over the land, threatening to storm. They reflected my thoughts.

Was Adam right? Was I an uncaring man? No. I had never killed except in self-defense or to protect others. There would come a time when great cities would spread across this country, a time when courts would settle disputes and men would not wear guns, but here and now, guns were needed. I'd wear mine until we had law.

Soon after sunup the next morning, I set out to find who was doing the hiring for the UP. Not having much luck, I finally found that if I followed the roadbed, I'd come upon the grading crew. I might find someone who was looking for a strong back and a weak mind.

This didn't bother me. I'd worked hard all my life, swinging an ax or sledgehammer, loading tobacco, and plowing. Sure, we had slaves, but I never asked them to do anything I would not do myself.

I worked right alongside them, and there were times they joshed me about working too fast. They wouldn't let a white boy outdo them, so they, too, worked fast.

I looked at Adam. "I need a job. My cash is getting low, but the railroad isn't paying much, thirty-eight dollars a month, a place to sleep, and three meals a day. Can't start a ranch on that kind of money."

Adam dug in his pocket and pulled out a rawhide bag. "My money, Mistuh Chance. You can have any of it or all of it, if you need it."

I looked at Adam a long minute, then shook my head. "No, Adam, I'll not take your money. If we're partners, I'm bringing as much to the table as you." I frowned. "Don't know how much you have, but don't mention that you have anything to anybody else. Most out here are hardworking, honest men, but there are those who'd cut your throat in a minute for a dollar, so keep quiet and keep it in a safe place."

"Yes, suh." He wiped his forehead. "What we gonna do now?"

"Let's go get a beer and talk about it. I believe I have a pretty good idea."

We went back to the saloon that had cold beer, got our beers, and sat at one of the two tables.

I took a long swallow, put the glass down, and looked at Adam.

"I think, from what you've said about keeping Mr. Creighton's books and the studying he made you do, that you have a better education than most." I drank again. "Me?

Well, I have one of the best engineering educations a body can get. West Point did that for me."

"Yes, suh, I can't differ with you on that, but what does it all mean?"

"What I'm trying to say, Adam, is this. The good-paying jobs are the ones that don't require a strong back and a weak mind."

I leaned against the back of my chair. "Ah, hell. I know there are a lot of people out here, darkies like yourself, newly discharged Union and Confederate soldiers, disgusted farmers, even some Indian squaws. They're people who need any money they can get, because there are not many jobs to be had back East. There are damned few weak minds among them, but you and I have something special. We're trained to do particular kinds of work."

Adam drained his glass and put it on the table. "Yes, suh, but what is it gonna get us?"

"Adam, I'm not above doing track work, surveying, whatever it takes, but the money isn't there."

"Well then, where is it?"

"I'm going to ask General Grenville Dodge to hire us, you as an accountant, me, an engineer."

"But he's in New York."

I nodded. "Yeah, but he'll be back, and we're going to end-of-track to meet him. While we wait, we'll lay track."

Adam grinned. "You mean we're gonna saddle our horses and ride back the way we came?"

I shrugged. "Why not? We sure as hell haven't lost anything here."

"When we leavin'?"

"As soon as we have one more of those cold beers." I stood and walked to the bar.

chapter

four

WE LEFT TOWN without replenishing our supplies. By the fourth day, we were down to reboiling grounds from the previous morning's coffee and gnawing cold, hard biscuits. We chewed jerky and shaved some into water to make a thin soup. That kind of fare doesn't stick to your ribs very long.

I'd had several chances to shoot a buffalo calf, but I didn't take to the idea of my shot being heard deep in Indian country. We were in the middle of short-grass prairie with no way to hide our tracks. An Indian child could follow the trail we laid down.

Late afternoon of the fifth day, we topped out on a ridge. Not two hundred yards off, I saw four antelope and a nice-sized buck grazing. We were downwind so they'd not picked up our scent.

I shucked the Henry from my saddle boot, took careful aim, and dropped the deer.

I looked at Adam. "That meat may get us killed, but with it close to dark, we can skin him out and be gone before getting caught. Besides, I've seen no Indian sign in several days."

I'd finished skinning and cutting the chunks we'd take with us and tied them to my saddle when I saw the stallion's ears prick. He looked toward the way we'd come.

Not wasting a move, I slung the rest of the carcass in front of my saddle. "Mount up. We better get out of here."

Adam didn't question. He was abreast of me by the time I saw who our company was. I think they were as surprised to see us as we were them. There were only two that I saw, but there might be more. I didn't take a chance. We ran.

Our horses, who were bigger and better fed, gained on them from the outset. I noticed, in the quick glance I had before mounting, that they carried only bows. I saw no rifles, but their friends, if they had any nearby, might be better armed.

I frowned. They seemed content with keeping distance between us. They were not trying to catch up or get close enough for a shot. They must be the only ones in their party, I thought, but not wanting to take a chance, planned to stay ahead of them.

I signaled Adam to slow a little. "We'll try to keep this distance from them until dark. Then we'll change our route and head directly for the rails." I grimaced. "Looks like we got a long night ride ahead, so we'll take it easy after darkness settles in and they can no longer see our trail."

Another hour and it was too dark to see them, or for them to see any tracks we might leave. I kneed the stallion toward the south. Adam followed. We walked the horses until what I guessed to be about three o'clock, then stopped for a couple hours of sleep. I still didn't know whether there were more than the two Indians we'd seen.

Long before sunup we were back in the saddle, heading east but a little north. I wanted to cut across the rails as soon as possible, and I thought they should not be very far now. We'd killed the deer and hadn't had a chance to eat any of it. My stomach let me know it.

When I finally saw the cars lined up at end-of-track, there was no town, just the bunk cars and those with all the building materials. "Rail hands must be saving a lot of money with no town to spend their payday in."

Adam smiled and shook his head. "Bet you on payday they ride the freight cars back to Julesburg and stay till they've spent every last cent."

"Yeah, you've got a cinch bet there." I sighed. "Let's get on down there and see if there's a job. But first I'm going to get close enough to build a fire safely. Then I'm going to cook the biggest breakfast you ever did see."

Adam looked at the venison in front of my saddle and said whimsically, "You reckon chickens have quit layin'? Oooo, Lordy, I shore would like to see 'bout a dozen eggs fillin' my plate so full they'd be fallin' off the sides." He glanced at me, grinning. "Then I'd see how fast I could make them disappear."

"You saying you're not gonna eat any of the victuals I fix?"

"Ah, now, Mistuh Chance, you know I'm gonna eat. Fact is, if I don't get it cooked right soon, I'm tempted to start in on that haunch plumb raw."

"Well, let's get started gathering some buffalo chips for the fire."

Adam bent to pick up a chip and looked sideways at me. "When was it we last ate a cooked meal?"

I shrugged. "Damned if I know; five, six, seven days. It's been long enough that my backbone's grown solid to my navel. It will take at least half of that deer to push my front end back where it belongs."

We were two big men. Anybody who had seen us eat that breakfast would have figured that if we ate that way all the time, there wouldn't be a deer or buffalo left on the plains.

Thirty minutes after breakfast, Adam and I were sitting in Jack Casement's railcar. It served as office and sleeping quarters for him. He and his brother Dan were the construction bosses. From all I'd heard, they were tough but fair.

I studied him. He was short, not over five feet four inches, with a full beard. Anyone who worked for him would tell you that, despite his size, he stood ten feet tall.

"You're looking for a job? Hell, I have plenty of work. What can you do?"

"Well, sir, my partner here, he's a damned fine accountant and bookkeeper."

Casement looked at me a little closer, probably not accustomed to the run-of-the-mill worker being conversant of the capabilities of an accountant. He glanced at Adam, then back to me. "All right, we know what he does, what can you do?"

"I'm an engineer, sir, graduate of the United States Military Academy, but served in the Confederate Army."

Jack Casement blinked a couple of times. Mine was not a new story. Many of West Point's graduates had served the Confederacy.

He frowned. "It seems that I've seen you before, in a blue uniform."

"That's possible, sir, but it was probably my twin brother, Vance. When the war broke out, we figured that we owed the Union for giving us a good education and the South for being our home. Well, owing them both, we decided that one would fight for the North, and the other for the South. I drew the South." I didn't tell him the heartrending emotional scenes the decision incurred.

"You think you can come out here and get a soft job because you're educated?"

"No, sir. Neither Adam nor I expect that. We've both worked hard most of our lives and are willing to do so again, but if anything opens up while we're doing whatever you put us to doing, we'd appreciate a shot at it."

Casement's smile barely crinkled the corners of his eyes. "You've done all the talking. Doesn't your partner talk?"

Adam sat forward in his chair. "Yes, suh, I'm willing to talk for myself, but it seems that every time we get in a talking situation, Mistuh Chance just naturally takes over and deals me out of the action. What do you want to know about me, suh?"

Casement shook his head. "Nothing. I just wanted to hear you say something. Tenery was hogging all your time."

I felt like a kid that had been spanked. I was so anxious to have Adam get a good job that I made sure Casement knew his qualifications.

Casement stood, ramrod straight, and looked at us. Even though he wasn't wearing his uniform, he might as well have been. He was again John Stephen Casement, Brigadier General, Army of the United States.

"It happens that I'm a damn sorry man at keeping tally of the things that must be accounted for." He pinned Adam with a penetrating stare. "You've got the job of keeping me out of trouble. We'll talk about salary later." He turned to give me the same stare. "You·ever built a trestle or bridge before?"

"No, sir, but if engineering is involved, I can do it." I kept my eyes on his. "And, sir, what is even more important, in my opinion, I can handle men, get the most out of them without bullying them. I can do that, sir, and from what I hear of you, that's also the way you operate."

Jack Casement looked at me another long moment, then glanced at the .44 at my hip. "Can you use that?"

"When I must, sir, although I don't like to."

."Tenery, I lost one of my trestle bosses three days ago to some gunslinger up from Texas. I had to pull that crew off the line. They're here now. I want you to take them out." Casement walked around his desk. "There is one more thing you must do. When your crew goes to town, usually after payday, I want you with them.

"I put up with the fights, the cheating, whores, and card sharks, but now the sorriest element from New York, Chicago, New Orleans, and God knows where else have come out here. There are pimps, gunmen, thieves, all the ones who won't work for money but will take it from those who will. It's routine to find our people dragged off into an alley, streambed, or behind saloons and stabbed, shot, or simply beaten to death. I want you to see that it doesn't happen to any of your crew."

"If I have to kill someone, will the law or the railroad stand behind me? I'm not going to prison just for a job."

"We *are* the law, the *only* law out here, Tenery. If you're caring for your crew, I'll assure you the law isn't going to bother you."

"When do we go to work, sir?"

"Right now." Casement turned to Adam. "Stay until I get back. I'll show you my books then." He smiled grimly. "That is, I'll show you the pitiful records I've kept. You're going to have one hell of a job making sense of them."

"Yes, suh. I'll be here. I'll make sense of them" Adam's voice was sober.

Casement walked toward the door and said over his shoulder, "Come, Tenery. I'll get you and your crew acquainted." He stopped. "And by the way, you and your men keep rifles handy. The Indians figure we're destroying their hunting lands."

He led me to one of the bunk cars, entered, and walked to a bunk where six men were playing poker. They looked up briefly but went back to their card game.

"Men, this is your new boss, Chance Tenery. Mike," he addressed a brawny Irishman across the bunk, "round up the rest of the crew and have them fall in, military formation, outside."

I kept my face rigid to keep from smiling. It was true then, what they said about Casement, and General Dodge insisted on it. They drilled all of the construction crews as though they were a military unit, even had them take target practice with the new Henry .44 caliber rifles. I reckoned then he was serious about not losing men to Indians or the hell-on-wheels town bullies. Looked like I would fit in here like a hand in a glove.

"General, I—"

"Don't General me, Tenery. Call me Jack. Everyone else does."

"Yes, sir!"

He led me outside to the shade of the boxcar. We stood there, waiting for Mike to round up the crew. I watched them arrive one by one and fall in. There were men in the butternut gray of the Confederacy, Union blue, and many freed slaves. There were even a few Indian squaws among them, and the ever-present Irish. I was also to learn there were many German and English adventurers. All in all, they looked like a tough, hardworking crew.

Mike reported when all were present. Casement looked them over, then turned to me. "A motley crew you have here, Tenery. They'll fight a buzz saw, drink more whiskey than would fit in one of these cars, go to town on payday and blow their whole week's pay." He stopped and looked at me through narrowed eyes. "But they are the hardest-working lot you'll find on the face of God's green earth."

I smiled. "Jack, you've obviously never seen a roundup crew at work. Since the war, I've done about every kind of job a ranch hand is expected to do. Roundup is hell."

He turned and swept the line of workers with an arrow-like gaze. "Men, this is your new boss. I'll not bother to call each of you by name. He'll get to know you soon enough. His name is Chance Tenery. That's all." Jack Casement walked away, leaving me with them.

"Hold it, men," I yelled when they started breaking ranks. "Be ready to leave at five in the morning, and I mean ready with all your gear. Leave nothing you might need. Clean your rifles and draw ammunition for two weeks. Who's the cook here?"

A wizened little man in a ragtag Confederate uniform stepped forward.

"I expect you to see that your chuck wagon is fully supplied. It's your job, and I'll not interfere unless these men don't get enough to eat."

"Yes, sir." He stepped back into the ranks.

"I want to see all the foremen. The rest of you men be ready to go in the morning. Fall out."

I wanted to get to know my foremen and let them get to know me. Mostly, I wanted to learn from them. I'd seen the way the men worked together as a team and how the teams worked together as a complete unit. The rhythm with which they worked was every bit as musical and cadenced as those of galley slaves. Every moment was sparing in motion and precise in intent. I wanted to know all these men knew and more.

After introducing ourselves, I led them into talking of themselves, their crew, and the specifics of their jobs. I told them I wanted to have a talk every evening after supper. They nodded in unison.

"That's all for today then."

I'd turned to walk away when Mike Mulroon, the same man Casement had round up the crews, touched my arm. "Chance, I want to talk a minute more."

I stopped. "Sure. What do you want?"

"Well, it's like this; every new boss we've had has had to prove how tough he is sooner or later. Can you fight? No, now I don't mean the sporty kind o' fightin'. What I'm talkin' about is knuckle an' skull, get 'em down and kick 'im, gouging, punchin', chokin', buttin' kind o' fightin'.'"

I let a sliver of a smile crinkle the corners of my lips. "You challenging me, Mike?"

He grinned back at me. "Not right now, boss, but I might be the one. Who knows?"

I studied him a moment and realized that, win or lose, these men would want to know whether I was a fighter. They'd follow me as long as I proved I had guts. And, even if they knew what I was made of, they'd still want to see a good fight to break the drudgery.

I stood there a minute, just looking at him, smiling slightly. "Mike, whoever takes on the job, you be sure they bring a lantern and their supper, 'cause they're gonna be there awhile."

That big, brawny bastard stood there grinning at me, then he laughed. "Boss, it might be me. I've whipped every man in your crew, so to be sure you get the best, I have a hunch it'll be you and me one o' these days."

"I'll look forward to it, Mike, but I don't want to hurt you too bad. I'll need to get a good day's work out of you when it's over."

"Don't worry 'bout me, boss. If you whip me, I'll give you my week's pay and work as hard as ary a man."

"Start saving then," I told him. "Right now, I'm going to see if Casement has any special word for me."

The next morning, we saddled in the dark and rode out. The trestle construction site was about twenty miles ahead of end-of-track. We'd ride out, and the crew we relieved would ride the horses back. Not keeping horses, except the huge draft horses needed for pulling equipment, gave the Indians less reason to attack.

We let the horses walk, not wanting to outpace the chuck wagon. I figured we'd get to the construction site about dark, but still in time to get grub cooked before crawling into our blankets.

About five miles out, we passed the laying crew. They laid five ties to a twenty-eight-foot length of rail. Out here where timber, food, everything was scarce, tie cutters traveled creek banks and cut pithy cottonwood. Five cottonwood ties were laid, then an oak or cedar tie, with the idea that they would hold until trains could bring good ones later.

A constant stream of huge freight wagons followed the roadbed, dropping their loads at intervals so there would not be a hitch in the work.

I knew the wagons we passed, piled with long, heavy timbers, would be unloaded at the trestle site. I was anxious to get there and see how much of everything we'd need. When the last structural member was in place, I wanted a very thin pile of equipment left to pick up and haul to the next site.

When we stopped for a nooning, we had long since left the foremost wagons behind. I had sixty men in my crew and didn't think we'd have Indian trouble with that many rifles, but after eating, I told the men to ride with rifles across their pommels. Mike, riding alongside of me, asked, "You expecting a fight?"

"Don't know." I shook my head. "It never hurts to be ready, though. I'm going to scout a circle around us, see if there's any sign."

Mike looked at me, a question in his eyes. "You ever fought Indians?"

"Yeah." I nodded. "The Apache, Comanche, Kiowa, Sioux, most all of them east of the Rockies."

He looked at the .44 Colt at my side. "I figured that was just for show, but I suppose after what you told me, you know how to use it."

"Yes," I responded quietly. It was a thing a man needed to know, whether the man he traveled with could use a gun, if he figured to stay alive.

Most who wear guns hope they won't need them, but there are others who like the feel it gives of being a great big man. Resignedly, I thought those were the ones who made it necessary for the rest of us to carry a gun.

My being a big man physically made it even more necessary, because the little men like to show that they're big as any, so long as they have a gun.

Before reining my horse to ride out and scout the area, it seemed Mike looked at me differently. Apparently he had thought Casement brought me out from the East, and to be flashy, I'd strapped on a gun. Now he had cause to wonder.

I circled my crew, riding far enough out to lose sight of them. There was no sign of Indians, no tracks, nothing. A glance to the west showed a huge buildup of black, roiling clouds. We were going to get some weather soon. I headed back to the roadbed.

chapter
five

RAIN FLEW LIKE wash water thrown from a bucket, blown horizontal. Lightning stabbed jagged lances at the ground, then thunder crashed across the heavens. We were soaked through our slickers in seconds. The big danger was the lightning; it always picked the highest object on which to vent its power.

"Get off your horses and walk!" I yelled over the noise. The wind tore the words from my mouth, seeming angry that I'd deprive the storm of its vengeance upon us. The smell of brimstone burned my nostrils.

Only a few heard me above the turmoil. I dismounted, waving at those nearest to me to do the same. Lightning, now a constant, awesome display of heaven's anger, lit the plains to the horizon, and the storm's roar crashed and exploded across the grass sea.

Leading my horse, I ran along the column, yelling and motioning the men off theirs. I reached the end, and in the next flash, saw all saddles were empty.

A fiery dagger from hell speared the middle of our column. A horse screamed, and I saw him go down. Before the next flash, I caught the sickening smell of burned hair and flesh. I ran, stumbling toward the horse. It was too late for the horse, but I wanted to know about the rider.

He lay alongside the horse's head, his hand gripping the

bit. Had he gripped the reins instead of the metal ring, he might have been all right. In an area twenty feet wide, steam lifted from the ground. Even the wind could not blow it away fast enough. In a lightning flash, I saw the men staring at the downed horse and rider. That quick glance showed them wide-eyed, rigid, terrified.

I bent at the rider's side for a closer look. He blinked up at me, alive.

The crew gathered around. "Kneel down . . . all of you," I yelled. "Get close to the ground and stay there. Don't touch any metal." I turned my attention to the injured man.

Carefully, I pried his fingers from the ring of the bit and examined them. They were charred. "Get cook to bring me some of that grease he saves from the bacon," I told the man squatting next to me. As soon as he left, I again gave my attention to the man lying so still and silent.

"Can you hear me?"

He nodded.

"If you can talk, tell me where you hurt."

His lips moved but uttered no words. He tried again. "Hand and both feet." His words were strained, reedy.

"All right, now lie still. I'll see what I can do."

I looked at him, front and back, all the way to his feet and saw no smoldering clothing, so I figured the bolt had gone straight through him, from his hand to his feet and into the ground. I took my knife out to cut the laces on his boots. The soles were gone. They'd blown free of the uppers when the explosion of energy left his body. I cut laces and leather until I was free to peel the boots from him.

Damn, I wished the doctor had come out with us instead of waiting to ride one of the supply wagons. I looked up to see Mike standing with a double handful of bacon grease.

The storm continued to crash about us. Shelter, any kind of shelter, would have been a godsend. This man was in shock and needed to be kept warm and dry, which was as impossible right now as asking him to stand and walk.

"Mike, take some of that grease and carefully spread it

over his hand. That flesh will peel right off the bone if any pressure is put on it." He nodded and slapped a handful in the hand I held out to him.

I picked up one of the burned feet and inspected the bottom of it. Every bone in his foot showed. His boot soles, when blown off, had taken the flesh with them.

Not knowing anything better to do, I spread a layer of lard on both feet and wrapped them in a soggy cloth. There was nothing dry. I removed my slicker and covered him with it.

I turned to one of the men. "Tell cook to bring the grub wagon and drive it as close to this man as he can. We've got to get him under something, out of this weather." I knew, with the force of the storm, there was little chance the wagon would be dry inside, but I had to try.

"Mike, tell the men we'll stay here overnight. We have no choice."

The wind died a little, and it began to hail, large, jagged chunks of ice. I'd seen this type of hail only a few times, and it was as brutally destructive as a ricocheting minié ball. As many as could got under the chuck wagon. The remainder of us used our saddles to cover our heads. A hit by one of these chunks of ice could kill a man. The horses had only a little better chance.

The sky lightened. Many, thinking the storm was through, stood. My guts, tight with fear, controlled fear, forced me to think. There had been many similar situations when I'd had to keep my head clear. My men were in danger, and I couldn't let them be hurt by my inability to function.

"Get the hell back on the ground and stay there," I yelled frantically. As is usually the nature of these storms, there are tornadoes buried in their backsides, and this one was no different.

I saw a pencil-like finger dip out of the clouds. Sometimes they came out like that, then drew back into the angry gray layers and hid for awhile. This one didn't withdraw. It reached closer and closer to the ground.

Its tip touched a swell of grass, and then it spread,

seeming to cover a couple of hundred yards. It roared like one of the big belching engines that pulled freight cars. We cowered flat to the ground, as though trying to crawl into it.

The horror lasted only a few seconds, but it seemed a lifetime.

The tornado ripped, tore, and sucked its way for a quarter mile before I saw it leave the ground and disappear into the clouds. Then the chuck wagon pulled up beside me. I'd been lying across the hurt man, sheltering him as much as my body afforded.

I looked at the suffering man to ask if he wanted anything. His eyes gazed at the sky, but they were now unblinking. I squeezed my eyelids tight to hold back the tears. Here lay an honest, hardworking man, maybe a family man. Like so many others, he would be buried with a wooden marker over him that would soon rot. The grass would grow, and no one would know he'd passed this way.

"Get some shovels," I told one of the men nearest me.

We buried him, burned letters in a marker, set it in the ground, and kept him company during the night.

The next morning, we reached the work site. Since leaving the burial place, the men had looked at each other with sliding glances, still terrified at what had happened. Many had seen death in its most brutal forms, but the awesome manner in which one of them died during the storm would not leave them.

While waiting to meet the engineer in charge of the crew we were relieving, four of my men came up to me and quit. They said they were going home where the weather wasn't so sudden. I told them I was sorry to lose them and for them to ride back to end-of-track with the crew going that way.

I found the engineer, Red Brady, and had him brief me on where they were with the job and the state of materials.

He walked me around and introduced me to the key people. He gazed out at the land that seemed to have no beginning and no end.

"Chance, we've seen some Indian sign." He nodded.

"Yeah, I know, that's not unusual, but seems like there's more than we're used to, so keep a sharp eye out."

"Yeah."

He grinned and squinted at me. "You had to fight any o' your crew yet?"

I tilted my hat back and smiled. "Not yet, but it's coming."

"You can bet your next payday on it. Don't make no difference whether you win or lose, it's just that they gotta take your measure, or just plain enjoy a good fight."

"Some things never change, Red, whether it's a cow camp, mining camp, or a railroad. They have to see if a man has any sand."

"Well, lots o' luck. I'm gonna get my crew back so they can blow their payday. The way they're growlin', you'd figure they hadn't had a woman or a drink in a year." He flipped his hand in a farewell gesture. "See yuh."

I nodded, watching him walk away.

Work quickly fell into a routine. With sentries posted, I stayed busy checking that each beam and cross member were secure. Where I figured we might need extra strength, I had the trestle beefed up.

When supply wagons rolled in, I made sure they off-loaded at places where it would require the least effort to get the material when needed.

A couple of cowboys drifted about ten head of cattle to the side, and I assigned men to see the cattle didn't stray too far. Watching them with the small herd, I found myself wishing they were my cows, on my land. But that day was a long way off. The rain broke the intense heat. It was still hot but not as oppressive as it had been.

Every evening, around the campfire, I saw the men studying me. I knew they were figuring which one of them could whip me. I didn't know when it would come, but come it would.

They'd not been able to estimate my weight very well because I carried none extra, was tall, and big-boned. I'd boxed some at West Point, but in a knuckle and skull fight, that wouldn't count for much.

Since the War Between The States, I'd had to fight in Mississippi River towns and tough border towns between Texas and Mexico. We'd used fists, knives, or guns, whichever came to hand. The cow camp fights were mostly from sheer boredom. I figured this crew had a surprise coming. I didn't figure to lose a knuckle and skull fight to anyone.

Finding whether I had guts was no longer the issue. They'd had ample opportunity to observe that. They just wanted to see a good fight.

A week passed with work going smoothly. The second week, one of the hands fell from near the top of the trestle to the dry creekbed below. We buried him, and after his death, I made a rule that all who worked off the ground would wear a safety rope around their waists, the other end secured to a structural member at track level. The crew grumbled at the loss of freedom of movement, but they wore their ropes.

Fresh Indian sign showed two or three mornings a week, but no Indians rode where we could see them. They seemed more curious than hostile, but knowing they were close gave me reason to use extra caution.

The sentries kept their horses' reins in hand while on lookout. The cow herders grazed our small herd close to the trestle, and all workers at ground level kept rifles within easy reach.

My guns got attention every night. I carefully cleaned and oiled them, and I whetted my knife, too, even though it cut hair with either side of the blade. With all the caution, it still wasn't enough.

Two days before we were due to be relieved, a delicate, rose tint in the eastern sky signaled the coming day as men growled and rolled out of their bedding. While most of them were taking care of their personal needs before heading for the coffeepot, a shot sounded, ripping the morning stillness. And with it, high-pitched yells of an attacking war party.

Men ran for their bedding where their Henrys lay. Spencer

rifles were more dependable, but Henrys fired faster. Whatever we had, we were better armed than Indians.

I'd been up and had a cup of coffee before the shot. I ran to the crest of a rise, peered over, and saw we were in real trouble.

About a hundred Indians were riding, forming a circle around us. My men began to hit the dirt, striving for shelter of any kind.

"Don't fire until they're in range," I yelled.

In the dim light of dawn, I waited until I could see the bead on the front of my barrel. I centered it on the closest Indian's chest and squeezed the trigger. He fell off his horse. By then I'd fired again and another fell. I didn't know whether my shot got him or a bullet from some other gun. The men were all firing.

There were not many shots fired from the Indians, but judging by the hail of arrows, they didn't need anything more than their bows. A man close to me stood, clutching an arrow sunk almost to the feathers in his chest. Before he could fall, he had four more sticking in him.

My rifle hammer pounded on an empty chamber. I dropped the Henry and pulled my six-shooter. An Indian pony coming right at me jumped and cleared my legs. A hoof struck the ground not an inch from me. A look at the rider showed hate-filled, crazed eyes glaring into mine, and his right arm extended toward the heavens. I fired and missed.

He spun his horse on its hind legs and came at me again, trying to get me under his horse's hooves.

The rifle fire of my crew was taking its toll. Some of my men were lying flat, firing up at point-blank range into horses and Indians almost on top of them.

The Indian I fought wheeled his horse again and tried to get me under its hooves. I rolled aside, and again the pony's deadly feet missed.

I stood and threw a couple of shots toward the warrior's back before he could turn again. He threw his hands wide and lurched off the side of his horse.

I twisted and fired into a rider coming from the left. He fell.

A shrill yell took my attention to their leader. His arm waved toward the horizon, and as suddenly as they had come, they were gone. Some of the men chased them on foot, firing insanely, until I called them back.

As if on signal, the crew collected about me. All were reloading.

I finished reloading while telling the men what to do next. "Check those who are down. Be damned sure all Indians are dead before you turn your backs to them. You four," I pointed, "get on that ridge and keep a lookout. They might come back. You, O'Leary, give me a count of how many we lost. The rest of you start digging holes downwind of the trestle. It won't take these carcasses long to start smelling in this heat."

I looked up, saw the chuck wagon, and remembered we'd not eaten breakfast. "Hold up a minute. A few of you eat. Take turns. All of you, whatever the hell you're doing, keep your rifles handy." I smiled grimly. That last order was dumb. Right now I couldn't pry those rifles from them.

A count showed we'd lost four men dead and six wounded. The sentry who'd fired the warning shot had twelve arrows in him and had lost his scalp, but it was his shot that had warned us.

The Indians had left eight dead warriors and had carried some from the field. We'd hurt them.

That night, after we'd eaten and were sitting around the fire smoking, I tapped the dottle from my pipe and stood. "I want to say something." I paused and looked from face to face. "This is probably the first contact many of you have had with Indians. If you want to quit, I'll understand."

"I didn't figure on no tea party when I come out here," one man growled.

"Me neither. I come to build my wife and kids a future," another chipped in.

Most of them had a few words to say, but none of them said they were quitting.

I looked around at them and saw nothing but determination on their faces. My chest felt tight, and a lump swelled my throat. I was so damned proud of them right then I could have yelled like one of those Cheyenne. I looked at them a moment longer, gave them a slight smile, and nodded.

chapter

six

THE RELIEF CREW showed on time, and we went back to end-of-track.

I rubbed my horse down and fed and watered him before Jack Casement sent for me.

He looked up from a stack of papers on his desk. "Have a seat, Chance. Hear you lost some men this time out."

"Some."

"Tell me about it."

I told him about the storm, the Indians, the man who fell from the trestle, and the order I'd given for safety ropes. I didn't leave anything out.

"Good move." A thin smile crinkled the corners of his eyes. "If you keep losing men at this rate, we'll soon run out of them."

"Reckon you're right." I held his gaze with a steady one of my own. Hell, if he wanted to fire me, he could do it, and I'd feel well rid of him. A man did what he had to do.

Casement held my gaze a moment longer. "No excuses, Tenery?"

I shook my head. "I'm sorry those men got killed, but that's the end of it."

Casement picked up a quill pen, dipped it in an inkwell, and wrote something on a piece of paper. He held the paper out to me. "Give this to Adam. He'll see that you get more men."

Taking the piece of paper, I turned to walk away.

"Oh, Tenery, I don't want you to get the idea that every time out will be as rough as this one." He nodded. "Good job, son."

"Thanks." I walked to the end of his car and left, feeling ashamed that I'd not given him credit for being more understanding. He had most likely experienced about everything this country could throw at a man. I straightened my shoulders; Jack Casement was a man to work for.

I found Adam and was surprised at how glad I was to see him.

"Shore good to see you, Mistuh Chance. I was about ready to ask Mistuh Casement to send me out to the trestle to see if you were all right."

I grinned at him. "Yeah, I'm all right." I handed him the note. "I'm taking my crew to Julesburg on the supply train in the morning. When I get back, I'll need those men ready to ride."

Adam glanced at the note, frowned, and looked at me. "Reckon you had some trouble out yonder."

"Some." My look told him more than the word.

Adam smiled that wide smile of his. "I s'pose you were right glad I wasn't along for you to take care of."

"Ah, c'mon, Adam. I felt kind of lost not having to look around to see if you were all right, but I found enough to do without you."

Adam looked down at the note again with a somber expression. "Yes, suh, I shore reckon you did."

"You think Mister Casement will give you a couple days off? If he will, why not come to town with us?"

Adam shook his head. "No. Think I'll stay here." He tapped the note. "I'll take care of this for you though, and maybe next time you head that way, I'll go."

"Good."

Leaving Adam, I rounded up my crew and told them to drop their gear anywhere they'd be comfortable, but to try to stay in the same area as we'd be leaving for Julesburg early. I wished the work train had enough bunks to accommodate my men, but they were taken by the track workers.

My crew dropped their bedrolls close by and spread blankets for poker games. By nightfall, I noticed several of the men had gone to spread their bedding. Broke, I figured.

When it grew too dark to read cards, they broke up the games and gathered around the fire. Not long after, sitting with a cup of coffee grasped in my hands, I noticed that more than the usual number of glances were cast my way. This was it, I knew, and wondered who they'd picked for me to fight.

It caused me wonder that after the Indian fight, I'd have to prove myself. It occurred to me it wasn't so much proving I had guts; they knew that. They just wanted to see a good fight. Well, I'd have to accommodate them.

My coffee finished, I stood, thinking I'd spread my blanket and get a good night's sleep. I wasn't too keen on having to fight tonight.

"Hold on, Chance. What's the hurry?"

I turned to him, knowing he was the one. "No hurry, Mike." I grinned at him. "So it's you they picked, is it?"

"Yep. They figured if you could take me, there wouldn't be any need for you to fight them, 'cause I've already fought 'em all an' whipped 'em all."

"Well, what they say is right. You're the bull o' the woods here, so after you lose to me, I won't have to fight the others, right?"

Mike grinned. "That's right, except you should of said, after *I* whip *you*."

Almost on signal, the men formed a ring around us. I shucked my shirt and handed it to one of the men. Mike did the same, and I saw then that this might take longer than I'd thought.

Mike's chest, which seemed to roll out from his throat, giving the impression of fat, was not fat at all, and his arms looked like tree trunks. I felt skinny by comparison.

In the background, I heard the men begging for bets, but

there were few takers. All the smart money was on Mike. No one seemed to think I had a chance. They weren't betting on who would win, but on how long I'd last. I smiled grimly. This wasn't the first time the odds had been stacked against me.

A man from the crowd stepped forward. "This here fight goes all the way. No rounds, no time-outs. They ain't no rules. Fight any way you want, do anything you figger'll win for you. Fight till one o' you cain't git up, unerstan'?"

He looked over his shoulder and said to no one in particular, "Throw some more wood on the fire so's we can see good."

Both Mike and I nodded.

"All right, git at it." His words brought a roar from the crowd. All seemed to be yelling for Mike.

I circled warily, wanting him to take the first punch, wanting to see how fast he threw that big fist, but not wanting to experience the feel of it.

He stepped quickly toward me, his fist coming at me all the while. I ducked and sidestepped, but that big ham of a fist caught me on the shoulder and knocked me to the edge of the ring of men. The noise of the crowd swelled. Like I'd thought, Mike had a helluva punch.

I figured right then I'd better use what boxing skills I had. In a slug-fest he'd make short work of me.

Mike turned, moving like a big cat, and came at me again. He threw another right. I slipped it over my shoulder, went in fast, and pounded a right and a left to his gut, then danced back out of his reach, feeling a roundhouse right split the air a breath away from my face.

I thought I had found a weakness in his attack. Every punch he'd thrown so far had been a right. I danced to his left, hoping if he connected with that big club of a fist, I'd be going away from it.

I went in fast again and landed a hard right to his nose. It flattened and poured blood. I whipped a left to his gut, then stepped back too late.

His right found me, and it was steaming. It lifted me off

my feet and slammed me into the men. They seemed to think Mike had me then. The din in my ears was almost physical.

They threw me back into the ring, and he hit me again. He used no science, no finesse, just brute strength. That one hurt; it got me right in the wind. He shuffled forward, always forward. He was quick, but he obviously thought that with his strength, he could whip anybody.

I danced around him, trying to keep away until I could suck air back into my lungs. The crowd screamed for me to stand still and fight.

Seeing an opening, I darted in, pumped a right to his gut, and got out of reach again.

Enough blows to his wind and he'd weaken, but a couple more like he'd stung me with, and I'd be in for a long, hard night.

The months and years I'd spent bulldogging cows, in the saddle from morning to night, and swinging an ax or sledgehammer in woods crews and mining camps, had made me as tough as any.

Regardless of how tough or lasting my condition, one solid blow could win it for Mike. I had to keep him from beating me that way. I had to wear him down so I could exchange punches with him, punches that had to be every bit as hard as his.

A slicing left jolted me. I staggered, almost went down, but got my balance in time to roll away from another right that whooshed up from the ground.

He caught me with another left then. God. There was little difference between it and his right. I went to my knees and saw his big work boot swinging at my crotch. I grabbed his foot, rolled to my feet, and twisted.

He went down, and I gave his boot another twist that brought a groan. Another wrench on the boot and I turned loose to try a kick of my own. It missed. I danced back out of the way, glanced around the circle of men, and saw Jack Casement standing in the foreground. He grinned and shouted encouragement, but I couldn't tell who it was he encouraged.

Mike regained his feet and limped toward me. That twist of his foot had done some damage. The lust for battle still showed in his eyes, but now they showed more. They showed the glow of caution and respect, too.

I slammed a right and a left, a right and another left at his head. I had him bleeding above both eyes, the blood from the cut over his left eye blinding him. He wiped the back of his fist across his eyes. My blows didn't even slow him down. He continued to shuffle toward me.

I knew he wanted to get me in his grasp. I danced back out of reach, the men constantly yelling for me to stand and fight, and then quickly darted in. I hit him again, but again he kept coming. He brought his arms together and had me. They wrapped around my chest and squeezed. My back arched, feeling like it was breaking.

My sight dimmed. I felt he was squeezing all of my blood into my head. Another few seconds of this and I'd black out. He was as strong as most bulls I'd had hold of, only now he had hold of me and would break me in two if I didn't do something fast. I felt myself weakening.

He lifted my feet clear of the ground and I knew he would drop with me underneath.

He'd kill me. I swung my right into his body, low down, and grabbed his crotch.

"AAAaaah!" His moan, filled with agony, accompanied the opening of his arms. I dropped, landing on my feet.

While he clutched himself, his face the color of biscuit dough, I hit him alongside the head with a left hook, then brought my right up to his chin. He staggered.

I had him then but kept pounding. Couldn't let victory get away from me; I might not have another chance. A second or two to get his bearings and we'd be at it again.

I feinted a left to his head and followed it with a hard right to his wind. It brought a moan, and a left to his head rocked him to his heels. My next blow came from down around my knees. It caught him square on the button. His arms dropped to his sides.

His eyes blank, he stepped toward me. I hit him again, my

blow on the same track as the one I'd fired to his chin. He stopped cold and stared, although I knew he couldn't see me. He swayed like a giant tree, then dropped like a patty from a tall cow. He didn't twitch.

I stood, waiting for him to get up but knowing he couldn't. Blood dripped into the dust at my feet, rolling up in little mud balls.

I had not been aware that he'd landed any blows to my face, but he must have, because my right eye was swollen shut. It wasn't what was bleeding. My right hand went to my face and felt a cut under my left eye. Then, looking at my hands, I saw they were cut, with skin peeled back from my knuckles.

The excitement of the fight left me feeling that there had been a buffalo stampede, and each buffalo had taken its turn stomping me. God! I hurt all over.

A glance at the ring of men showed them obviously stunned. Their champion had lost. Every man had been yelling at the top of his voice only a moment before, but they were silent now. Not a man jack among them uttered a sound.

Fatigue engulfed me. I could hardly talk, but I did. "This fight's over. Any of you don't figure it that way, hit the ground stompin'. There's enough left to kick your ass, too."

No one moved. If anyone had stepped into that ring, I don't think I could have lifted a fist.

"I say it's over." Jack Casement stepped into the ring and swung his gaze around it. "I never expected to see it, but Mike's been soundly beaten. You men clean him up and bring him to my car for a drink." He turned to me. "Tenery, you come with me." He grinned. "I figure we can be three drinks ahead of Mike by the time he gets there."

Somewhere, on the way to Casement's car, Adam joined us.

"Mistuh Casement, if you don't mind, I'd sure be beholden to you if you'd let me come along and tend to my partner."

"Come on then, Adam. You can most likely do a better job of it than me."

Casement led us to his sitting room. He and Adam carefully pushed me into a chair. I sat there while Adam found a cloth and started sponging my face with cold water.

Jack poured a water glass full of rye whiskey and handed it to me.

I held it in both hands, not trusting one to do the job, and tilted the glass until it was half empty.

"Damn, but that big bastard can hit," I mumbled when I got my breath back from swallowing the fiery whiskey.

Casement leaned against his bar with an amused smile. "Tenery, you just whipped the toughest sonuvabitch on the Union Pacific."

"Jack, even the thought of fighting him again would make me saddle up and get the hell out of here. He's one tough dude."

"If you didn't leave, I damned sure would," Mike bellowed from the end of the car. He limped the length of the car, his hand outstretched. "I want to shake the hand of the only man who ever whipped me. You're one tough bastard, Chance."

He looked at Casement. "You sure hired yourself a trestle boss, Jack. Me an' my crew'll work our asses off for this man."

Mike turned my hand loose and took the drink Casement handed him.

After one more drink with them, I told Adam to stay, but I was going to find some salt and soak my hands.

"No, suh, I'll get some salt and help you." He shook his head. "Lordy, just don't know what to do with you. All the time in trouble."

My sour look told him what I thought of his remark. "You think I asked for this, you're crazy."

My eyes shifted to Casement. "Thanks for the drink, Jack. I needed it. Mike, meet you at the supply train in the morning. Now, my poor beat-up body needs some rest." I nodded and left.

My hands felt better after soaking them for about an hour, and then I crawled, with a good bit of pain, under my blanket and went to sleep.

chapter

seven

THE NEXT MORNING, Mike and the other foremen gathered their crews and climbed aboard a flatcar, knowing it would be cooler than a boxcar, for our ride to Julesburg.

The men had plenty of room to spread out, but they collected around me. Today, I was one of them. I was still the boss, but to their thinking, I was now the boss by *their* choice, not Casement's nor anybody else's. I had won the right.

Every muscle in my body hurt. I noticed that Mike wasn't moving with much enthusiasm, either.

A twist to settle more comfortably on the wooden surface brought a groan from me. "Next time, Mike, I think I'll charge admission."

He looked at me and grimaced. "Next time, hell; if it looks like I'm gonna get in a screwdy-woody, knock-down, drag-out fight with *you,* pull that six-shooter you're wearing and knock me in the damned head. That way I'll only hurt one place."

My laughter was swallowed by that of the crew.

I lay back, resting on an elbow, and listened to the good-natured banter around me. Soon, the clickety-clack of the wheels over the rails lulled me into other thoughts.

I wondered what the girl on the train was doing and where she might be now. I'd not had a night since seeing her face framed in the window that I hadn't thought of her. I decided then to find her when we finished building the Union Pacific. It might take a long time, but I would find her.

The train slowed, and I roused enough to see we were pulling into Julesburg. When we off-loaded, I called for the men to gather around. "I want you to stay in groups. If you have trouble, gun trouble, with anyone, leave it alone and find me. Yeah," I nodded, "I know it'll be hard to do, but I want all of us to get back.

"I don't want some gambler or gunslick killing you. Let me take care of it. Nobody's gonna question your guts. There are a few things, though, that you're not equipped to handle. Let me take care of those things. All right, go have a good time."

We'd been standing alongside one of the private cars used by the railroad's big bosses. When the men scattered, I gave the car a closer look and saw it was the one that passed Adam and me when we were heading for end-of-track.

Not daring to hope that *she* would still be aboard, I scanned the row of windows. The third window framed her halo of dark hair just as I'd seen her before. My chest felt as though cinched with a tight belt.

I wondered at the strong reaction. What made her different? I'd thought of her often after crawling into my blankets, but had shrugged it off as being a natural reaction to a beautiful woman. Now I knew better.

Discounting her beauty, an attraction I couldn't identify pulled me to her. I had never met her, never been within twenty feet of her, didn't even know her name, but she pulled on me as had no other woman in the world.

I smiled and tipped my hat. She nodded and smiled in return. I turned to walk to the main street.

"How in the jumped-up hell can a man like me meet a woman like her?" I mumbled.

I settled my Colt more comfortably against my thigh and walked on, knowing that if I had to, I'd simply go aboard and introduce myself.

What was she to the general? His wife? His daughter? Hell, I didn't know, but I'd sure as the devil find out.

Julesburg, the same noisy, dirty hellhole that I remembered from a few weeks back, still filled me with disgust. Men going from one saloon to another, from one whorehouse to another, all looking for something. I knew from experience in cow towns, border towns, and mining camps they'd never find what they looked for in a place like this.

They were tough, rough men, but all had left a home somewhere. Many were not here by choice, but by necessity. This was where the money was.

I walked into a couple of saloons and realized quickly that was a bad move. In each of them were some of my men, and without exception, they all wanted to buy me a drink.

"Men," I told those in this last saloon, "a drink with each of you, and my middle name would be Drunk. Wouldn't make it until noon. Gonna wander around some. We'll drink together tonight."

Going back to the street, I loafed along, watching the crowd, smelling the stink, and feeling the din of street noise beating my ears. Damn, for all the enjoyment in this, I might as well be working. For that matter this *was* work.

Seeing a café and thinking a cup of coffee would give me a chance to sit for awhile, I went in. Only five people were there. It was nearly noon, so I decided to eat.

For Julesburg, it wasn't a bad place, and the food was good. There were only two tables of rough-hewn boards. They were long, with benches on each side, and room for about eight people to a side. The floor, probably wet down daily, was hard-packed earth.

I'd eaten and had a huge slice of apple pie sitting in front of me when two people came in, a man and a girl. Even though the light was bad and they were silhouetted against the open door, I knew she was the one from the train.

They came to the table where I stood, hat in hand. I recognized the general, and watched as he seated the young lady.

She wore a summery light blue dress, fitted at the waist

and with a high collar all trimmed with lace. I thought it the most beautiful dress on the most beautiful girl I'd ever seen.

She looked at me, a mischievous twinkle showing in her eyes. "I believe, sir, that we've met three times."

I felt my face flush, but nodded. "That we have, ma'am, although I never expected to see you in the same room with me. I'm Chance Tenery, and you, General, I'm sure you'll not remember it, but we've met, also."

He looked puzzled, but only for a moment. "Ah yes, you're the young Johnny Reb colonel who had pity one miserable rainy day and didn't kill me, even though I was at your mercy." He extended his hand and I shook it. "You seem to know my niece, Miss Betsy Travis."

After shaking hands, we took seats at the table.

"Well, sir, we've met, sort of."

"Oh, Uncle, this is the romantic-looking cowboy I told you about, the one on horseback beside the tracks that day. Surely you remember."

The general cleared his throat. "Oh, oh yes."

He was embarrassed, but I didn't know what to do about it. I figured he'd give Miss Travis hell once he got her back to his car.

"Oh, Uncle, don't be so stodgy." She turned to me. "Uncle's going to tell me when he gets me back to the train that nice young ladies don't introduce themselves to young men."

"And it'll do not one whit of good," the general interjected.

I looked from one of them to the other and smiled slightly. "General, you should know that my mind was already made up to meet your niece some way, even to the point of just walking aboard your car uninvited. You see, she's going to be my bride."

My face felt hot, and I knew I was blushing furiously. If willing it would have made it happen, I'd have evaporated into thin air. I couldn't imagine why I had said such a thing.

An unmistakable gasp told me I'd gotten Miss Travis's attention.

"Why of all the . . ."

"Unmitigated gall?" I asked, finishing her sentence.

I would have thought General Dodge would be on the verge of apoplexy, but I hadn't figured him right. He looked at his niece, leaned back, almost falling off the bench, and laughed until tears came to his eyes.

"J-just bet you think you can do it, too," he choked out the words. "If you do manage it, somehow, you have my deepest sympathy. You don't know what you're asking for."

I looked at him a moment. "Yes, sir, I think I do. There are things that must be done first, though. This railroad must be finished, mine and Miss Travis's ranch built, some serious courting, and getting her consent. We'll be married then. I'll get it done, General. You can stake your life on it."

I didn't mention there was still a man out there who'd killed my brother and would have to pay for it. That was another job to add to the things that must be done.

He sobered. "By God, I'll just bet you will." His voice had no doubt in it.

"Don't I have a dam—uh, darned thing to say about all this?"

Our eyes locked. "Yes, ma'am, but you're gonna have to have time to get used to the idea. Don't want you to give me an answer now that'll have to be taken back later on."

Not giving her a chance to say more, I bid them good-bye and left. This way, she'd think about me. All her thoughts would not be good ones, but she'd think about me, just the same, and some of those thoughts would be in my favor.

Out on the street, I pondered what had happened, shrugged, and knew that, given another chance, it would be the same. I knew it must have come as quite a shock to her, but hell, the only thing I'd ever sneaked up on was an Indian. Miss Travis, I thought, would be hard to sneak up on, so I just said what had to be said straight out.

The fact that she remembered the times we'd seen each other showed more than just a passing interest.

The street was still crowded. I pushed my way past a cluster of people and stopped in front of a saloon. The sound of a ruckus inside got my attention. I went in to see what it was about, thinking it might be some of my men.

There were two men rolling on the floor, punching and gouging. Both were dressed in coveralls and heavy work shoes. There was no doubt they were railroad men. Let them fight, I thought, and turned to leave when a man dressed in a black broadcloth suit fired a shot into the dirt floor by them. They stopped fighting at the sound of the shot, rolled over, and stood.

The man with the gun waved it back and forth at them. "You men want to fight, c'mon," he waved the barrel of the pistol at himself, "c'mon and fight me."

"Hell man, we ain't got no gun, but you put yours down an' me or my buddy here'll fight you."

The gunman shook his head. "No, I'll not put it down. I'm damned tired of you railroad scum coming in here and tearing up my saloon. So you're gonna fight me, gun and all."

"I'm railroad scum, as you call us. If you want to fight somebody, fight me. I have a gun." I stood there ready to draw and kill him if I had to.

The room quieted. I heard tobacco juice ring a spittoon across the room.

The gunman started to turn toward me. He still had his gun in his hand, so I drew mine. "If you turn even a whisker farther, I'm going to blow you to hell, so why don't you holster that gun."

To my surprise, he did just that, then smiled at me, a patronizing twist of his lips to be sure, but still a smile. "Perhaps I was a bit hasty. We need have no trouble here." His gaze traveled around the room. "You men go ahead and have a good time."

"No!" My voice rang loudly in the quiet. "This place is closed to all railroad people. Find somewhere else to drink."

"B-but you can't do that." The man in the black suit stammered.

"The hell I can't, and I'm going to stand outside your door and keep *all* UP people out of here. You'll have to hunt

someone to shoot or threaten with your gun next time."
I cocked my eyebrow at him. "And while you're looking,
see if you can find others to patronize this dump of
yours."

His hands trembled, wanting to reach for that hideout gun
he carried, but he just didn't have the guts.

His place emptied fast, and while backing out the door, I
taunted him once more. "See how much money you make
now, you crooked sonuvabitch."

Good as my word, I stayed outside the saloon for a couple
of hours, told each UP man that showed up not to go in, told
him why, and instructed him to spread the word.

After awhile, when no one even attempted to come in, I
went back to the café and ordered a cup of coffee. Sitting
there, I mulled over the things that had happened since I
first arrived in Julesburg. Aside from meeting the girl I
intended to marry, I'd made three bitter enemies; that Texas
gunslick, Snake Thompson; the Cheyenne, One Hand; and
now the saloon owner; but I'd made more friends than ever
before.

Men came and went, most of them Union Pacific hands.
No women came in. The few who lived here didn't dare
come out on the streets. Julesburg courted only the rough
ones.

The coffee in my cup grew cold. I'd wasted more time
than comfort would allow. I wished the men would get their
fill of rotten whiskey and painted women. I'd already seen
more of it than I wanted.

It would be nice, I thought, to walk down to the tracks
and drop in to visit Betsy. She'd probably throw something
at me, and the general was one of the highest UP officials,
so I stayed in town.

A bench spread across the front of the general store, its
wood surface highly polished from much use. I sat at one
end. A couple of whittlers idled there, but they paid me no
mind.

A small boy rounded the corner of the store, stopped, and
stood looking at me. His gaze traveled from my boots to my

head, but hesitated a moment at the .44 slung from my waist.

"Hello, boy. Who're you?"

"I'm Billy."

"You live here?"

He hesitated a moment. "Yes, sir. Round abouts here. Wherever folks don't throw me out."

I looked closer. He was the dirtiest, skinniest kid I'd ever seen.

"Where are your folks?"

"Got no folks. Sioux killed 'em on the way out here." He said it matter-of-factly, standing as straight as his thin little body would let him.

This little boy had pride. I decided to use care with my words, because if, somehow, I lessened his pride, I would be taking all he had left.

"Come sit by me and let's talk," I said, and moved over to make room.

He backed up to the bench and had to jump to get on it.

He looked up at me, his face serious. "Heered some o' the men talkin', said you wuz one o' the bosses on the railroad."

I nodded. "That's right."

"I could work for you."

Surprised, I said, "You could?"

"Yes, sir. I could carry water to the men and collect buffalo chips fer your fires, and wash pots and pans for the cook, and—and . . ."

"Whoa up there, youngster. You've already put your rope around a whole bunch of work, maybe more'n most could handle."

"I could handle it and more, sir, if you'll take me on. All I would ask would be to be with you. You wouldn't have to pay me nothin'."

I swallowed, and for some reason had trouble doing so. This little boy seemed to embody all the homeless children I'd seen during the war; ragged, hungry . . . hungry for someone to belong to as well as being food hungry. I wanted to put my arm around him and draw him to me.

I looked at him, my eyes narrowed. The chores he'd outlined needed doing. Suddenly I knew I couldn't leave this kid in Julesburg. He was alone, dirty, hungry, no clothes, nobody that gave a damn about him, and winter was not too far off.

"How old are you, boy?"

"Ten."

"Ten, huh? Well what do you know? I was thinking, just yesterday, that when we got to Julesburg I'd have to find me a hardworking youngster about ten years old. I figured I'd have him do the jobs I didn't have time or men to do."

I pulled my pipe from my shirt pocket and filled it with rough-cut tobacco. After putting a lucifer to its end and puffing fire into it, I looked at Billy, frowning. "Now, boy, this job's not an easy one. You'll have to carry your weight."

His face serious, he stared me right in the eyes. "Sir, I wouldn't have it no other way. I always do my part. My pa taught me a man had to do that or he wasn't no good."

"Your pa was right, son." I didn't say more. If I had, I believe I couldn't have held back the tears.

"You got any gear you want to bring with you, Billy? We'll be leaving day after tomorrow, sunup."

"I got what I got on, sir. Are you sayin' you gonna hire me?"

"I surely am, starting now." I stood. "C'mon, we'll go buy you some work clothes, underclothes, the works. We'll have to get you a bath, too, before we go across the street here to eat supper." I looked down at him. "Forgot to ask. Think you could eat some steak and brown gravy with me? I haven't had a bite to eat all day," I lied.

Solemnly, he stared at me. "Yes, sir. Reckon I might handle a little bit to eat, but I ain't got no money."

"Shoo, now, you're working for me. I pay the bills."

Sunshine came into that little boy's face. He reached out and put his hand in mine, trusting me to lead me wherever I went.

Going from the store where we'd outfitted him to the

barbershop so he could take a bath, I looked over the bundles to see his little hand clutching mine. In only a few hours, I'd told my woman I was going to marry her. And not even married, I had a kid to take care of.

chapter
eight

AT BREAKFAST THE next morning, Billy didn't look like the same boy of the night before. He was clean from the skin out and wore new clothes. He'd gotten a haircut, too, although he didn't cotton to the idea much. I explained to him that part of doing his job was to keep himself as clean and neat as conditions allowed.

We had flapjacks and buffalo steak. I had coffee, and Billy had water. He told me his mother never let him drink coffee unless the weather was real cold, and then she put a lot of milk and sugar in it.

"Well, when it gets cold, I reckon we'll go by the same rules. That all right with you?"

"Yes, sir, I'd like that."

Billy attacked that stack of flapjacks as though fearful there would not be another. The night before, he'd eaten as much as I had, only then I'd thought it was because he'd not eaten in awhile. Now, I remembered, boys ate a lot all the time. Some seemed never to get enough. I had been that way.

We were hardly into our breakfast when the general and Miss Travis came in, walked right to our table, and seated themselves next to us. I stood and waited for the general to seat Betsy. I'd started thinking of her as Betsy, although I wouldn't dare call her that to her face. I introduced Billy. He hadn't given me a last name, so I couldn't pass it along.

"Billy's my new hire," I said, hoping the general wouldn't take exception, but he did.

"We have no room for kids at any of the construction sites, and we don't have the budget for them." He looked at Billy, who had grasped my hand and held it tightly as though afraid I would disappear. Once again he'd have no one.

The general cleared his throat and continued. "I might add, it's too dangerous out there, and Indians aren't the only thing to worry about; there's the danger of the job itself."

I squeezed Billy's hand to let him know not to worry. "General, this lad will cost you nothing. I'll take care of any expense he might be. And he will be of help to us."

"No. I'll not permit it."

I felt my face harden and blood rush to my head. I controlled my anger and said, "I'll not leave him here alone. I'll tell Casement when I get back to end-of-track he's one trestle boss short."

Dodge frowned. "What do you mean?"

"Bad as I hate to, I reckon I'll have to quit." I shifted my gaze to Betsy. "Ma'am, I hate to do this. Now it's going to take me longer to fix things so we can be married."

If Betsy had any doubts before, I knew now that she would take me seriously. I had restated my intentions when angry.

Dodge and Betsy sat there, stunned. Neither said anything, but I thought I saw disappointment in Betsy's eyes. She turned to the general. "Uncle, please don't think I'm interfering in your business, but let Mr. Tenery do this. I'm certain he will take care of the boy."

Dodge's face looked as though chiseled from stone; there was no give in him. "No. I'll not have it."

I tugged on Billy's hand. "Come, Billy, we have some traveling to do." I tipped my hat and nodded.

Still holding tightly to my hand, Billy stood and walked out with me.

I went to the edge of the boardwalk and stopped,

wondering what the hell to do now. I looked down at Billy to find him staring up at me. "You gonna take me with you, sir?"

I winked at him. "Well, now, Billy, I'm sure not going to leave you here. You're my friend. I'll not leave you, but I think we'd better think about finding me a job. We'll wait until morning to saddle up, though. I have to find my foremen and let them know what's happened."

That little boy's eyes misted up, and the way he smiled at me made giving up a job to keep him seem a small price.

I searched from one saloon to another, looking for Mike and the other foremen, Billy walking proudly beside me.

Mike spotted me before I saw him. He yelled from the end of the bar, "Hey, Chance, c'mon down. I'll buy you a drink."

"You stay here, son, I'll be back in a minute."

His small hand didn't release its pressure on mine. I looked at him and saw his eyes wide, lips pressed together, and realized that he was terrified that I might leave him for good.

"On second thought, you belong with me." I stepped into the saloon, feeling his hand tightly clutching mine.

At the bar, I declined Mike's offer of a drink, bought a sarsaparilla for Billy, and a beer for me. I explained all that had happened.

"Well I'll be double-damned!" Mike exploded. "Jack Casement might answer to Dodge, but by God, he ain't gonna stand still for this. Jack figgers you as one of the best trestle bosses he's ever had." He shook his head. "No, sir, he ain't gonna stand still for this a'tall."

I grasped Mike's shoulder. "Thanks, Mike, but it's already done. I'll ride to end-of-track with you tomorrow. My horse is out there. I'll get my gear before we head out." I looked down at Billy. "Come on, son, we'll find a place to bed down tonight, and we'll have to find you a horse."

On the way out, I heard Mike bellow for the men to gather around.

On the boardwalk again, I looked up and down the street and decided to head toward the tracks. I hadn't gone far when one of the railroad men stopped me. I didn't recognize him, so I knew he was with another crew.

"You Mr. Tenery?"

"Yes." I nodded. "I'm Chance Tenery."

"Jest wanted to tell you, sir, to be careful. Heared tell that saloon owner, the one you kept from shootin' our men, well, he's done hired somebody to kill you."

He pulled his cap off and swiped sweat from his brow. "Don't let nothin' happen to you, sir. We all kind of taken to you right off, so be careful."

My feelings right then were in a tangle. With me, the boy might get shot. Alone, he'd be back where I found him. Inside me, a cold, hard knot formed, and it pushed angry blood to my head. I knew one damned thing for sure: Billy was staying with me.

I didn't know who or what to look for. A man had been hired to kill me. A shot from an alley would do the job, or some gunslick might challenge me in a saloon or on the street. If it happened to my face, I figured I could take care of myself, but there was no way but caution to defend against an unknown assailant.

I felt a tug on my hand and looked down. The boy looked at me, his eyes wide. "Somebody gonna try to kill you, Mr. Tenery?" He tried to be brave, but I felt the tension in his little hand grasping mine. His voice quavered.

I squatted there on the boardwalk so as to look straight into his eyes. "Billy, don't worry about me. There are those who've tried to kill me before." I smiled, although I didn't feel much like doing it. I spread my arms. "You can see they haven't had much luck so far."

Doubt flickered in his eyes and he cast me a tremulous smile. "Yes, sir, but like that man said, sir, you be careful."

I wanted to reach out and hug him to me, but knew it would embarrass us both, so I patted his shoulder and ran my fingers through his hair. "Good boy. Now, I think we'll find something to read. If we're to be friends, I want you to learn to read real well. It'll make you able to do a lot more things that'll help when you grow up."

"I can read already. Ma an' Pa used to teach me every night by the fire."

"Good, but it's something you can't stop doing, or you might forget how." Seeing he accepted that, I stood and led him toward the general store.

To have him with me every minute was dangerous. A shot meant for me might hit him, and I'd never forgive myself for that. But, what in the name of jumped-up hell could I do with a ten-year-old until we left Julesburg? I pondered that while we looked for a book.

The store had a poor stock, nothing for a kid, so I bought a book by Scott, *Guy Mannering*. I'd read it a couple of times but figured he hadn't.

From wondering what to do with Billy, I settled in on who was gunning for me. I knew that whatever happened, I was not going to jeopardize a child's safety.

"Come, Billy. We're going to see Miss Travis." It was a helluva chance, but a chance I had to take.

A knock on the door at the end of the car brought a darky, dressed in a white waiter's jacket and black trousers.

"Miss Travis in?"

"Yes, suh? Who shall I say is calling?"

"Tell her that Chance Tenery is here, and that it is urgent I see her."

His gaze shifted from me to Billy. He sniffed as though smelling something bad and replied, "Yes, suh. I'll see if she's receiving visitors."

Only a moment passed before Betsy came to the door. "What is it, Mr. Tenery? I thought you had terminated your business with the UP."

"Miss Travis, I need help, need someone to look after Billy for awhile."

Her eyes cool, she looked at me. "And so you came to me."

"Yes, ma'am. You're the only one I know in this town. I wouldn't have bothered you otherwise."

She stared at me a moment longer, then stepped aside. "Come in, Mr. Tenery, and you, too, Billy."

That woman hadn't forgotten the manner in which I'd

expressed my intention of marrying her, and the guard she'd thrown up between us was cold enough to freeze hell a mile. She told us to be seated, then asked for an explanation.

I told her as briefly as I could about the probable gunfight and my fear for Billy.

Her gaze never shifted from mine, and in it there was no give. "Suppose you are killed." I heard her voice catch on the word and realized that her iciness was only a facade. "What will I do with a small boy?"

"Miss Travis," Billy cut in, "you can just push me outtn that there door, and tell me good-bye. I ain't never had nobody since my folks got killed, until Mr. Chance came along. I reckon I won't have nobody after he's gone. I ain't gonna be no trouble to nobody. Just let me stay here till Mr. Chance gets back so he won't worry none."

Betsy frowned. "You're worrying that he'll be concerned, and you don't want him to be?"

"Yes'm. Reckon he's got enough on his mind 'thout that."

Unexpectedly, she reached out, pulled Billy to her, and hugged him. "Bless you, Billy." Still hugging him, she shifted her eyes to me. "Is this trouble something you can't avoid?"

"Well, ma'am, I told Mr. Casement I'd take care of the men. I can't . . . won't run, and I owe Jack Casement. So I'll see this through."

She released Billy, who was red as an Indian. I suppose it had been a long time since a woman had hugged him.

"Mr. Tenery . . ."

"Ma'am, I'd sure take it kindly if you'd call me Chance. I know of no one who puts a handle to my name since I left the military service."

The icy facade behind which she'd been hiding disappeared. She laughed. "All right, mister, but only if you'll call me Betsy."

It didn't seem right, what with my not knowing her any longer than I had. I grinned. "Yes, ma'am, it'll be an honor."

She stood. "You go take care of your business." She held out her hand like a man to shake hands with me. "And," her face sober, she added, "don't worry about Billy. I won't push him out the door."

I bowed above her hand and kissed it. I don't know why, but for some reason, it seemed the thing to do.

Our eyes locked. Neither of us spoke for a long moment. "Betsy, I appreciate this. I'll get back as soon as I can, but I'll say honestly that I don't know how long it will take. I don't even know who's hunting me." I realized that I still held her hand and released it. She had not tried to pull it from my grasp.

With high color in her cheeks, she said, "I know. Don't worry."

Stepping out the door, I couldn't help a parting shot. "Betsy, I think it will only be a year until I come courting. That's plenty of time for you to think on it."

Her face flushed even more. I didn't know whether it was from anger or embarrassment. So, not waiting for a scathing remark, I hurried down the steps.

Walking toward town, I wondered where General Dodge had been, then thought that he must have been at the work site. I pondered the way Billy had responded to Betsy's initial hostility, probably not realizing that it had been aimed at me. That little boy would make quite a man.

The sky had clouded over while I talked with Betsy. Good; we could stand some rain. I continually cast glances down the street and into the spaces between stores for anyone who might have a weapon ready to fire at me. I didn't really expect to see anyone. I didn't think they'd be that obvious.

The saloon I'd staked out the day before was on my left. On impulse, I turned toward it and went in.

It took only a glance to see everyone in the room. There were three people present. None of them were UP personnel. The man with whom I'd had trouble was behind the bar.

"Aren't you satisfied you've ruined me? This is all the business I've had in two days."

"You asked for it." I walked to the end of the bar so as to keep the room in front of me, then motioned the bartender to me and said quietly, "Word has it you've hired someone to kill me."

"No, I . . ."

"Don't lie to me, you sonuvabitch," I ground out. "Whoever you hired is going to have a helluva time collecting from a corpse."

"Wh-what you mean?" he squeaked. "Y-you can't do this."

"The hell I can't." Anger rode me with Spanish spurs. I was ready to shoot him where he stood. I inhaled, slowly, forcing myself to calm down. I couldn't shoot any man in cold blood. My anger didn't subside, it just changed from white hot fury to a cold, calculating one.

The three men at the table stood and started to spread out. "You men separate any farther and I'll drop you where you stand."

They stopped, dead still. My gun, still in its holster, gave them an edge, they being three to one. I knew they wondered if I could outdraw them, and if I did, who I'd shoot first. They were certainly wondering at the fact that I wasn't afraid of them.

"In case you're wondering," I smiled grimly, "the first move any of you make I'll kill all three, so stop wondering which of you it'll be. I'm not partial." I looked directly at the bartender and said, "And after I take care of them, I will put a slug through each button of your shirt pockets."

They stood there, frozen.

"Now, tell me who you hired to come gunning for me."

"I didn't—"

"One more chance. Whether you draw or not, you'll be so full of holes you'll leak syrup at forty below."

His face twisted into that sickening smile I remembered from before, and then he reached for his gun. His .44 came from somewhere under his coat and swung toward me.

I palmed my .44 and put two rounds into him, one in his brisket and the other in the middle of his forehead. I turned my gun on the three standing by the table. None of them had moved. Their hands were held shoulder high.

"All right, so I lied to him about where I'd put my slugs."

"Don't shoot, mister. We ain't buying chips in this game."

I held them with my gaze. "I don't know who he hired, but I'm sure you do, so find him and tell him he hasn't got a payday coming." I motioned toward their gun belts. "Now, unbuckle those and let them drop to the floor."

I watched the gun belts hit the floor, and told them to walk out ahead of me.

On the boardwalk, I let them go. The man who had been hired to gun me down was still a mystery, and if he'd taken advance money from the saloon owner, he would still come after me. The boardwalks and all in between was filled with people. I stepped off into the dust and headed down the street. Staying in the crowd was no problem, and that was good. I didn't think the gunman hired to kill me would be fool enough to fire into that many people.

I thought I'd walk until time for supper, then I'd go back to the railcar and get Billy. I didn't worry about the man I'd killed. *Somebody* would bury him.

chapter
nine

BETSY LOOKED THROUGH the window and watched Chance walk away. Unconsciously, she brought the hand he'd kissed to her face and pressed the back of it to her cheek. Then she held it out and looked at it, expecting to see the brand of his lips there, almost hoping she would. She felt guilty. A nice girl wasn't supposed to have such thoughts.

Billy stood beside her. Glancing at him, she saw him blink hard and squeeze his eyes shut. She knew he did it to keep back tears.

"He'll be all right, Billy." She put her hand on the boy's shoulder, pulled him closer, and was surprised he didn't resist. Instead, he put his arm around her waist.

"Yes'm, I s'pose he will. I think I'd just want to die if somethin' happened to him." He looked up at her. "Miss Betsy, why don't you like Mister Chance?"

Surprised, she thought a minute before answering. "Billy, what makes you think I don't like him?"

"Well, uh, the way you looked at him when he brung me for you to look after. Yore eyes, Miss Betsy, well they wuz cold as winter winds. You jest didn't look friendly at him a'tall."

She studied him a moment and again looked out the window. "Billy, grown-ups aren't as honest with each other as you young folks. I do believe, though, that Mr. Chance says and does what he thinks is right. He takes most people by surprise, even makes some angry. We counter by acting and saying things we don't mean so he won't know how we really feel."

He looked puzzled. "Golly, ma'am, why'd you want to do somethin' like that?"

She smiled, knowing it was bittersweet. "I guess we can't stand too much happiness. Perhaps we're afraid if we get it, we'll lose it."

"Well gollee, Miss Betsy. Looks to me like if you could have happiness, you'd jest naturally be glad an' never let go of it. I reckon if Mr. Chance had it, he'd fight like an old he coon 'fore he'd turn loose."

"Yes, I think you're right. I think Mr. Chance would fight for anything he wanted. As for children, well, for some reason we grown-ups aren't as honest with each other as they are." She rumpled his hair.

They watched until Chance disappeared into the crowd. "Come. Mr. Chance left a book for you to read. You start it, and if you have any questions, I'll try to answer them."

Betsy went to the kitchen, an efficient little cubbyhole with a place for everything. She poured herself a cup of coffee and brought Billy a glass of milk. She sat across from him, leaned back, and closed her eyes.

She did admire Chance. He was bold, and she sensed his arrogance was brought on by urgency. He was the most handsome man she'd ever seen: tall, with blue eyes and black hair, wide shoulders, and narrow hips.

Just looking at him stirred feelings she'd never experienced. Looking at him made her feel warm all over. At first glimpse, her breath had caught in her throat, and she'd wanted to feel his hard body pressed to hers. She'd wanted his lips on hers.

She tried to deny these feelings, opened her eyes, and sat bolt upright. What in the world was she doing, sitting here daydreaming about a man she'd known only two days? And such shameful thoughts.

She leaned back again and closed her eyes, allowing a slight smile. *But no one else knows, and I guess I'm a hussy 'cause I like my thoughts. Heaven forbid that Chance should find out.*

Then she wondered if he really meant to try to marry her, as preposterous as it seemed. By his own admission, he had nothing to offer a bride, but that, somehow, didn't bother her. She shook her head, thinking he'd probably given her the same blarney he gave to all women. He couldn't possibly mean what he said.

She drew a mental image of his eyes and thought they didn't look like those of a man who said anything but what he meant.

Betsy toyed with the idea that maybe he did intend to marry her, but she refused to take him seriously. What man would walk up to a woman he scarcely knew and express such an intention? She knew the answer to that question as soon as she posed it; Chance Tenery would. Although she tried to cast her arguments aside, she hugged her answers tightly inside, and her smile broadened. The door at the end of the car opened and closed, and she looked up to see her uncle. She heard him tell Tom to bring him something cold to drink, and he walked into the sitting room.

Dodge looked at Billy. His face clouded over like a thunderhead. "What's the boy doing here?"

"Mr. Tenery had some railroad business to attend to, something he'd promised Jack Casement, and he had nowhere to leave Billy while finishing the job." She looked at her uncle, knowing her voice had an edge to it. She knew her expression was stormy. "As far as I know, he hasn't changed his mind about leaving."

Dodge stood there a moment, staring at her. Betsy knew the war going on inside him for he was a stubborn man, but a fair one. And she knew also that he didn't want Chance to quit.

His frown deepened. He cleared his throat. "Well, I suppose he can stay until Tenery gets back. How long's this business of his going to take?"

Her chin came up, and her face set into stubborn lines. "I don't know, but however long it takes, I intend to care for the boy."

Dodge looked at her a moment longer, apparently realizing that to argue with her would be futile. They had butted heads before, and he seldom won. She knew it unfair to take advantage of his affection, but in this case, she'd do whatever was necessary.

"Humph," he snorted. "Well, if you're set on him staying, get him something to eat. Don't you know boys are always hungry?"

Betsy threw her arms around Dodge's neck and kissed him on his cheek. "Oh, Uncle, thank you for being an old softy."

He grimaced. "Only where you're concerned, little one, only where you're concerned. Now, you two get on with what you were doing. I'm going to have a cigar and a drink."

Dodge eased tiredly into his favorite chair and removed a cigar from the humidor at his side.

Betsy turned to ask Billy if he wanted something to eat. He wasn't in the room. She searched the rest of the car, bedrooms, kitchen, and bathroom, knowing she'd not find him. Tears welled up so she had trouble seeing. The spat with her uncle had torn at the little boy's pride. She ran to the steps while her gaze searched the street toward town. No Billy.

Betsy jumped to the ground and looked down the length of the train. She stooped to check the other side and saw no sign of him. Then she looked under the general's car and saw Billy's small form sitting on the nearest rail. His face set, proud and determined, he stared back at her.

"Come, Billy, let's go back in the car and get something to eat."

"No, ma'am. Reckon I'll wait here for Mr. Chance. Ain't gonna put you and your uncle out none."

Betsy walked to where he sat, crawled under the car, and sat on the track at his side. She put her arms around his shoulders. "Billy, Uncle didn't mean that you were in our way. He's a stubborn man, and I know it seemed to him that Mr. Chance and I were bucking him. After I talked to him, I think he believed we didn't mean to disobey his orders.

Matter of fact, he likes you. Won't you come with me? I really wish you would."

"No, ma'am, reckon I can sit here and watch for Mr. Chance just as well as from up there."

Cinders crunched and they both glanced up to see the general swing off the steps.

"Here we are, Uncle."

Dodge bent to peer under the car. "What are you doing under there?"

"Billy thinks he's putting us out and is in our way, so he says he'll wait here for Chance."

Dodge glanced at her. "'Chance,' is it. Hmmm. Son, sometimes I act like an old bull; don't get upset when I act like that. I talk when I should be listening, and up there in the car awhile ago was one of those times. Come now, forgive me."

Billy looked at him wide-eyed. "Sir, there ain't nothin' to forgive. I wuz there, an' I wuzn't doin' nothin' to earn my keep, so reckon I had no right to be there. Reckon I'll just wait here for Mr. Chance."

Dodge frowned and scratched his head. "Yep, I suppose you're right. Know most of us men like to earn our keep. What would you think if I gave you a job until Mr. Chance comes for you? I think Tom could use a little help, don't you?"

"Yes, sir, reckon he could." Billy's face brightened. "Does this mean Mr. Chance can take me out to the trestle?"

Dodge shook his head, frowning. "No, son, it doesn't. It's just too dangerous out there for a small boy."

The sun left Billy's face. "Reckon I'll stay here then, till my friend comes back." He looked at Betsy. "I promised I'd be here, and I will. I ain't leavin' till he shows up."

Betsy's eyes locked with Dodge's. He shook his head. "He means it. Why don't you go aboard and have Tom make sandwiches? Bring them back, and we'll sit here and have lunch." He chuckled. "Won't be the first time I sat in the shade under a car and ate."

Betsy crawled from under the car, her thoughts stormy. Why, she wondered, were men so damned stubborn?

When she stood on the top step, she turned and looked toward town, hoping to see Chance returning. Instead, she saw Mike and the other two foremen followed by the trestle crew walking—no, marching—toward the car.

Betsy watched as the general crawled from under the car and turned to look from his approaching men to Billy. "Stay here, Billy, I think those men want to see me." He walked out to meet them.

When they were close enough, Betsy saw that every face was set in hard lines, tight jawed. She listened.

"You men looking for me?" the general growled.

Without preamble, Mike answered. "General, we hear you fired Tenery. Any truth to it?"

Betsy saw her uncle's hands, folded behind him, clasp into fists. She knew he held a tight rein on his temper and was glad. It wouldn't do for all of them to be angry. Every man he faced was riding a hair trigger. "No. I didn't fire Tenery. He quit."

"Same as fired 'im. That little feller ain't gonna hurt nothin' out there. They ain't a man jack o' us what won't be looking out for him."

Dodge's fists opened and clutched tighter. Betsy had seen these signs before. His temper stretched thinner. "You men trying to tell me how to run my railroad?"

"No, sir, by God we ain't. It's just that Tenery had done killed one man in this hellhole doin' what Mr. Casement told him to do. We reckon he deserves more consideration than you're showin' 'im."

A long silence followed Mike's words. Betsy gulped, trying to swallow the knot of fear in her throat. She heard Dodge ask the question she wanted to ask, but feared the answer. "He killed a man? Is he all right?"

"He's all right. Don't figure there's anybody in this town big enough to hurt 'im, less'n they got him from behind. He's too careful a man to let that happen." Betsy sighed, rooted to the top step.

"Where is he?" Dodge asked. Betsy saw that his hands were hanging at his sides now, but he leaned toward the men and she knew he understood and feared that Chance might be hunted down and killed at any time.

Mike glanced over his shoulder and looked down the street. "Don't know. The man he killed hired another to kill him, but Chance figures the one hired to do the job has already been paid and will still try. So he's makin' hisself available."

"Mike, Jake, Bill, take your men back to town. Spread the word in every whorehouse and saloon that if they let anybody, and I mean *any damn body,* lay a scratch on Tenery, we'll tear every rotten board of this cesspool to the ground. We'll break every bottle of watered-down whiskey, and then we'll throw every one of them, including women, in boxcars, lock the doors, and ship them back to Council Bluffs."

The men turned toward town. "Hold up a minute. I'll get my gun. I'm going with you." Dodge ran to the steps. As he stepped aboard, Betsy heard Mike yell for the men to draw ax handles from the supply car.

Betsy followed her uncle into the car.

"I hope I've not unleashed a mob," he said. "If they start tearing the town apart, every railroad man there will join in. I'll play hell stopping them once they start." He frenziedly buckled on his gun. "I'd better be there to lead them. I might be the only one able to hold a tight rein on them."

Before leaving, he yelled for Betsy to get Billy aboard and stay there until he got back.

She walked back to Billy and coaxed him from under the car. "Come, I'll make sandwiches. We'll eat while we wait to hear from uncle."

chapter

ten

I WALKED THE length of the street twice and wondered what good it did. I could walk this town until Christmas and might be no closer to the identity of the hired killer.

My mind kept slipping back to Billy. There were many like him in this war-torn nation. I couldn't help them all, but if I took just one and helped him to manhood, it would be a start. There were others doing the same thing. Like my father told me, it takes the first step to begin a journey.

I thrust Billy and Betsy from my mind. To think of anything other than the one who meant to kill me would only help him get his job done. I didn't intend to help.

I ambled along, passed a couple of saloons, and walked into Rose's House of Pleasure. What did I expect to find in here? Maybe the gunman had a woman; most men who hung out in towns like Julesburg did. I asked to see the madam.

"You wanted to see me?"

Surprised at the soft-spoken words, I removed my hat, and nodded. "Yes, ma'am, if you're the proprietor here."

"I am."

I guessed her at about forty years of age, and except for too much face paint, I'd say she was pretty.

"Ma'am, I'm not here for service. I want to ask something of you. Don't know how you'll take it, though."

She smiled, but I saw that she'd raised a wall between us. "Wouldn't do you any good if you wanted *me,* but I'll be happy to steer you to a woman willing and able. As to how I take what you ask, I don't suppose we'll know until you ask, will we?"

A wry smile creased my lips. "You're right, of course. Well, here it is. Someone's been hired to kill me. I have no idea who, and I thought, perhaps, you'd be kind enough to try and find out if your girls might know anything."

"Why come to me?"

"I know you have no reason to help me or even believe me, but I'm just trying to cover every possibility of finding out. Thought you might help."

Her gaze traveled my full length and registered approval. "Hmmm, you're one handsome dude. Be a shame to waste all that man to a bullet."

She was trying to throw me off-balance, but despite knowing her reason, I felt my face redden and turn hot. "Ma'am, you've already told me that you didn't want a man, and I told you that I wasn't looking for a woman. I asked for your help. If you will not provide it, I'll not trouble you further." I turned toward the door and said as I stepped toward it, "Don't know about my being handsome, but I do know I'm no dude, and think you do, too."

Before I could open the door, she placed her hand on my arm. Her face showed no expression. "No, you're no dude." She played a mental poker game with me, still trying to make up her mind whether to buy chips in this game. I could almost see the cogs turning. If she made a friend of me, perhaps I could help her somewhere down the line.

Her eyelids lowered, shading her eyes, so there was no chance to try to read her thoughts. "Why should I help you? There are two categories of people here I can't count as friends: the law and the railroad bigwigs. You're no lawman, but you are one of the rail bosses."

Surprised that she knew I worked for the railroad, I told her, "No. I'm not. I no longer work for the railroad. Fact is, as soon as I find who's hunting me, I'm leaving, heading for Cheyenne."

She studied me, her gaze that of a cold, calculating businesswoman. She still tried to decide whether she could trust me.

I wondered how she knew I had worked for the railroad, but I understood the distrust. The law or the UP could shut her down in a minute, and she'd not be able to go into business in any other end-of-track town. If she knew anything and told me she would be putting herself squarely in the middle if the gunman found out.

"Is your heading for Cheyenne supposed to mean something? You could be going out there to set things up for the UP. I only have your word that you no longer work for the railroad, and I can't think of any reason why a man would give up a good-paying job to go wandering again."

"Yeah." I rubbed my jaw, studying her. I had no reason to think she'd have a soft spot in her heart for homeless kids. I told her about Billy anyway and that Dodge refused to let me take him to the work site. As I talked, I thought I saw the hard facade she showed the world breaking down. At one point, I was certain I saw moisture in her eyes. Her face took on that frozen look again. I thought I'd lost.

"All right, so you took on the job of raising a kid. Is that supposed to engender trust in you?"

My face hardened. "No, ma'am. You asked why I quit the railroad, and I told you."

She made up her mind. It was like reading a book; her eyelids lifted, she looked straight at me, and a resigned smile flitted across her lips. "Come, we'll go in my room where we can talk."

I hesitated.

"Oh c'mon, handsome. You can keep your clothes on." She cast me a calculating glance. "I think, though, it'd be interesting if you didn't." She laughed. I realized she was trying to get my goat and had almost succeeded.

Following her into the room, mild surprise flooded me when I saw it was nicely furnished. A closer look at her made me think she'd probably been a proper lady in some other place and at some other time. It was hell, the things the war had done to people, but the strong survived and fought their way back. I would not deal out the possibility of someday finding her in a proper lady's role again.

She handed me a drink. "Sit down." Her voice sounded like the businesswoman I'd first met. "I can't say that I know anything, but I'll tell you what I've heard and what I've seen, although it isn't much. This has to be between us. If it got out that I told you anything, it could get me killed."

"Whatever it is, it's more than I have now, and I assure you I'm not a talker."

She stuck out her hand. "Call me Charlotte."

I cocked an eyebrow and smiled, taking her hand. "Somehow I thought you'd be Rose. Well, Charlotte's a mouthful. How about Lottie?"

"I'd like that. My friends and family called me Lottie a long time ago." Sadness crossed her face. "Rose got the lung fever and died. I took over her business."

"All right, Lottie, let's hear it." I tossed off my drink. It was good whiskey. She motioned toward the bottle, but I shook my head. "One's enough. Thanks, anyway. And, if you're of a mind to, call me Chance."

"I know who you are. Knew you when you came in." She crossed her legs.

She dressed fashionably and modestly. Nothing about her fitted my picture of a madam.

She continued. "You became well-known when you helped the big Negro man and broke Snake Thompson's jaw."

"I wouldn't think a fistfight would be noticed in Julesburg."

"You'd be surprised how efficient our grapevine works in this town."

She described seven men in town who she thought would take money for any kind of job: murder, robbery, anything. Three were from Texas, which included Thompson, and the other four were from Kansas and Missouri; she thought those four had probably ridden with Quantrill.

She spread her hands and shook her head. "That's all I know."

"Lottie, thanks. I'll not take up any more of your time.

Maybe I can do something for you someday. You're carrying my IOU, and I always pay my debts. So, if you need anything, send for me. I'll come."

She turned a crooked smile on me. "Yeah, maybe someday you'll be lonesome enough and with an itch in the right place, to come see one of my girls." She sobered. "Really though, I'll probably move this operation to Cheyenne when the track reaches that far, so come see me. I'll buy you a drink."

With a nod, I said, "You can bet on it."

I left thinking she'd make a helluva friend and knowing she'd be just as good a poker player.

Stops in other houses got me no more information. I'd not seen any of my former crew in an hour. *What the hell's going on*, I wondered. *Maybe they're all broke, or maybe they're bedded down with some women. Yeah, bet that's it.*

At the far end of town, away from the tracks, I went in another saloon, the shabbiest one I'd seen. A glance showed a sparse crowd, mostly railroad men. Under the circumstances, I kept the whole room under my gaze while walking to the bar, a wide plank laid across two barrels. I asked for a beer, "But only if it's cold," I added.

The bartender raked me with piglike eyes buried in a tub of lard. He looked like he wanted to put out a smart answer, but he looked at the tied-down .44 against my thigh and seemed to think better. He turned to the keg and drew a beer. I noticed that two of the men I'd seen attacking Adam were sitting at a back table, and they were giving me their undivided attention. I mentally shrugged. I'd finished my business with them when I broke Snake Thompson's jaw, but being careful, I moved my beer from my right to my left hand.

"You scum see something that interests you?"

The hatchet-faced one squinted and stared at me. "It's a free country. I'll look any goddamned place I want." He pushed his chair back.

"Unless you got business you can't handle sitting down, stay where you are."

Hatchet Face stood abruptly, knocking his chair over. The

short, blocky one hadn't moved. "You ain't tellin' me what to do. Who the hell you think you are?"

"Just trying to do you a favor, bucko, trying to keep you alive."

"You ain't gonna be around long, anyhow. You gonna be buzzard bait by sundown."

"Goddammit, sit down and shut up," the stumpy one said and pulled on Hatchet's shirt.

I felt myself go still inside. If they figured I'd be dead by sundown, they knew who would do it.

"You talk too sonuvabitching much," the stumpy one growled deep in his throat, but I heard him.

I'd never have a better chance than now to find out who was gunning for me, so I pushed. Maybe they'd spill something. A glance to the side showed me the bartender, his hands flat on the bar.

"I ain't buyin' chips in no shootin'," he said.

"Now, I'd say you're a man with a lot of sense," I replied. My gaze had already returned to the two men at the table. "You said something about me being turned into buzzard bait? You figure to be the one to do it?"

"Aw, he wuz jest jokin'," Stumpy mumbled.

"No. Don't reckon that's a joking matter." I looked directly at Hatchet Face. "Stand up. Let's see if you can cut my demise short of sundown."

I didn't think he was the one hired to come after me, but maybe he would let it slip, or I could force it from him. "When you get out of that chair, don't make any sudden moves. I'm a right nervous man. I wouldn't want to kill you before you had a chance to draw."

He slowly stood, his hands wide of his side.

"Looks like it's you and me, bucko. You going to try buying the pot, or are you throwing in your hand?"

Hatchet Face, seeing that I stood ready and seemingly unafraid of him, hesitated.

"I ain't lookin' for no trouble with you. You brung it to me." Hatchet's voice squeaked, higher than the last time he spoke.

I nodded. "You bet I brought it to you. Way I have it

figured, your partner, the one whose jaw I broke, has been hired to kill me. I want you to take him a message, if I don't decide to let Stumpy there do it. In that case, I can't see any reason for you to go on taking up space."

"I ain't no damned messenger boy," he growled. "Besides, that dumb bastard paid Snake to do what he wuz gonna do for free." He realized he'd said too much and clamped his jaws shut.

"You'll do as I say, or I'll break both your goddamned kneecaps." Anger fed into my voice, despite my effort to control it.

Hatchet stood there, his trembling hands held far from his body.

"Now, you, too, Stumpy. With your left hands, unbuckle your gun belts, easy like, or my nerves will likely get the best of me."

Pure contempt welled bitterness into my throat. Any man too cowardly to back his own play was no more than human garbage. Their hands trembled while they followed my command. Their guns made a thunk against the floor and they turned and hurried from the saloon like scalded cats.

Even though I now knew who had been hired to kill me, I had no idea where he was or where he'd make his play.

Four men filed through the door. Dodge stood just inside with Mike and two other men. Each carried an ax handle except Dodge; he had a holstered six-shooter hanging from his belt. Dodge smiled, a question showing behind it.

"You push pretty hard, don't you? I heard it all and saw most of it." I kept quiet and stood looking at him, keeping my face devoid of expression.

He continued, "You weren't the same man as that proud young colonel who walked away from me on the battlefield that day. You had gentleness in you then."

I stared at him only a moment longer. "Think what you like," I said, and turned to look at Mike.

"Were those two the ones?" Mike asked.

"No. If they were, I'd have killed them." My voice sounded flat, even to my ears. "But they know who is the one. They'll get my message to him."

"Why don't you just leave town?" Dodge asked.

"Well, General," I drawled, "I figure if a man's got trouble, the sooner he faces it, the sooner he can quit worrying about it. Would you leave town? Would you ride out and look over your shoulder the rest of your life?" I shook my head. "That's not my way or yours, either."

"Give these men a beer," Dodge said to the bartender, "and bring a couple to the table over there."

"Come," he said to me, "let's sit down. I want to talk to you about your job."

"I have no job."

"The hell you don't. You've got a job if I have to have your whole crew whip your ass. Now, let's talk."

Behind me, I heard Mike say, "You ain't gettin' me in no damned fight with Tenery again."

I felt a crooked smile twist my lips.

chapter

eleven

I FOLLOWED DODGE to a table, sat down, and waited for the bartender to bring our beers. While waiting, I packed my pipe and lit it.

"You know your job is still there. Your men show you a degree of loyalty I've seldom, if ever, seen. I believe they would follow you to hell. And, every bit as important, Jack Casement swears by you. So why don't you reconsider?"

Buying time, I puffed on my pipe. I wanted this job. In fact, I needed it to reach my goals before becoming an old man. I wanted a home to take Betsy to and a place to raise Billy. But the conditions I'd spiked out in the café were still the only ones I could see that made sense.

Billy's firm little grip on my hand had told me the fear he carried of once again having nothing. I would not, could not, abandon him.

I looked at Dodge. "You saying I can take the boy with me to the site?"

Dodge's face flushed. "No. I'm not saying that at all. What I'm saying is that there may be some alternative."

"Don't see that changes anything."

"Chance, don't be so damned stubborn. It's dangerous out there."

"General, I'm willing to listen, but I don't see any way other than keeping the boy with me."

Dodge frowned and took a couple swallows of his drink. "I've given this some thought. In the next day or two, I'll be headed for Cheyenne to hook up with my survey crew again. We'll be working west, up toward South Pass, and we'll be gone a pretty good while."

He leaned toward me, resting his elbows on the table. "Now, here's what I came up with. Betsy's going to be alone and would probably appreciate company. Why not leave the boy with her when you're at the construction site?"

Hope surged in my chest. On the surface, it sounded like a good, logical solution, but the key players were not sitting at this table. If both of them agreed to Dodge's proposal— *both* of them—then I could agree. Besides, it would give me an excuse to see Betsy every time I came to town.

"Sounds too easy, General. I'm willing to give it a try, though." I added, "But both of them are going to have to agree. If not, I'll take Billy and ride."

Dodge downed his beer, waved for another, and told the fat bartender to keep Mike and the other two men supplied. "Tenery, what's that kid to you? Why did you take him in?"

I had thought about that a lot, and offered myself many reasons, but wasn't sure any of them were the real ones. Maybe all of them together weren't. Perhaps, if I said them out where someone listened, it would help.

"General, I've covered a lot of territory since the war. Much of it left a bad taste in my mouth. I've seen kids from both North and South without families. When I went home, even though I am a grown man, I felt deserted with both Mama and Papa gone. I wanted to sit right down on an old log and cry."

The bartender placed two beers in front of us. "Well, I got to thinking; if a grown man felt that way, how must those little ragamuffin kids feel?

"When I first saw Billy, he asked me for a job. I couldn't turn away from him. I took on the task of raising that little boy right then, and I'll get it done."

I leaned forward and tapped on the table. "And somehow, General, I'm already getting more than I'm giving. He has a home with me as long as he wants it."

"Even at the price of giving up a damned good job?"

"Yes, sir. Even at that price, and that price is more than you can imagine. It'll mean that marrying Betsy and being able to provide for her will take longer."

His smile reflected puzzlement. "I haven't been real sure until now that you really meant your intent to marry her. You're not just whistling Dixie, are you?"

I tried, but I couldn't keep from breaking into a big grin. "Don't ever doubt me when I make a statement of that importance. Yes, sir, I sure do mean it. It might be an uphill fight all the way, but that is something I'm going to do."

He tossed down the rest of his drink. "Let's go back to my car. We'll talk to them about this." I suppose he read the puzzlement in my expression. "What's the matter?"

I grinned ruefully. "Somehow, I suppose I thought you'd raise Cain, protesting that you would see me in hell before you let Betsy and me marry."

He frowned, but he looked at me straight-on. "Tenery, Betsy's folks died some time ago, and I took on the job." He shook his head. "No, not job, that's not the word. I took on the pleasure of raising her. She has a good head on those pretty shoulders. If she sees something in you that's worthwhile, and you can convince her to say yes, then I'll guaran-damn-tee you I'll not stand in the way." He chuckled. "I wouldn't dare."

He said again, "Let's go talk to them."

"No. I'd just as soon you went on ahead. Walking with me might get your breathing stopped permanently. Go ahead, sir, I'll be along after awhile."

"Stop my breathing? What about your breathing? You're the one trying to get himself killed. No. Damned if I'll leave in order to keep my hide safe. We came out here to make sure you were all right, and we're going to do just that."

"We? General, who's we?"

"Your whole damned trestle crew is patrolling this town right now, Tenery. They're threatening everyone they see that they'd better leave you alone, or they'll take this town apart."

I turned away from him so he'd not see how much his

words affected me. I tried to swallow the lump in my throat without much success, and a deep breath didn't help much, either. How could I ever think of leaving these men? But I knew I would if I had to make a choice between them and Billy.

"You go on back," I said quietly. "I know who's been hired to kill me. I don't think he'd be fool enough to try it in town, in full daylight. Besides, I'm not sure Snake Thompson's a back shooter. I think I can handle him head-on."

I walked to the bar and told Mike to round up the men before something set them off. We didn't want to tear up a town unless we had a good reason, and nothing had happened yet to justify it.

Dodge and Mike grumped and growled, but they left. I stayed behind long enough for them to put some distance between us before I followed.

I had not walked a block before I saw Betsy and Billy, talking to the general. As I walked up, I heard Dodge tell Billy, "See, son, there he is and he's all right." He glanced at Betsy. *"Now* shall we go back to the car?"

At her nod, we turned toward the tracks and almost bumped into Lottie, devoid of face paint. She really was a pretty woman. I tipped my hat. "Afternoon, Lottie."

She nodded. "Afternoon, Mr. Tenery." She tried to walk around us.

"Oh, Lottie, I'd like you to meet General Dodge, his niece, Miss Betsy Travis, and my buddy here, Master Billy." I looked at Dodge and Betsy. "This is Miss Lottie, uh, I'm afraid I didn't listen very well. What is your last name, Lottie?"

Her smile was almost cynical. She covered it with a laugh. "Probably because I didn't offer it, but, yes, I'm Charlotte McKinsey." Her voice, genteel and well-educated, had nothing of the madam in it.

I couldn't read her thoughts. With a very slight curtsy, she said, "Nice seeing you again, Chance." She nodded to Dodge and Betsy, ruffled Billy's hair, and walked away.

Betsy's smile looked forced. "An old," she emphasized the word *old*, "girlfriend, Chance?"

I couldn't keep from grinning. "No, ma'am, she's a right new acquaintance. I'll tell you about her later."

We were only a short distance from Dodge's car. After making certain that Mike gathered our ax-handle-carrying crew and got them off the street, we walked the rest of the way in silence. As a matter of fact, Betsy's attitude was downright chilly.

Although I felt guilty, I was mighty happy about the way Betsy acted. To my way of thinking, if she didn't care just a little for me, she wouldn't give a damn about how many women I knew, and she sure wasn't elated about Lottie being a friend. There was no way she could tell that Lottie ran a houseful of shady ladies. For that matter, Lottie dressed as well as and looked like any other upstanding pretty lady of the town.

Helping Betsy mount the steps to Dodge's car, I hid a very satisfied smile.

chapter
twelve

On the platform before entering the car, I whispered to Betsy, "If you disagree with what the general says, please don't say so in front of Billy."

Her glance anything but reassuring, she nodded.

On the way through the kitchen area, Dodge told Tom to make a pot of coffee. After all of us were seated except Dodge, he stood in the middle of the floor, holding his hands behind his back like a politician ready to address Congress.

He cleared his throat. "I'm heading back to the survey crew in a couple of days." He looked at Betsy. "You'll have to stay here all *alone.*"

Frowning, she stared back at him. "Well, la-di-da, isn't that unusual?" she chirped. Then, with a look that said, *Don't flimflam me, Uncle. I'm onto your little game,* she nodded. "All right, you're steering your engine somewhere, so let us all know where."

"Why do you always think I'm trying to put something over on you?" Dodge asked, but his red face said he knew she could read him like a book. "Oh hel—uh, all right, yeah, I've got something in mind, something I've given a lot of thought and want to see what you think of it. I've already tried it on Chance."

I felt Billy scrunch up closer to me as though he knew

something affecting him was about to be proposed and was fearful of it.

My arm around his shoulders, I tightened it to reassure him. He looked up at me with trust in his eyes, making me feel like a turncoat. I almost called the whole thing off, but a glance at Betsy changed my mind.

I felt like a bear in a trap. I stood to lose everything, even the chance to make a home for Billy, if this didn't work out.

"All right, let's hear it." Betsy's words came out flat, without promise of agreement, as though she braced herself against whatever came.

"Well, we, no, *I* thought maybe, as lonesome as you get when I'm gone, that Billy could be a lot of company for you." Dodge's words tumbled over each other, obviously trying to get the whole idea out before she could veto it. He continued, "I thought if you'd take care of Billy, Chance could continue working for us and could come see Billy when his crew comes to town."

Betsy didn't give an inch. She smiled that chilly smile she'd given me when I introduced Lottie. *"And,"* she pinned Dodge with a no-slack gaze, "you wouldn't have to lose face by backing down on your word that Billy couldn't go to the job site with Chance, *and* you still would have Chance working for you." She leaned back and smiled angelically. "Did I hit that spike on the head dead center, Uncle?"

Dodge cast her a chagrined smile. "Someday, I'll learn that you know what I'm going to do before I do it. All right, that's the plan, for whatever reason. Now let's talk about it."

"No. Chance and I will discuss it *in private*. Come, Chance, let's step out of the car for our little caucus."

I opened the door for her. She stepped through and whirled on me, her eyes blazing. "What do you mean putting Uncle up to this? You might at least have discussed it with me first."

Blood surged to my head, and I tasted angry bile boil up in my throat. Then, getting my temper under control, I stared at her a moment. "I'll get the boy. We won't trouble you again." I pulled the door open. She caught my sleeve.

"Wait. Chance, I don't know why I blew up at you. It's, well, it's just that Uncle and I clash all the time. Oh, I don't know why. We love each other so much, but we rub each other the wrong way a lot." She made no effort to hide the moisture in her eyes.

"I suppose, with me, much of it is cabin fever. I'm cooped up here in this—this car without much chance to get out in the town. And, well, I need a break once in awhile. I'm sorry. I had no cause to blow up." She nodded as though reassuring herself. "This was Uncle's idea."

I wanted to reach for her, take her into my arms, and wipe away any hint of tears, but I lacked the courage. Instead, I shuffled my feet, not knowing what to do or what to say.

Betsy still held my sleeve between her fingers. "Thank God you were thoughtful enough to warn me to keep quiet until we could talk alone. It would be terrible for Billy to see a scene like this. He'd think he wasn't wanted anywhere."

My face felt stiff, devoid of expression. "Miss Travis, I thank you for being considerate of Billy's feelings, but I'm certain I know how you feel. I'll collect Billy and leave. Thanks, too, for keeping him while I took care of my business in town." I pulled the door wide to step through.

Turning the sleeve loose, she clutched my arm and, despite my feelings of the moment, her hand on my arm sent a tingle through me.

"Oh, Chance, you're angry with me. Please don't go back to calling me Miss Travis. And yes, I'd love to have Billy with me while Uncle's gone. It wasn't you or Billy or even Uncle, really. I suppose it was the suddenness of the idea that caused me to act as I did."

The anger washed out of me. I felt stupidly mushy inside and reached across my chest and placed my hand over hers. I looked into her eyes. "If you're *real* sure, all right, but I'll understand if you don't want him. It's just that I didn't understand your animosity. Be sure, very sure, Betsy. Having him here will surely cause you trouble."

"Not trouble I wouldn't enjoy." She smiled, then nodded. "I'm sure, Chance. Let's go tell Billy." She walked through the door ahead of me.

Dodge looked up when we came back. I'd seen far less anxiety in his eyes when I had my bayonet at his chest during the war. He cleared his throat. "Well?"

Billy didn't utter a word, but crowded back into the cushion of his chair as though that would give him security. I tried to imagine how he must feel, perhaps like a pawn in a chess game. Here were three giants deciding things about him that he had no control over. But he had strength, that little boy did. I'd seen it when he asked me for a job. He was proud and brave. I would be honored to call him son.

Betsy explained what we'd decided. Dodge beamed, but Billy didn't show his feelings at all. His eyes never left my face. Then it hit me.

Warmth flooded my body, my throat swelled almost shut. Billy didn't just want to have someone, anyone, to call his own. He wanted *me*. My God. I couldn't account for why, but if I felt about him the way I did, it surely made sense that he could have the same feelings toward me.

Tom served us coffee. Billy had milk. We talked awhile, then I suggested that Billy and I had more shopping to do and that we had some man-to-man things to talk over. I winked at Betsy to let her know that we were to go alone.

When we were off the train, I led Billy to the café, thinking that we could eat and talk at the same time. I'd take him to the store later and buy one Sunday-go-to-meeting outfit for him and a couple more pairs of Levi's and some shirts.

"You hungry?" I asked.

He looked up at me. "Yes, sir. Seems like I'm always hungry." He grinned, seeming happy just to be walking with me. We were still fifty yards or so from the café when the aroma of roast, coffee, and freshly baked bread wafted past my nose.

"Boy, that food smells good. I think even if I had just eaten, those smells would make me want to eat again." I sniffed. "Hmmm, seems I can smell an apple pie there somewhere, too. What do you think?"

Billy gave an exaggerated sniff, looked thoughtful, then grinned at me. "I kinda figure maybe you're right, sir."

I looked at him with a puzzled look and shook my head as though with a great problem. "You think after we put some of that roast away we might still have room for pie?"

Billy sucked his scrawny little stomach in and gave me a big-eyed, honest look. "Mr. Chance, I jest plain ain't gonna eat so much I can't stand some of it."

I can't remember ever feeling so good. I laughed. "All right, if you figure it that way, reckon I'll try to leave room for it, too."

We had eaten and were having our pie when I decided it was time to talk to Billy. I looked at him, hating to get started. This had all been fun so far. "Billy, we need to talk."

He gave me a straight-on look, fearless, yet hesitant. "Yes, sir, I know. You want to talk 'bout leaving me with Miss Betsy. Well, I want to go with you, Mr. Chance."

I frowned, wanting to put this off, but knowing it had to be done. Stalling, I asked, "Billy, if we're going to be friends, seems like you should call me something besides Mr. Chance. What do you think?"

"Yes, sir. But what could I call you? That there's your name."

"Yep, so it is. What would you like to call me? Chance? Partner? What?"

He looked at me, down at his plate, sipped his hot chocolate, then cast a sideways glance at me. "Well, sir, I surely would be beholden to you if you'd let me call you—nah," he shook his head, "you wouldn't like it." He shook his head again and sat back.

"How do you know I wouldn't like it? C'mon, let's hear it. Can't decide if I don't know what you have in mind."

"Uh, well, I always called my daddy Pa. I, uh," then with a rush of words, he said, "I surely would like to call you Papa."

His words, each one, shot straight into my heart. Quick tears welled to my eyes. I swallowed a couple of times, then reached out and pulled him close. I didn't give a damn if everyone in the café or the whole town saw, but we were the only ones there at the time.

I sucked in a deep breath to steady my voice. "Son, I'd be

proud for you to call me Papa. If I ever have a little boy, I want him to be just like you. Now, let's talk about what you'll be doing while I'm on the job."

Billy nodded. "Yeah, reckon that's what we come out here fer."

I explained to him that I wanted to have him and Betsy with me for the rest of my life, but I had no home now. For that I must work and earn money, so I could make a home for them.

I told him that the general was a good man, but he was responsible for the safety of everyone on railroad property. He just couldn't let me take a little boy to the danger of the trestle site. The job I had was a good one, an important one, and the pay was very good. I explained that, with what I made, I thought we could have our home in a little over a year.

Finished, I glanced at him out of the corners of my eyes to see how he'd taken it. I hoped I'd convinced him he must stay with Betsy or we'd be a lot longer having our own place.

"But, sir, we don't need much else besides you an' me. We could hunt buffalo an' build us a dugout in the side of a hill. We'd be warm and have plenty to eat."

I sucked in a deep breath. How did you make a ten-year-old understand about the feelings men and women have? Mentally, I shrugged. I had to try.

"Billy, having you with me makes me happy, maybe happier than I've ever been, but I need one more thing to make me as happy as a man needs to be." I stopped, tamped roughcut into my pipe, and lit it. My mind going like the wind, I tried to decide what to say next.

"You see, there are two of us who want you with us, Miss Betsy and I. We both want you so bad it almost hurts us to think that either won't have you." I puffed on my pipe, watching him through a cloud of smoke.

"But, being big people, it takes more to make us all the way happy. We want to be with each other, too." I couldn't help wondering what Betsy would think of my argument if she could hear it. I smiled at the thought.

"You see," I continued, "she and I really need each other almost as much as we want you, and in order for all of us to be happy, it'll have to be the three of us. The sooner I earn the money, the sooner we can be together."

I sat back and studied him to see how he took it. He seemed to be doing all right, so I continued. "Now, I've laid it on the line with you, little partner, except for one thing. Maybe the most important one. The real reason I want you to stay with Miss Betsy is, well, there won't be a man left here to protect her, keep her safe, and keep her from being lonesome. Don't you think you could stay with Miss Betsy and take care of her while I'm gone?"

He sat there, frowning. Knowing he mulled over the things I'd said, I waited for him to respond. Finally he looked at me, his face serious. "Mr.—uh, Papa, I'm gonna miss you worse'n apple pie, but I don't reckon you'd feel very good if you wuz out there knowin' they wuzn't a man here to take care o' Miss Betsy. I like her, too, but bein' with her ain't gonna be like it'd be with you."

He toyed with his fork a moment. "Yes, sir, seems the least I can do. After all the things you done fer me, reckon I'd be right proud to take care o' her fer you."

I gripped his shoulder, and feeling how frail it seemed in my grasp, quickly released it. "Thanks, Billy. Knowing you both are here taking care of each other will let me do my job better. This way we're all there working toward getting us a home. Let's go back and tell Miss Betsy and the general."

On the way back to the train, Billy kept up a constant stream of chatter. He asked me questions about my job, Indians, cowboys, bears, and mountain lions. And, without taking a breath, he launched into wanting to know how to rope a cow, track animals, shoot a gun, and seemingly a hundred other things.

I realized that the world I would be taking him and Betsy into was foreign to both. I'd have to find time to teach him how to shoot, build a fire without matches, and finally, how to survive with little but his brain to aid him. I looked down at his tousled head bobbing along at my side. Showing him those things would be fun.

Back aboard Dodge's car, I spent a little time with Betsy, showing her the clothes I'd purchased and finding things to fuss over. Finally, she stood, hands on hips, and smiled at me. "Chance Tenery, will you please stop fussing around. Billy and I are going to be perfectly all right. Now, you get on back to your men. Go build a railroad and come back to us safe at your every chance."

A rueful grin forced its way to my lips. "Yes, ma'am, I suppose I just wanted to make certain you were all right before I left."

She looked at me, shaking her head, and said, "We're *all right*. Now, go. I have to get Billy and me ready for bed."

Looking down, I ran my hand over Billy's head. "Be good, son. Take good care of Miss Betsy for me."

"Yes, sir, you got nothing to worry about. I'll do just like I said I would."

I turned to Betsy, wanting to take her in my arms and kiss her good-bye. Instead, I tipped my hat and said good night.

Stepping off the platform to the ground, I heard my name called and looked up to see Dodge coming down again behind me.

"Tenery, I'd like to make a suggestion."

"All right, sir."

"If you really want to save money, and even have it work for you, why don't you take most of it and put it in UP stock? It's doubling and tripling in value every two or three months."

Grinning and frowning at the same time, I asked, "Where in the hell could I find a broker out here, General? Your idea sounds good, but I have no idea how to go about it."

He gave me a jerky nod. "I know how. There are a couple of fellows, George Francis Train and Thomas Durant, who have created a construction company by the name of The Credit Mobilier of America. It's the company that's building the railroad. Those who've bought stock in it are getting rich. I can get you in, if you'd like."

I shook my head. "General, I'd like to get in on it, but I doubt that I could scrape together enough right now to make it worthwhile."

"Why not draw only thirty dollars of your salary each month and have Casement send the rest to me. I'll invest it for you."

I grimaced, scratched my head, then nodded. "I'll do it. Look for it every payday. And thanks, General. This'll make my wedding day a little closer."

He grinned. "I heard a little of that rawhiding Betsy gave you out there on the platform. Seems like you don't know when you're well off." He shrugged. "Suppose a man's gotta break his own trails."

"Yep, I suppose you're right. I do, anyway." I shook his hand. "Thanks again, sir."

I walked toward the construction train that tomorrow would take us to end-of-track.

I marveled at the many things happening to me. My life had direction. My only goal, that of killing the man or men who had murdered my brother, didn't seem to be my prime driving force any longer. It was still there, but other things, other people were important to me now.

I wondered what Adam would say when I told him about Billy. I knew that whatever his response, it would be good. That big man had a heart as large as his body.

The flatcar loomed in the darkness, and I walked to it. Several of the crew were stretched out on its bed, already asleep. They were probably already broke, or maybe just tired of this town. If it weren't for Betsy and Billy, I'd never find a reason to come here again.

I climbed to the bed of the car, lay down, and soon slept.

chapter

thirteen

THE SHRILL BLAST of the train whistle woke me. Although the sun was not yet up, the engineer blew the whistle to call the crew from town. They straggled up, some cursing, some stinking and dirty, but they came.

Once aboard, most of them lay down and immediately went to sleep, others sat holding their heads with both hands, cursing the day whiskey was invented, but all seemed glad to be going back to work.

A jolt signaled the engineer taking up slack between cars. Slowly the train inched ahead, building speed.

I looked aft and saw Betsy holding Billy's hand. Running toward the train, both waved.

Standing at the edge of the car waving to them, I choked up, knowing they had run all this way just to tell me good-bye. It had been a long time since I'd had anyone who gave a damn whether I came or went. A shrill little voice called, "Bye, Papa, I'll take good care of Miss Betsy for you."

Well, dammit. I must've gotten cinders in my eyes right then because they teared up so I could hardly see.

The wheels clickety-clacked faster until the two people I cared most for in all the world were just tiny specks in the distance. I stood there all the while, watching until they disappeared from sight.

When we approached end-of-track, I called Mike over and told him to be sure the men packed everything they needed while I reported to Jack Casement.

"Yeah, he'll have our horses ready at railside when we get in. It shouldn't take us long to move out."

"Okay, you tell the other foremen. When you're ready, head out. I'll catch up with you. It'll probably take awhile for me to brief him on our trip into town."

True to Mike's prediction, the horses were waiting for us when we arrived.

I swung down from the train and headed for Casement's car.

He looked up when I entered. "How'd things go?"

"Fine." I nodded. "No one hurt, no one dead, the men are all right except for a few headaches here and there. Good trip."

He stared at me a moment, a faint smile showing at the corners of his eyes. "Good trip, huh? No trouble." He laughed. "Damn you, Chance, we never had a crew go to Julesburg but what they had trouble, a bunch of it. Don't tell me you had no trouble."

I grinned, then admitted, "Yes, sir, we did have a little problem, but I stopped it before it got started."

I told him about shutting the saloon down to UP personnel, the killing, and that Snake Thompson had been hired to see that a funeral was held in my honor. I shrugged. "That's about it, but the important thing is that none of our men were hurt or killed."

A furrow creased the center of Casement's forehead as he smiled. "I can't say you don't follow orders. By damn, if we had more men like you, we'd tame these end-of-track towns before trouble could start festering." He poured me a cup of coffee. "Sit down. We'll talk awhile."

I picked up my coffee, sat, and tasted it. If I'd had a good sharp pair of scissors, I could have strung it out, clipped off a hunk, and chewed it.

Casement told me that things were relatively quiet at the trestle site. He'd had a couple of men hurt from falls, but not badly. He said that tie and trestle timber was getting scarce.

The pithy cottonwood we used, lacking good timber, had been cleaned out of all the creek banks close by. We burtnettized it with zinc chloride to protect against rot.

Then he told me about the Plumb Creek Massacre where a young Englishman, William Thompson, lost his hair to the Cheyenne but lived.

Finally, after giving me all the UP news, he sat back in his chair, patted the arms, and smiled. "Chance, I want to thank you for steering Adam to me. I never had a moment to relax like this before he hired on. He has the records, orders, everything so shipshape it'd probably take me all of a week to mess them up again."

We chuckled. I told him about how Adam and I became partners, and I told him about Billy. I left out my intentions toward Betsy, but did tell him about Dodge's refusal to let Billy come to end-of-track with me.

Casement nodded. "I understand his reasons, but if it would cause me to lose you, I'd have let the boy come out."

He stood. "Before you go visit Adam, I want to show you something." He slanted a questioning look at me. "You ever watch the pure symphony of a track gang at work?"

I shook my head. "No, sir."

"Come along then. I'll explain it while we watch."

We left his car and walked past a supply train dumping mountains of ties, rails, spikes, fishplates, and the hundreds of other items it took to build a railroad. The work train was ahead of it.

We passed the work train engine and headed down the length of its more than twenty cars. Casement waved toward the cars as we passed them one by one.

"Once we have the supplies, this train takes over. The machine shops, carpenter shops, saddlery, kitchens, telegraph, general store, water cars, and sleeping accommodations, divided, of course, by rank, are all part of this train.

"The dining cars have tables and benches that run the entire car length. Plates are nailed in place so the swabber can come along and wipe them out between feedings." He laughed. "Can you imagine what the ladies' finishing schools back East would say to *that?*"

We walked far enough to the side so as to not interfere with the hundreds of men working close to the train.

Casement peered ahead. "Ahh, now you're going to hear the pure music of building a railroad."

Looking ahead two car lengths, I saw the last one in line. The engine was attached to the other end of the train, to push or pull it as necessary. Then we came up on the track-laying crews. Between them and the last car of the train were small flatcars pulled by horses. They were driven by boys not much older than Billy.

"You see here, Chance, the *real* end-of-track. Those little cars stayed right up on the last rails that have been spiked down. Notice that they're loaded with rails, spikes, everything it takes to secure a rail in place.

"Those men on each side of the track are called iron men." Casement chuckled. "Although they'd qualify for the term in lots of ways, they get their name from handling the big iron, the rails. There are five men to each twenty-eight-foot rail. Those rails weigh between five hundred and seven hundred pounds each."

I tamped my pipe with fresh tobacco, watched, and listened. Hammers ringing against spikes provided the timpani, bass voices issuing commands furnished the violas, and the wind whispering across sun-cured grass, the violins. Even the groans of men straining to their backbreaking jobs furnished a rhythm. Although Casement had planted the thought, these sounds played a symphony of their own.

On command, each team of five would heft a rail, walk forward, and at the word *down,* they'd drop it right in place, or close enough that with little effort it fitted to the gauge: exactly four feet, eight and one-half inches apart.

I saw the spike men go to work with their sledges, hitting each spike three times. That done, another rail extended the track another twenty-eight feet. For every four hundred rails in place, the track stretched a mile longer.

I marvelled at the precision, the music of it all, but mostly at the incomprehensible task of pushing a railroad across a vast continent.

Casement kept glancing at me, I knew, to see if I appreciated the teamwork, the effort, and certainly not least, the backbreaking labor that went into making this country's dream come true. I allowed a slight smile, knowing he was trying his very best to make a railroad man of me. He wanted me to feel the beat of it, the thrill, the pride of being a part of it all.

I looked at him, my face sober. "Jack, you called it right. It *is* a symphony. This is the first time I've had the opportunity to see it up close. It's truly magnificent."

Casement was like a little boy looking for approval of something he'd done well. "You like it, Chance? By golly, I can see you do!" He nodded. "Yep, being an engineer, and having worked hard, you understand what it takes to have an operation like this."

"Jack, I can honestly say that I've never seen anything to compare with it; the logistics, the teamwork, the planning is almost beyond believing."

We headed back toward his car. "I've got to see Adam, then I better get going. My crew is getting far ahead of me."

I spent only a few minutes with Adam, but I had time to tell him all that had transpired in town.

When I told him about Billy, I thought his grin would go all the way around his head. "Oh, now, Mistuh Chance, that's about the nicest thing I can imagine." He shook his head, marveling at what I'd told him. "What do you know, we got us a little boy."

He grasped my shoulder. "You always doing somethin' nice for somebody. You're a *good* man, Mistuh Chance. God bless you."

Blood rushed to my face. I felt confused, embarrassed. I'd never before been told I was a good man. "Aw, c'mon Adam, I sure never thought of myself as being good."

"Well, suh, reckon you can take my word for it. You are."

I explained the Credit Mobilier to him and told him about putting my wages into it, and said that, if he liked the idea, I'd ask General Dodge about him getting in. "You think about it and let me know when I get back from the trestle next time. If we make enough out of it, we'll have our ranch before we meet up with the Central Pacific."

"I'll do that. Now, you better get going, or you'll be out there with the Indians all alone."

We shook hands and I rode out.

I let my stallion set his own pace. Knowing the crew would be slowed by the chuck wagon, I thought to catch them shortly after high noon. Might even catch them during their nooning, I thought.

The sky, clear and brassy hot this late August day, showed no sign that autumn hovered just around the corner. My shirt clung to my back, no longer soaking up the sweat; it was already saturated. I reached for my canteen, took a few swallows, again hung it from the horn, and then saw the tracks. A small party pulling a travois had crossed my trail. The gouges of the travois wended their way over the ridge.

I looked at the sign for more detail. There were six of them, maybe seven, if what the travois carried was an Indian. They had only one horse. I figured three children and three women—women because of the depth of the tracks, short steps, and small feet. The children's tracks were much smaller and didn't make as deep an imprint.

Frowning, I stood looking at the sign. Were they headed somewhere to join up with a larger party? If not, what were they doing out here without warriors? My curiosity got the better of me. I mounted and turned the stallion in the direction they traveled. I could catch the crew at the work site later, in time for work at daylight.

Careful to stay off the skyline, I cast back and forth until I heard voices. I crawled to the top of the ridge and peered over.

I had calculated right; three children, young, less than five or six years old, three squaws, and an old man, very old. He lay on the travois. They had stopped to eat, apparently, for I saw a squaw, the oldest of the three, picking around in a deerskin bag. Finally, she pulled a strip of jerky about six inches long from the bag.

She divided the strip into six equal pieces and handed each of them a piece, taking none for herself. I waited for her to dip into the bag for more, but there must not have been any. She sat and stoically watched them chew the dried meat. Still curious, I stood and walked toward them, hand held out in the universal peace sign.

They didn't take alarm but sat there, staring at me. Although I couldn't speak their language, I knew sign language as well as any. I asked where they took the old one.

"He is dying and wants to go to the sacred grounds," the one who had apportioned the jerky answered.

"In the Black Hills?" I asked.

She nodded.

"Are you Lakota?"

"Yes. We go home now."

"Why do you not eat?" I asked.

"We have no more. I will eat when we have plenty."

I looked at the children, then at the grandfather lying there so weak and helpless. My first reaction was anger that I'd been so foolish as to leave end-of-track without provisions. I had nothing to give them. These people were hungry, and I could not help them.

I told them good-bye, went to my horse, mounted, and rode slowly to meet my crew.

Those people were hungry. Sioux or not, they needed help, and I had nothing to give. I wondered if one of those kids were Billy or if one of those women were Betsy, what I would do. *To hell with it,* I thought. *I'll ride all night if I have to in order to get back to the crew. Right now, I'm going hunting.*

I reined my horse into the wind. There would be greater chance that I'd find game ahead of me that way, and being downwind of it, I'd be able to get closer for a good shot.

The sun reached its height and swung on its downward journey. I hadn't seen even a jackrabbit. But, on the good side, I hadn't seen sign of a war party, either.

The rolling, sun-browned plains stretched to the horizon in every direction. A faint scent of dust intruded on the cured-on-the-stem aroma of the grass. The wind had died to a breeze that hardly stirred its blades.

I reined the stallion in, pushed my hat off my forehead

and wiped my brow, sipped stingily from my canteen, and when hanging it back on the pommel, I saw them.

There were six antelope, a spike-buck, and another deer, about a six-pointer. Careful to make my moves slow and fluid, I dropped off my horse. I wanted that six-point buck, but I still stood too far away for a sure shot.

Knowing where they fed, I worked around the swell of the hill. When I again spotted them, they had grazed farther from me. A glance showed the stallion, head close to the ground, pulling the tough bunch grass off in chunks, and moving on to another.

A mental nod gave my approval. Good. He'd stay until I returned, unless some Indian took him for his own, and I'd not seen sign of an Indian since leaving the small band of Lakota behind.

I continued stalking the deer. Antelope was food, but nothing I cared to eat unless it was all I had.

The next time I saw them, the distance had closed by about fifty yards. The shot I wanted, one of about one hundred fifty yards, stretched in front of me. I moved slowly, knelt, sighted just behind the left shoulder of the six-pointer, and squeezed off my shot. He bounded forward, all four feet off the ground, then crumpled. The other animals, at the sound of the shot, left fast.

Warily, I approached the downed buck. I'd seen hunters hurt badly by the hooves of wounded deer, but when I was within only a few feet of him, I saw that he didn't breathe. To be sure, I walked closer, stuck the barrel of my rifle toward his eyes, and touched it. He didn't blink.

Although I hadn't seen sign of Indians, I didn't take time to dress the buck. I brought the stallion to him, draped him across my horse in front of the saddle, and cut out of there. I aimed to cross the route the squaws and children had taken.

Sundown overtook me and melted into twilight, with distant purples and soft yellows and browns, tinted by shadows of ground swell. I caught a whiff of smoke before I saw the glow of their fire.

Being as silent as when stalking the deer, I drew closer. I

counted the figures moving about and gauged the size of each. One horse for the seven of them told me they were the right party.

Boldly, I rode to them, my arm again extended in sign of peace. Dismounting, I pulled the deer from my horse and proceeded to skin and cut the carcass into chunks. After taking a small steak for myself, I made sign that the rest was theirs.

The squaw who had not eaten when the others had their pitiful nooning looked squarely into my eyes and smiled.

"Thank you, friend of the Lakota. You are welcome to stay at our fire tonight." She spoke in perfect English.

Showing no surprise, I nodded solemnly. "Thank you, Grandmother, but I have a long ride and must leave now." I glanced at the old man. "Take care of Grandfather, and have a good journey to the sacred land of the Lakotas." I mounted and rode into the darkness.

Maybe, just maybe, I'd made a friend. A rueful grin creased my lips. In a Sioux camp you'd not be harmed, but away from it you again were a hated white man. Only time and another meeting with them would tell.

chapter
fourteen

"You move one muscle and you're dead," a quiet voice said from close to the ground, not ten feet away.

"Chance Tenery here," I said, knowing the one who spoke stood watch at the trestle site. I had been expecting a challenge for several minutes.

"Where the hell you been, boss? We been a mite worried about you. This is Slagle, sir."

"Just took a roundabout way of getting here, Slagle, but thanks for worrying about me. Any coffee at the fire?"

"Reckon so, sir." He chuckled. "You take a cup o' that stuff and you won't have to eat. It's really got body; been on the fire since supper."

"Can't be any thicker'n Casement's. God, that man makes the worst coffee I ever tasted." I laughed and reined the stallion toward camp.

After a couple of swallows of coffee, I crawled into my blankets for an hour or so of sleep.

I dozed off, thinking that this trestle should be finished before long, and then I'd put my plan into motion. It should save us a lot of time and material in the future.

Two days later, we had the last timber in place and were ready to move to the next site.

A mound of material to be loaded and moved with us lay alongside the roadbed. I frowned and called my foremen to

114

me. "Do we always have this much left to reload and move when we finish a job?"

Mike answered. "Yes, sir, this much or more."

Nodding, I said, "All right for this time, but we'll have damned little left in the future. After we get the job started for the next trestle, I'm going to the next two or three sites and try to estimate a hell of a lot closer the material we'll need for them. We're wasting a lot of time with this reloading."

Jake Brindley grimaced. "You're right, boss, but it's gonna be almighty dangerous out there alone. You figure to take anybody with you?"

A swipe at my hat pushed it back so I could wipe my brow. "Don't know right now, Jake." Including the three of them in my glance, I frowned. "If someone goes with me, it'll save a lot of time when we get to the new sites." I worried a rock with my boot toe while trying to think of some way to get the job done alone.

"With me, a man's going to have his neck stuck out a mile. I'll not ask anyone to do that. Figure I can estimate the material pretty good alone. The only reason for taking someone would be to handle the chain and sticks." While talking, I made up my mind. "No. I'll handle it. You men are needed here. Another thing, one man won't draw as much attention as a larger party. I'll go it alone."

Mike said nothing, but shook his head, and I thought I heard him mutter, "Damned fool." At the same time, I heard Jake and Bill agree.

With the wagons strung out behind us, we passed several places eroded so badly they'd have to be graded, but grading was cheaper and quicker than constructing trestles. We moved on, following the survey flags, and were close to twelve miles from our last trestle before coming on a ravine.

"All right, men. This is our next job. Mike, Bill, Jake, get the wagons unloaded. Stretch it out so we won't have to haul this stuff again while we're here."

They had the wagons pull up to the roadbed at intervals and had their crews off-load them.

While they were engaged with that chore, I went to the

wagon where I'd stored the theodolite. Taking it from its case, I handled it with great care. If it got damaged, we'd be really hamstrung. It was our only instrument for measuring angles and elevations without a great loss of time, not to mention backbreaking labor.

Seeing Mike busy with the wagons, I called Jake Brindley to help me. With the theodolite we shot the ravine, locating positions for each of the pilings. Jake had men mark the locations while I jotted down the height for that particular piling. By sundown, we had finished shooting the ravine and unloading the wagons. We were ready to start work the next day.

By firelight, I sketched the trestle, made notes of timbers and their lengths, sketched in cross members, distances apart, and the angles at which they were to be bolted to the pilings. I poured a cup of coffee and sat by the fire to study my drawings. Satisfied that my foremen could follow them, I unrolled my bedroll, stretched out, and went to sleep.

The rattle of pans signaled the cook had started breakfast. I crawled from my blankets. Coffee boiled on coals by the fire. I poured a cup and sat sipping it, waiting for cook to call us to eat. Groans from the men indicated they'd soon be joining me. When my foremen were up, I called to them, "Grab a cup of coffee and come look at this drawing. It's rough, but it'll tell you how I want the trestle put together."

I explained each notation, bolt size, and timber dimension, until I was satisfied they understood exactly how I wanted it. "All right, this'll keep you busy until I get back. This is the kind of planning I intend to do while I'm gone. You men are needed here."

I looked at Mike. "You're the senior man here. You're in charge. Keep sentries out so you don't get surprised by the Cheyenne."

That Mike was senior of the three wasn't my only reason for picking him as boss in my absence. The men respected him and would obey him without question. Besides, he could whip the hell out of any man here.

My gear packed, I looked longingly toward where the theodolite lay snug in the wagon bed. I had decided to do my estimates by educated guess. An even better reason for not taking the theodolite was that it required two men to shoot a site.

"You be careful, boss," the three said, almost in unison. I waved. "Look for me when you see me." I kneed my horse into a trot.

. Headed west, I followed the survey flags. They didn't allow the comfort of riding below the land swells, or that of taking advantage of the safest route, but this job had to get done. We wasted too much time by oversupplying every construction site. I hadn't been hired to waste time.

By midmorning, the sun beat down mercilessly. I squinted to see through the shimmering heat waves. The plains stretched beyond forever. No sign showed that I wasn't the only human in the world. I liked it out here alone. If I saw another man, the chances were he'd be Indian. I could do without that kind of company but would be prepared.

Regardless of his tribe, the Indian had been a warrior long before the white man came to this land. He'd fought and defeated other Indians to get hunting land. He'd fight to keep it until others defeated him, be it Indian or white man. The Indian never understood the notion that anyone *owned* land.

He was courageous and brilliant on the field of battle, but he didn't understand the white man's need to kill, especially from a distance. To him, touching an enemy showed courage. He called this counting coup. Hand-to-hand combat gave him opportunity for bravery. He didn't understand us whites, nor we him.

Many whites thought of the Indian as an uneducated savage, mostly because he wouldn't adapt to our ways. *Why, I wondered, should he become as we were? His ways had served him well for hundreds of years. And as for being uneducated, well, he was as educated as any white, only in a different way.*

The education of the Indian started at birth. His learning centered on survival in a very hostile environment. *How long, I wondered, would a white man survive in the Indians' world?* The Indian attended *nature's* school and learned by observing.

I pulled my shirt from my skin, letting the air between cool me. My horse responded to my knees and walked on, shied, and almost threw me when a prairie hen flew from under his feet.

A small gully cut diagonally across the survey line. I studied it a moment and calculated how much dirt we'd have to move. I concluded we'd have to move too much. Taking out my sketch pad and pencil, I started earning my pay. By nightfall, I had this trestle documented and materials estimated.

Having seen no sign of life throughout the day, I gambled and built a small fire at the bottom of the gully, cooked supper, and boiled coffee. By the time I'd finished eating, a chill breeze brought goose bumps to my arms.

A glance around the horizon satisfied me there was no storm brewing. I spread my bedroll in the bottom of the gully, crawled between my blankets, and lay there looking at the sky.

Bracketed by the sides of the gully, the stars seemed closer and larger and my world lonelier. I missed Betsy and Billy. I finally slipped into sleep thinking of them.

My eyes opened. Knowing I'd been asleep only a short time, I wondered what had awakened me. I lay still, hardly daring to breathe. I heard no sound, but there was danger here, I didn't know what it was. I breathed in shallow breaths, not wanting my body to move or my breathing to make noise.

Then I felt it, a long, slithery movement that touched my side and seemed to move away, only to touch me again in a different place. Frozen with fear, I finally felt the whole length stretch out close to me. I had company in my blankets.

Knowing I must lay still until the sun came up, and then move only if what was in the blankets with me had left, I lay rigid. I had no idea what kind of snake cuddled beside me. Odds were it was a rattler. A man could count hundreds of them in any small area out here.

I thought about slapping my arm down on the blanket hoping to pin him. I cast that thought aside. Hell, any snake could strike faster than a man could move his hand.

I lay there sweating, even though the night was chill. If the snake had snuggled to me looking for warmth, I gave him plenty.

Watching the stars, hardly daring to breathe, time stopped. Every second seemed a year. I wondered if my hair turned white. I'd always heard it could happen to a man in situations like this. Goddammit, why didn't the sun hurry and rise? I knew that wish wouldn't come true. Hell, that old sun couldn't be hurried by a mere man, and my best guess said it was no later than midnight. For me there wouldn't be a sunrise for a couple thousand years the way time passed tonight.

The snake wriggled. I gasped. He quieted, again stretched close to me. He had moved, I suppose, to get more comfortable, because he again lay still. If I'd had a weak heart, I knew it would belch a couple of times and quit beating. A woman would wet her pants, so would a kid in this situation. I thought I would do the same if it would help any, but it wouldn't.

My mind raced. What in the hell should I do? I drew a blank.

I continued sucking slight breaths into my lungs, hoping for enough air to live. Then the thought struck me: *Jesus Christ! What if I have to cough?* I trained my thoughts in a different direction, hoping the power of suggestion didn't hold true in this instance.

That cold-blooded bastard would stay right where he was until the sun warmed him enough to move, but I had no assurance that he'd move even then. He might wait until night again to do his hunting.

I swallowed a lump as big as my saddle. Scared? Hell no. I always lay in my blankets, sweating, not daring to breathe or move. I prayed that I didn't start shaking. That would sure as hell get his attention.

Frantic, I tried to think of something, some course of action, but came up with nothing. I lay stretched out, north to south, my head south. I saw the North Star with the Big Dipper to its left. It was twelve o'clock.

In the next hour, that damned snake wriggled twice, each time creating hope that he'd leave. He didn't, but he didn't strike, either. I suppose there's some good in everything.

Anger began to replace fear, and with it I started thinking rationally. Both my arms were under the blanket. I didn't dare try to move the one laying across my chest next to the snake for that would quickly draw a set of fangs. My left arm stretched at my side. I wanted it free of any encumbrance.

Maybe, just maybe, if I got it out from under the blanket, I could bring it across my body quickly enough to push the blanket between me and the reptile.

I thought back on my moment of being awakened. At which end was his head? *Think, Tenery, you gutless bastard, think. Where was he when you first felt him?*

Sweat trickled in ever-increasing rivulets from my body to the ground. I smelled of cold sweat and fear. Jesus, I thought, I hope he's not attracted to human stink. But there was nothing I could do; my juices continued to flow.

Nerves and muscles taut, I slowly, very slowly, moved my left arm. The scaly bastard wriggled. I froze.

Lying stiff and still as a corpse, I held my position for another fifteen or twenty minutes. Oh, Christ. It could have been only that many seconds, but it seemed to the end of time.

I again moved my arm toward the edge of my blanket. This time I knew how long it took. I gauged time by the stars, and it took me the better part of an hour before I felt cool air on my fingers. Another hour went by before my arm was free. The dipper lay straight below the North Star.

Now what should I do? Think, Tenery, think. Was I willing to get bitten? What were the odds that I'd get out and away from the snake before he struck? Better yet, what odds did I have of living if he hit me? I was a long way from the trestle crew. Could I make it back to them with a leg or arm or neck filled with venom? I didn't think so.

I felt a rock under my left hand and grasped it tightly.

Should I throw it to my other side? Maybe he'd attack it. Yeah, and maybe he'd crawl up on *me*. Snakes didn't look for trouble. As a matter of fact, they avoided it whenever possible. But they always struck when threatened, and he'd recognize me as a threat because I was encroaching on the territory he'd chosen to take a nap in. No. The thrown rock wouldn't work.

Finally, I decided what to do. I might get bitten, but I was damned if I'd stay here all night with that bastard for a bed mate. I convinced myself that fear was as bad as a bite, almost.

I again tried to think where his head might be. When first I felt him nudge me, it had been along my thigh, then farther up my body. I decided his head was in the direction of mine. This made a strike more dangerous, but it also made the possibility greater of my plan working.

Still holding the rock, I inched my arm across my chest. If I misjudged where his head was, a long painful journey awaited me. I damned sure didn't want to pin the blanket ahead of him. This would give him an unfettered length to coil and strike.

I decided to grab the blanket almost at my waist. I thought I should have sweated my last drop, but I continued to pour perspiration. My nerves tightened to the point that I started trembling.

My God! He's going to feel me. Taking a tight grip of my emotions, I realized it was the inside of me that quivered. I still lay quiet outside.

My hand clutching the rock reached the other side of my body, just above my waist. I slowly took the first deep breath I'd taken in hours.

Chance Tenery, you better make this a good estimate. You're not going to have a second shot at it.

I slammed the rock against the blanket. Using the hand with the rock as a fulcrum, I forced my body sideways, to the left. The blanket came alive, writhing like something gone mad beneath it.

Cursing, sweating, pounding, I pummeled that blanket

like a bull gone berserk. Not one inch of it escaped my fist and the rock.

Long after all movement ceased, I continued to beat it.

Out of breath, I squinted through the darkness at what had once been my bed and realized through the fog of crazed fear that the snake had either left or lay smashed under my blanket.

Sleep this night had ended. My coffeepot came out, and I stoked up the fire. Only after I had a cup of the steaming liquid in my trembling hand did I go to the blanket and cautiously lift it by the corner.

I gazed, hypnotized, at the pulpy body of a large rattler, over four feet long.

My bowie knife made short work of taking the rattles, thirteen of them and a button. Sticking them in my shirt pocket, I again set by the fire. I felt weak and still trembled. When the bottom of my coffeepot was dry, I felt just as dry, drained, wrung out, weak. I shook my head in disbelief. I'd not known before that I was a coward, and I didn't like the feeling.

chapter

fifteen

AFTER THROWING MY gear into the filthy blanket, I saddled and rode up the gully. There might be a sump filled with water along its course, and I wanted to wash everything I owned.

I had often heard that the smell of one snake would bring another. The faintest smell of that big rattler on my blankets or gear had to go, or I'd never use that equipment again. Snakes stink. I couldn't describe the smell, but it is an evil, flesh-crawling odor.

I'd face shivering, bone-freezing cold before I'd tolerate any semblance of snake smell in that blanket. After it was washed, I'd throw it away if any odor remained. I wondered why I hadn't smelled him the night before. Too, I'd been asleep and the coating in my mouth kept tastes and odors from being recognized.

A glance at the brassy sky behind showed several buzzards circling over my camp of the night before. They brought a shiver despite the heat.

My search paid off. I came on a pool even larger than I'd hoped to find. I drank, filled my canteen, let my horse drink, and dumped everything I owned except my rifle, pistol, and saddle into the water.

For the second time this day, I took a smooth rock and pounded my blanket with it. Satisfied after beating every inch of it that I had purged it of any snake smell, I stood knee deep in the pool and rinsed it until my back muscles kinked.

My cooking gear came next. I scoured it with sand, spread it all out on the cured grass, and waited for the sun and wind to soak up the moisture. Later, aboard my horse, I found the roadbed again and followed it.

My cowardice of the night before nagged at me. Would not most men have reacted in a similar way? I'd never before questioned myself about this. I had known fear before, but never to the extent that it caused me to freeze. In war, in hand-to-hand combat, and when necessary, in gunfights, I'd always done what was necessary.

A rueful grin twisted my lips. *Well, I suppose I've learned something else about Chance Tenery,* I thought. "There's just one thing I'm damned glad of," I told my horse, "and that's you're the only one that saw me beat the hell out of my blanket in the middle of the night. We'll keep that a secret between you and me, old partner. That all right with you?" He twitched his ears.

Toward late afternoon, the wind shifted, clouds formed, and a coolness came on the air. By sundown, a steady rain fell, and I had seen no place to camp. The thought came to ride on, but I cast the idea away. Night riding would only blind me and would likely cause me to miss seeing places that needed bridging.

Soaked, cold, and miserable, I looked for a place to bed down. The thought of spreading my blankets caused a knot to form in the pit of my stomach.

This is stupid, I thought. *I've slept on the ground for years and never before had a snake crawled into my covers. Stop at the next likely looking site.*

Finding a slope, I set up camp and crawled between my blankets. I had no fire. The buffalo chips were sodden and there was no wood. It was a wet, miserable night filled with dreams of endless miles of rattlesnakes. The rising sun brought joy.

Eight days were spent away from my crew, and when I joined them, I had planned and estimated five trestles.

They were a day away from finishing the job I'd left for them when I slipped down from my horse and shook hands all around.

Tired of my own cooking, scant as it had been, I went to the coffeepot, poured a cupful, and sat on a pile of timber to await the call to supper.

"How'd it go?" I asked Mike.

He shrugged. "No trouble. Almost ran shy o' bolts before the supply wagons showed up with more. Other than that, there ain't been a hitch in the drawings you left us to work by."

"Make sense to try estimating these sites ahead of time?" I studied his face, waiting for a reply.

He frowned, walked to the fire, poured a cup of coffee, and returned to squat by me.

"Yeah. No question about the estimatin' bein' needed. And even the rough drawin's you give me to work by was good." He swiped at his red hair. "Hell, boss. Jobs like this are okay, but I don't figure I'd be worth a damn on a big job. If we had a bridge to put up across a good-sized creek or river . . ." He shook his head. ". . . Well, reckon I'd want you there."

"Ah, hell, Mike, you just want me in the frying pan or in the fire alongside you."

"No. It ain't that. I just ain't got the 'rithmatic behind me to keep from making mistakes."

"Okay. When I take this to Casement, I'll tell him he'll need to hire another engineer if he likes my suggestion. I'll be free to go or the man he hires will be."

Mike grinned. "Makes me feel a lot better. I'd rather you stayed here, though, and sent the new man out."

My knotted fist punched him lightly on the arm. "We'll see what Jack says about it."

"Everything go all right with you?"

"Yeah," I answered, rubbed the set of rattles in my shirt pocket, and left that story untold. I grinned into the darkness. Hell, I had even washed the rattles.

When our relief crew came, we had finished two more small trestles and were having to load very little excess material after finishing them. My idea worked. For that matter, Gabe Johnson, my relief engineer, told me we'd gained about five miles on end-of-track, so we were gaining time, as well.

I showed Gabe the estimates I made and told him how we were working the plan. He agreed to go along with it.

The next morning, I rounded up the crew and we headed out. I wanted to try my idea out on Casement and see what he thought of it. It took us the full day to reach end-of-track. After unsaddling and taking care of my gear, I went straight to Jack's car.

"Jack, I've an idea I want to bounce off you. Seems good to me, though. We tried it on a small scale this time out."

He poured me a drink and sat down. "Sit. Drink your drink and tell me about it."

When I'd told him what we'd done, how it worked, and Mike's reservations about not wanting to be held responsible for a big job, I sat back expectantly.

Casement pulled on his beard and stared at me. He stared so long that I squirmed in discomfort. Jerkily, he nodded. "Sounds all right. Worked this time, huh?" He poured himself a cup of coffee and again sat looking at me. "You ever think maybe you could get killed out there alone?"

"Long as I'm alone, Jack, I'll be all right. It's only when those plains get overpopulated with Indians that I'll begin to worry." I rubbed the rattles between my fingers and felt guilty for lying.

He leaned back in his chair. "Let me think about it awhile. I'll be hard put to find an engineer to replace you. Yeah, let me consider it."

I stood, prepared to leave.

Jack stood with me, frowned, and said, "I almost forgot to tell you. I suggested to Betsy that Dodge's car move closer to end-of-track, maybe around Sydney, but she'd not hear of it. Said she wanted Billy to have every opportunity to visit with you. They're still in Julesburg."

I felt blood surge to my face. "Yes, sir, I appreciate your letting it stay there. I'm looking forward to visiting with them."

"*Both* of them, I presume," Jack said, and laughed.

Christ! My red face shouted the answer to him. Grinning, I knew my actions were those of a schoolboy. All I had to do was shuffle my feet and say "shucks." Instead, I said, "Yes, sir, I'll be happy to see Betsy as well."

Casement laughed as though he'd caught me with my hand in the cookie jar. "Sometimes I envy you young people the fire of new love, but then"—he frowned—"I think of all the heartache attendant with it. No, I don't envy you, boy. But good luck." He clapped me on the shoulder.

I left him, feeling he'd treated me as my father would have only a few short years ago. I liked the feeling. Picking up my bedroll, I threw it onto the flatcar we'd ride to Julesburg the next morning. I'd sleep on the flatcar, giving in to my newborn fear of sleeping on the ground.

By the fire that night, I visited with Adam until some in the crew growled at us to go to bed so they could get some sleep. Adam had Casement's permission to go with us this time, so we saved some of our conversation until later.

After breakfast, we loaded on the flatcar and headed out. When we pulled into Julesburg, Betsy and Billy stood at trackside. I knew they waited for me.

A couple of hard swallows rid me of the lump in my throat but did little to ease my churning stomach. Hell, this feeling was similar to the one I used to have when going into combat. Maybe love was like that.

I swung down from the car and Billy hit me like a small tornado. He jumped into my arms, even though he weighed quite a bit to be doing that. Betsy stood to the side, smiling.

Holding Billy close to me and looking over his shoulder, my eyes locked with Betsy's. God! I wanted to drop Billy right there, pull her to me, and kiss her right in front of all the men.

Instead, I put Billy down, took her hand in mine, and thanked her for taking care of Billy and bringing him to meet me.

Her eyes seemed misty to me, but I laid it to train smoke.

"I'm glad you're back, Chance. We've missed you."

"We? You've missed me, too?"

Defiantly, her chin raised. "Yes, Chance Tenery, I've missed you, too."

I looked into her eyes a long moment and saw there what I wanted to see. Adam stood at my shoulder. I remembered my manners and introduced him to both Billy and Betsy.

"This is the other partner we'll have on our ranch. He has only one problem. He turns white when he has to kill anything."

Adam chuckled. "Yes, ma'am, reckon Mr. Chance is right about that. I just haven't got it in me to kill. I don't know that I turn white, though. Whooee, don't reckon anything could do that. My old master used to tell me I was black clean to my bones and that even they might be black."

While they got acquainted, I walked over to the crew and told them to stay out of trouble. I'd stop in a few of the saloons and buy the drinks after dark. "Go have fun."

They didn't need a second invitation and, walking past, they greeted Billy and Betsy.

"Let's not bother Tom. We'll go to the café. I think Billy is hungry again," Betsy said dryly. "As a matter of fact, I believe Billy is always hungry."

A study of Billy showed that, in the short while Betsy had taken care of him, he'd gained weight. Again, he held tightly to my hand, but this time there was a difference. With his other hand he grasped Betsy's. Adam walked right along with us at Betsy's side. Pride swelled my throat and tightened my chest. This was as it should be. We were a family, and we'd walk like this through life. A voice, surly, nasty, cut into my thoughts.

"So the big nigger's got hisself a white woman now. We kill niggers who think they're as good as white folks around here."

A chill settled over my entire body. A cold, controlled fury laid a grip on my brain. I looked to see who had said those hateful words.

One of Snake Thompson's men leaned indolently against the front of the feed and seed store. He'd been there the day I broke Thompson's jaw, but I hadn't seen him during my last visit to Julesburg.

I herded Betsy, Billy, and Adam into the feed store and noticed a surprised look from Betsy. She had never seen me angry or in a dangerous situation, but I could tell from her look that she expected something from me other than just getting them off the street.

She had no way of knowing I'd brought them in here to ensure they'd be out of the way of a stray bullet, if it came to that.

I looked at Adam. "Keep them in here. Don't come out until I call you. Understand?" My voice was harsh.

"Yes, suh. I understand."

I looked at them a moment before walking outside.

"Did you address us?" My voice was quiet when I spoke to the man still leaning against the building.

"No." He sneered. "I wuz talkin' to the nigger in yonder."

Seldom have I ever wanted to kill a man, but this one I did want to kill. I wanted to hurt him first, hurt him with my fists. My brain had ceased to function as anything but a control for destruction. He had not only cast filthy words of hate at Adam but at Betsy as well.

When I was within arms' length of him, he straightened from his slouch. His hand dropped close to his right side, fingertips brushing his gun butt. "Looks like you gonna try to take up fer the nigger agin."

"No. I'm not going to take up for him." My voice came out quiet, not because I wanted it that way, but because the anger in me choked it off. "If you get him mad he can take care of himself. What I'm going to do is teach you some manners." My voice lowered even further, and with it, I showed him a gentle smile, taking him off guard.

Without further words, I drove my fist into his stomach. He bent at the waist, and I brought my clubbed fists down in back of his neck, driving his face against my rising knee. I didn't permit him to fall. Grabbing the back of his shirt collar, I jerked him upright and hit him with a right that jolted my arm all the way to my shoulder.

Still not permitting him to fall, and slamming my right into his face time and time again, I cut him with each blow. He bled from cuts above and below each eye. His nose, already broken when I slammed it into my knee, took another shot from my left. It flattened even more.

It filtered into my clouded, frozen brain that I no longer punished him. He was out cold, not feeling my punches. He slid down the wall to the boardwalk.

A crowd had collected. My gaze swept them, looking for more trouble. I found it. Two of his friends were among the cluster of people. They moved through the tightly packed group, obviously trying to get in the clear so they could use their guns.

Without willing it, my .44 slipped into my hand. "You two come out here where I can see your hands." The crowd melted away from them. They moved toward me and stopped when they saw my gun had them covered.

I motioned them against the wall with my pistol. "Now, stand there, against the wall. Keep your hands above your shoulders, or I might get nervous and send you to hell."

They did as I ordered.

"Adam! Come out here," I shouted. "Tell Miss Betsy to keep Billy in the store for awhile."

Adam walked from the store, and I pointed to a bootblack stand at the other side of the door. "Climb up there and sit down. You're about to get the best shine of your life."

Looking puzzled, Adam did as I bid, but he studied my face. I realized this was the first time he'd seen me truly angry.

I dug in my pocket and flipped the shine boy a cartwheel. He caught it gingerly and stared at me. "What's this here for?"

"I want to rent your stand and equipment for a few minutes, all right?"

"For this much money, you can use it the rest of the day." He grinned widely and pocketed the dollar.

The crowd seemed to sense the show wasn't over and stood fast. They didn't utter a sound.

Holding Thompson's two men at the end of my .44, I watched the one on the ground until he stirred and opened his eyes.

"Get up, you filthy sonuvabitch," I ground out. He stood groggily.

"Go over there to that stand. You're going to give the big 'nigger,' as you call him, the best shine he's ever had."

He looked from me to Adam, his face dripping poison. "I'll be goddamned if I will."

"You'll be a dead sonuvabitch if you don't." I squeezed off a shot that nearly clipped the lobe from his right ear. "Now, pick up the brushes and start spreading shoe wax. Be real careful and don't get any on his trousers. I might take a notion to take your other ear, your whole ear, with my next shot."

"Aw, Mistuh Chance . . ." Adam made ready to get up.

"Sit down, Adam."

He eased himself back onto the seat.

"Now, start shining."

Out of the corner of my eye, I saw the other two slowly lowering their hands. I triggered my .44 again. This slug blew splinters from the wall into their necks. "You lower your hands one quarter of an inch, and I'll clip the tag off your Bull Durham. Of course, along with the tag your heart will get in the way." Their faces turned the color of the gray dust that coated everything in Julesburg. They froze.

I watched Adam's boots come to a brilliant, shiny black. The bully placed the gear back in its receptacle. "You're not through yet. Get the backs of those heels. I want them to shine like the toes."

He picked up the polish and again went to work. When he finished, he straightened and pinned me with a gaze more deadly than a rattler's fangs. "This town, no, this whole damned country ain't big enough fer you. I'll have a bullet waiting for you. It might come from behind a rock, an alley, anywhere. I'm gonna see you fry in hell. No man's ever done to me what you just done and got away with it."

My anger, beginning to cool, again came to white heat.

"Adam, hold your gun on those two while I take care of my business with this gentleman."

I watched Adam pull his .44 and wondered if he'd pull

the trigger if he had to. I thought he would; I had to take the gamble, anyway.

If this man walked away from here, I'd never know when a slug would take me between my shoulders or from where it might come. Looking to my back trail the rest of my life didn't appeal to me. I intended to finish with him here and now. Snake Thompson and his bunch had given me the miseries and walked away from it the last time.

"You've still got your gun. Use it."

He held his hands wide of his side. "I ain't drawin' agin' you. That would be too easy, just blowin' you to hell and havin' it end. No, I'm gonna wait until I got you right off the end of my Spencer, right dead center on yore backbone. Then I'm gonna tell you all about dyin' slow like. Then I'm gonna cut you down one shot at a time till they ain't no more breathin' in you."

"No. You see, I'm calling the shots here, and if you don't draw, I'm going to kill you anyway. You might as well take whatever chance you have, because it's all you have."

His eyes widened, then slitted, and he drew. His gun came out of his holster and was coming level when I drew and drove the buttons on his shirt pockets into his body.

My slug knocked him back against the storefront. He twisted into it, clawing at the wall with hands already dead. He slid to the ground again. This time he wouldn't get up.

chapter

sixteen

My GAZE FLICKED to the two terrified gunmen against the wall. They hadn't moved a muscle.

"Adam," I said without looking at him, "you did well. Now, get Miss Betsy and Billy and we'll go have our coffee."

"Yes, suh."

Anger flowed from me. The cold, hard knot in my stomach melted. The chill holding my brain in a vise of fury thawed. I felt drained, very, very tired. I wanted to rid myself of this bunch that caused me trouble every time I came to Julesburg.

"You men, if you're smart, you will saddle your horses and head for parts unknown. I don't want to see you in Cheyenne or any other end-of-track town. Savvy?"

"Mister, I done seen most every gunfighter in the West. I figger you to stack up with any of 'em. Yes, sir, I'm leavin' right now."

"Me, too," the other echoed his partner's idea. "I'm gone. You ain't gittin' no trouble outta me."

"All right." I holstered my gun. "Now, go."

I watched them scurry off the boardwalk, headed toward the livery stable. Adam led the boy and my woman from the store. I waited for them to join me.

My legs felt as though each dragged a heavy weight. My

arms hung limply at my sides. I had not been hit or shot at, but I felt that I'd endured both.

Betsy didn't say one word until we had coffee and doughnuts in front of us. Finally, she said, "You are not the romantic cowboy-engineer that, until today, I've thought you. I watched the whole thing from the doorway."

"Betsy, I apologize. I didn't want you and Billy to see what happened."

"Chance, you made that man draw against you. You even let him get his pistol out and almost trained on you before you made a lazy move for your gun, lightning fast though it was. You taunted him into it."

My face hardened. Some of the anger returned. "I don't apologize for that. He would have killed me someday from ambush. I'm sorry, but I did it the way I had to."

She said no more. The atmosphere chilled, although I could tell she wasn't angry with me. She seemed more stunned than angry. By the time he had finished three doughnuts, Billy seemed to have forgotten the scene alto- gether. Adam kept sliding me glances and I read a sense of awe and a reluctance to believe what he'd seen me do. Yet, he'd seen me do it before.

Now, added to my weariness, I worried that I'd instilled fear of me in them. My God! I would rather have been the one lying dead out there than have that happen. We were not the jubilant foursome that left the train less than an hour ago, and I was sorry I'd destroyed the magic of it.

I had never thought of myself as a gunfighter, and didn't want the name. Gun practice was not a habit of mine. The fact was, I had never in my life practiced a fast draw. Good coordination was a God-given gift. I had always been good with things that called for use of my hands but was surprised at the speed with which my gun came to hand when needed.

My thoughts shifted to Snake Thompson. He was down to two men now. The odds were narrowing in my favor. That, at least, was something to feel good about.

I looked at Billy. "You finished that book yet, boy?"

He shook his head. "Not all of it, Papa. I read kind of

slow, but Miss Betsy says I'm git, uh, getting better. She's learnin' me how to talk better, too."

I smiled at him. "Billy, she's not *learning* you to do anything. Learning is what *you* do; Miss Betsy is *teaching* you. Think you can remember when to use the two words?"

He looked as though I'd scolded him. "Yes, sir."

I put my arm around his shoulders. "Oh, c'mon little fellow, I'm not fussing at you. I think you're doing really well. Gee, you want to know how old I was before I learned the difference between the two words?" Not waiting for him to answer, I said, "Why, heck. I was about fifteen. My mother used to fuss at me all the time because of it."

His face brightened. "You really mean it? You were fifteen when you learned?"

"Sure was. So you see, you're doing well." I smiled at him, and his little face glowed with the praise.

Adam and Betsy gazed at me. Betsy shook her head in disbelief. "Chance Tenery, you are the absolute in contradiction. The man I'm listening to now and the man I saw in front of the feed store just can't be the same man. How can you be totally ruthless one minute and so tender the next?"

Adam smiled at her. "Miss Betsy, I've seen both sides of Mistuh Chance. He scares me when he's like he was awhile ago. I been sitting here thinking about it. I reckon the only explanation is, if he's your friend, he'd do anything for you. Reckon he would anyway, so long as he figures you need or deserve help. But Lord help you if you're trying to take advantage of someone and they can't protect themselves."

He rubbed his hand back over his face and hair. "I suppose Mistuh Chance thinks I can't or won't take care of myself."

I grasped Adam's shoulder. "Ah, Adam, I don't think that at all. You see, men like those . . ." I stared at the table a moment trying to frame words in my mind that wouldn't offend him, then continued, "men like those, Adam, are used to guns. They practice with them daily. You just plain couldn't match them in gun skills." I grimaced. "They'd kill you. I'm not going to let that happen."

"What makes you think they can't kill you?" Betsy asked, her words coming as though she'd been running.

A long moment passed while I looked at her. "Betsy, since long before entering the academy, I've been handling guns of one kind or another. I don't know how or why, but I'm good with them. There are times that I'm very glad I am."

Absently, I picked up another doughnut and bit into it. I didn't want it. I needed something to do while trying to explain myself to them.

"Today, seeing the expression on your three faces after I made that man fight me, well, I guess I'd rather get shot than ever see you look at me like that again."

"Oh, Chance." Betsy grasped my wrist. "Don't ever say that, don't even think it." She tilted her chin in the way I'd learned signaled no one should argue with her. "What you did was terrible. Oh, no, not the act, but the fact that it was necessary for it to be done."

"Yes, ma'am, I'm sorry it had to happen, too."

We finished our coffee and doughnuts, and I walked them back to the train.

Helping Betsy mount the steps to the railcar, I asked, "You see anything Billy needs? I don't know whether we can find it here in this town, but we can try."

She shook her head. "No. He and I went shopping about a week ago. I bought him a few clothes." Her face brightened. "Oh, yes. The general store had a box of books come in, and I bought a few. I'll read them first to see if they're all right for a young boy."

Somehow, I felt disappointed that I hadn't shared that experience with them. After we talked awhile longer, I excused myself, saying I had better make a walk through town to be sure the men were all right.

Betsy walked to the door with me. When I opened it, she placed her hand on my arm. "Chance, please, don't get in any more trouble."

I tipped my hat. "Don't intend to, ma'am. I'll even *promise* that I won't if you'll go for a walk with me after we get Billy to bed. I'll be back in about an hour."

At the first saloon I went in, Mike and some of the boys sat at a table playing poker.

"Sit in. Take a hand," they all invited at once.

"No. Just walking around to make sure you men stay out of trouble."

"Who the hell are you to talk about trouble?" Mike roared. "Hell, you're the only man I know who could get in trouble in Sunday school."

He held his cards close to his chest and grinned up at me. "Gonna have a talk with Casement about you. I'm gonna see if maybe he'll send a couple o' the boys to mollycoddle you next time we come to town." He tossed off the rest of a beer. "Goddammit, Chance, you beat all. What caused the trouble? I heard you killed another man."

"You go on with your poker game. I'll tell you about it later." I really didn't want to discuss the fight. Every time I pulled the trigger against a man, it seemed to kill part of me as well.

"All right, but I want to hear about it 'fore sundown."

I knew I'd have to tell him about it. "You have a deal," I said and slapped him on the shoulder.

I walked on to the next saloon and found more of my crew, but no trouble. Next, I stopped in Rosie's House of Pleasure to see Lottie. I liked her. She talked right up to you man-style, yet retained her femininity. Hell, the way things were going in this town, every friend counted.

She met me as soon as I stepped into her parlor. One of her girls came up at the same time.

"This gentleman is here to see me, Shirley. Come, Chance, we can visit in the parlor."

As we walked off, Shirley said, "He could put his shoes under my bed anytime without payin'."

Lottie smiled at me. "See, I told you last time. You're a handsome dude."

"You do know how to make a man squirm, don't you."

She laughed a nice laugh. "Oh, Chance, I enjoy making you blush. It isn't often I meet a sophisticated man of the world who can still get embarrassed."

We went into the parlor. Lottie gave the girls lounging there some signal, I assume, because they left us alone.

"Drink?" she asked.

Sitting here with her was relaxing. I nodded. To my surprise, she seemed to guess what I had in mind.

She brought me a large glass of good rye whiskey. "You sit there and relax, Chance. Close your eyes and sleep if you wish. Your nerves must be as frayed as an old rope after what you've been through today."

Taking the glass, I smiled. "Lottie, even if I was rude enough to sleep, I wouldn't. I enjoy just being able to sit and talk with you."

She looked at me steadily for a moment. "You feel it, too. Oh, I don't mean we are likely to get involved in man-woman stuff. I know better. What I mean is, from the first, I felt I'd found a friend, a real friend."

My eyes staying locked with hers, I nodded. "Yes. I value first impressions." I allowed my eyes to crinkle into a slight smile. "You, my lady, I count as a friend, and have since I last talked with you."

She poured a glass of sherry, sipped it, and sat down in the chair next to mine. "Tell me, Chance, how far has the steel reached? When should I plan to move to Cheyenne?"

"If you could do it safely, I'd say to start moving right now. That town's growing so when you go to bed at night you hardly recognize it the next morning."

She grimaced. "About the way I had it figured. I don't want to wait for the rails, or all the good locations will be gone. What should I do?"

"Do you have a friend here, a man friend you can trust?"

Lottie nodded. "Yes, one. He's a gambler now, but he wasn't always. We have known each other a long, long time. I can trust him."

"If he can get away, why don't you send him ahead to buy the lot you need. If you have the money, let him buy building material and start putting up a really first-class establishment. By the time it's finished, I'm sure you and the girls will be able to ride the train to Cheyenne. You'll be in business as soon as you get there." I sipped my drink, studying her over the rim.

She frowned, and I saw that she gave my idea a good scrubbing down. Her face smoothed, and she smiled at me. "Good. I'll talk to him and see if he can catch on with the next wagon train that comes through."

She had toyed with the idea only a moment before making her decision. I liked that. If you have to do something, then do it, don't vacillate. Get the job done.

"Good girl! You should be in time."

Lottie smiled, and I thought I saw a bit of sadness behind it. "Chance, this will be my last investment in a business of this sort. After I get it running and making a lot of money, I intend to sell for a handsome profit."

"What then, Lottie?"

She shrugged. "I've thought of building me a nice home, at the base of a pretty mountain somewhere and being a lady again."

"You're a lady now. All you have to do is go somewhere where you're not known and join the sewing circle."

Lottie laughed, sipped her sherry, and said, "Heaven forbid. I don't think I could stand the boredom."

"Well, at least you could do anything you wished. Think I better leave now. Just wanted to see how you were." I chuckled. "And yeah, I wanted a sip of your good rye again."

While she walked me to the door, I asked, "You'll promise to call on me if you need me, won't you?"

"Just knowing you're there, Chance, is more help than you can imagine."

I tipped my hat and left.

After another hour of looking in saloons and finding things quiet, I walked toward the tracks.

Betsy and I talked while Billy read. This world with them seemed a million miles from the one just down the steps of Dodge's car. In here, I felt like a family man, no problems, no cares. To think life could always be like this was futile. Whether we went back east, or farther west, there were good people and bad. The bad had to be handled, often brutally, so that moments like this were possible. I sighed.

Duels were fought all over the world. The East had more than its fair share of them, but out here, scarcely populated as it was, fights were talked about more. A man could get a reputation as a gunfighter quickly, whether he wanted it or not. I didn't want it.

"That sigh sounded as though you had the weight of the world on your shoulders."

I looked at her and smiled. "Sometimes, Betsy, I feel that I do. I suppose I should leave well enough alone when I see people being stepped on. It's really none of my business what happens to them, but I stick my nose in, and find every time I've bought a bunch of trouble."

"You're thinking about what happened today?"

I shook my head. "No. That *was* my business. Adam is our partner. I'll take care to see that no harm comes to any of you."

"*Our* partner, Chance? You still intend to pursue what you said in the café when we met?"

I poured a cup of coffee. "Let's take a walk after we get Billy to bed. We'll talk about it then. All right?"

Her eyes wide, she nodded. I turned to Billy.

"You know how to shoot a rifle, Billy?"

"Some. I shot at the Indians when they killed my folks. I ain't, uh, I'm *not* very good with one, though."

"What do you think about the three of us going out to that ridge behind town and shooting some tomorrow? I'll teach you the right way to handle a gun."

His grin was my answer.

"Now, Chance Tenery, see what you've done. He'll never get to sleep for thinking about what you've promised."

I tousled Billy's blond hair. "Ah, he'll go to sleep like a good boy, won't you, son?"

"I sure will, Papa. Soon's I get in bed. Miss Betsy don't even have to read to me tonight."

"*Doesn't* have to," Betsy corrected automatically.

"Yes'm," Billy responded.

True to his word, Billy turned on his side after hugging our necks and made ready to go to sleep.

We told Tom we were going for a walk and left the train.

I offered my arm, and Betsy placed her hand in its crook. We went around the end of the car and walked out on the prairie. This night, the stars looked close enough to touch with a stick. Wind sighed across the sea of grass, and the heat of the day cooled. The shawl Betsy had thrown over her shoulders should be a comfort to her.

I wanted to put my arm around her waist but thought that would be rushing things. It didn't stop me from wanting to, though. Walking here, with only the night sounds breaking the silence, made me hesitate to say anything, but time alone with Betsy was rare. I stopped and faced her. She tilted her head to look at me.

"Ma'am, I know the way I surprised you at the café that day was not the accepted thing to do. I want you to know, though, that I meant every word of it." My voice came out raspy, betraying my fear of her reaction. She parted her lips as though to speak. I cut her off.

"Betsy, if what you're going to say is no, hold off on answering me for awhile. I promise I'll make you a good husband. I'll protect you, and provide for—"

"Chance Tenery," she interrupted me, "stop talking, and hold me close."

I must have looked like an idiot. I know I felt like one. I was afraid to believe what I'd heard.

She giggled and then tried to look very prim. "If you're such an impulsive man, you could kiss me, too, although I know it wouldn't be quite *proper.*"

I gathered her into my arms, held her close a moment, and lowered my lips to her slightly parted, waiting ones. I held her lightly, afraid I'd break her in my rough arms.

She pulled back from my embrace. "I'm not made of porcelain. Hold me tight, Chance." Her voice was breathy.

This time I held her the way I'd wanted to in the first place. Her body pressed to mine, promising things I'd only thought of in the deepest part of the night, and even then, I'd been reluctant to let my dreams go so far. I had thought it might be a year until I could convince her that we belonged together. This was more than I had dared wish for.

When we stepped apart, she smiled. "If you think this is sudden, I want you to know it isn't. I had my mind made up before you dropped out of sight behind the train that first day. I felt I had to meet you somehow and was terrified that I wouldn't find a way."

"Y-you don't mean it," I stammered like a boy of thirteen. "Why, that's when I decided to find you and court you. Betsy, I can't say I know what love is, but I know I *like* you. I know I'd only be half a person without you. I want us to share our lives until the end of our time on this earth. Most importantly, something inside of me says that my feeling for you, strong as it is, will grow even more."

"Kiss me again, Chance, and stop jabbering so much. Besides, that speech sounds like you've rehearsed it over and over."

I felt my face turn red. She guessed right. I *had* rehearsed those stiff words, but they said what I wanted to say. "You will marry me then?" I asked.

"Of course we'll be married." She placed her hands on her hips. "Do you think I'd be out here with you, letting you kiss me and hold me if I didn't intend to marry you?"

"Well, no, ma'am. I suppose I just can't believe it. I wanted you to accept my proposal so much I was beginning to doubt it could happen."

"Well, it's happened. I don't believe anything would dare stand in our way." She laughed. "I know Uncle won't."

I nodded. "No, he'll give us his blessing. I've already talked with him about it."

"You have?"

"Yep. He said if I got your approval that I had his condolences and to get on with it."

"Condolences? Oh, he did, did he? I'll just have to speak to him about that."

My arm slipped around her waist. "C'mon, Betsy, he loves you like a father, but I suppose he knows how strong-headed you can be."

"Why, he might have changed your mind."

"Not a chance." I pulled her close to me again, and this time I kissed her like I really wanted to. She didn't break, either, probably because she held me as tightly as I held her. The promise of much more was still there. That promise would carry me through many lonely nights, but at the same time it would torment me, make me want to stop what I was doing and ride to her.

chapter

seventeen

WE WALKED FARTHER from the town.

"What about Billy?" I asked.

"What do you mean? I love that little boy. I like caring for him. I thought you wanted to keep him, raise him. That's the idea he has, anyway."

I stopped and faced her. "That's the idea *I* have. It's the idea Billy has, too. But you're a partner also. I want to know how you feel about it."

"Chance, I believe if you cast that little boy aside, I'd go with him. Do you really think I could be that selfish?"

I shook my head. "No, but raising a small boy is quite a responsibility and a whole lot of work. Most of it'll fall on your shoulders for awhile."

She smiled up at me. "When you hear me complain, Chance Tenery, we'll talk about it." I tightened my hold on her waist.

"Oh, goodness, we better get back to the car or Tom will worry about me."

"I'd like to stay out here with you until the sun comes up, but you being a *proper* young lady, I suppose it just wouldn't look right." I cocked my head and grinned at her.

"You know darned well it wouldn't. Let's go back." She stopped and turned squarely to me. "Of course, we might take a little more time if you'd kiss me again."

The kiss didn't take long, not nearly as long as I wanted, nor did the walk back to the train.

With Betsy back aboard, I bade her good night. Tom took one look at her flushed face, tried to cover a smile, and muttered, "Young folks. Humph."

The night passed without trouble. I played a little poker with the boys, went to the flatcar, spread my blankets, and went to sleep.

We used my Henry out on the ridge the next morning. Before we fired a shot, I spent an hour showing Billy gun safety and watching him practice it. Betsy was just as interested as the boy. Satisfied they wouldn't shoot themselves accidentally, I set up a target against the side of the hill.

The Henry was pretty heavy for a ten-year-old, but Billy soon placed his shots close enough to the target to draw my praise. He glowed.

Standing behind Betsy, helping her hold the gun properly, tilted my temperature to the high side. She looked over her shoulder at me. "Chance, I declare, you know I did this right a half hour ago. If I didn't know better, I'd say you're enjoying this."

I laughed and whispered, "It's the only way I can get this close to you in broad daylight. You bet I'm enjoying it, and if you want to know what *I* believe, I'll tell you."

"All right, tell me, smarty-pants."

I grinned, wanting to kiss her. "Yeah, I'll tell you. You learned the right way to hold this rifle the first time I showed you, but you messed it up every time on purpose, just so I'd hold you."

She shrugged out of my arms, raised the rifle to her shoulder, and fired. She hit the target dead center. Turning to me with a smug smile, she said, "All right, Chance, you just cost yourself the opportunity to hold me like that the rest of the day."

I must have looked like a boy who'd lost his last marble to the big kids, because Betsy laughed. "Yes, you messed it up for today," she smiled, teasingly, "but wait until tonight. Maybe, just maybe, I'll make it up to you then."

I knew I had a lot to learn about this woman. I suspected there was a core of steel in her makeup that she'd need when we had our ranch.

After lunch, I took them back to the car and returned to the streets of Julesburg.

At the first saloon I went into, a nice-looking, well-dressed man of about forty walked to the bar and stood at my side. He slanted me a sidewise look and asked, "You're Chance Tenery?" Without waiting for my reply, he continued, "Lottie said for you to drop by; she wants to see you."

I tipped my hat. "Much obliged."

"I don't think it's anything that can't wait a few minutes." He chuckled and stuck out his hand. "I'm Randolph Donavan. Lottie is my friend, too." He smiled slightly. "If you were a little older, as good-looking as you are, I'd be jealous."

I cast him a crooked smile. "As pretty as Lottie is, if I wasn't already taken, you'd still have reason to be jealous."

He laughed. "Thanks for helping her. We are good friends from a long time ago. I appreciate your help. You'd better go see what she wants to tell you. It might be important."

I nodded and left. After meeting Lottie's friend, I felt good about what the future held for her. One of the girls let me in, and I went directly to Lottie's room. At my tap, she opened the door and came into the parlor to meet me.

"Have a seat, Chance." She walked to her bar. "Do you have time for a drink?"

I shook my head. "Thanks, anyway. Mr. Donavan said you wanted to see me."

"Yes, I told Randy last night what we'd discussed. The thing I want to talk to you about has nothing to do with that."

"All right, let's hear it."

She poured me a drink despite my refusal and brought it to me. "It's Snake Thompson, Chance. He has me worried. After you left town last time, he went around town making his brag about what he'd do to you when he caught up with you."

"Yeah, I've already heard his brags." I shrugged. "That's to be expected, Lottie."

"Yes, you're right, but that isn't what has me worried. You see, as long as he made threats, I knew where he was. Now the threats have stopped, and he hasn't been seen or heard from for over a week. *That* has me worried."

"Maybe he just decided to move on to the next town."

"Or," she cut in, "maybe he's out there along the right-of-way somewhere, waiting for a shot at you."

I sipped my drink, smiled, and shook my head. Pulling my pipe from my shirt pocket, I asked if she minded me smoking.

"No, of course not. I like the smell of pipe smoke. Go ahead."

After tamping tobacco in the bowl and lighting it, I peered through the cloud of smoke at her. "No, Lottie, I think Thompson is the kind who'll want an audience any time he does something he considers big." I exhaled another great cloud of smoke. "He knows I work for the UP, so he has a pretty good idea where I'll be. I think, perhaps, he's gone on to Cheyenne, knowing I'll be coming there when work progresses that far. Thanks for telling me, but don't worry about it. I'm a careful man."

"Yes, I know you are." She leaned toward me and placed her hand on my arm. "But be especially careful now."

I nodded, then changed the subject. "I like your Mr. Donavan. He seems the kind who'd stick with a friend."

Lottie smiled. "I'm glad, Chance, and yes, he will stand by through rough times, *especially* rough times."

"Thanks, thanks for everything. I had better leave now, or we might have some jealous folks spitting daggers at us."

"Ah ha. So what I've heard is true. You and the pretty lady I met the other day are working on a romance."

I felt my face turn warm. She laughed and led me to the door. I felt her watch me walk down the street.

The afternoon went quietly, and my walk with Betsy after Billy went to bed was even better than the night before. The morning would bring me back into the world of building the railroad. It would be filled with growling, cursing men, and the ride back to end-of-track.

A week later, I rode alone, far ahead of my own crew. The stack of planning documents in my saddlebags grew with each day. I'd left Mike and the boys plenty to keep them busy until I returned.

I constantly scanned every swale, ridge, dry wash, and arroyo. I had not seen anyone for days. I felt I was the only man in the world. A glance from horizon to horizon showed distance an Easterner would not think possible. In the middle of it all stood one lone man. In this vastness, I was as a grain of sand is to the oceans.

If a man had the inclination to think himself big and important, he should come stand in my boots. Only a few seconds would shrink him down to size in this huge expanse.

Early in the morning of the eighth day, I heard a rumble, like distant thunder. A glance at the sky showed only a brassy blue, not even a puffball of a cloud. Again, I scanned the horizon, then pinpointed a dark, sweeping mass rolling into view from the north. I didn't remember having seen a storm act this way.

The ground trembled. I stared aghast at the thundering mass roaring down upon me. For an instant, I froze. Now, the dark mass stretched as far as I could see. Fear clamped my chest in a vise. I rode directly into the path of a buffalo stampede.

A glance showed no hole, no ditch, nothing that could shelter me.

I reined my horse hard left, dug my heels into his sides, and headed south. A glance over my shoulder showed I wasn't pulling away from the thundering terror, and I rode at a horse-killing pace. Frantically, I searched for some kind of shelter, any kind.

The dry plains stretched ahead of me with no break in the smooth, rolling hills. I stared behind as much as I did ahead. The herd drew closer.

We must have covered a little over a mile when the gelding stumbled. He was tiring, but tired was better than dead. He didn't run nearly as fast now, and the monsters were almost upon us.

Then I saw it, a shallow ditch with undercut sides. I reined toward it.

The lowered, brutal heads, powerful humped shoulders, and pounding hooves of the beasts were almost on us when the ditch fell away before me. Pulling my horse down flat beside me and pushing my head close to the undercut bank, I pulled the length of my body in close to it. All I could do for me and my horse was pray that the momentum of the rampaging animals would carry them over us.

Grim darkness, and noise such as I'd never heard, even in the midst of all-out cannon fire, engulfed me, penetrated me. My guts, my flesh, all of me quivered with the vibrating roar passing only inches above.

The air, mixed with dust and dirt and the musky stench of the animals, choked me. I buried my nose in my armpit, gasping for air. Holding the gelding's head snubbed to the ground, I prayed he wouldn't rear up into the avalanche. One of the animals passed over me and fell.

If he caused others to pile up, I'd be crushed under tons of mangled meat. My horse would be the first to go, and without him, I'd be as good as dead, anyway.

I had never felt heat like this. The combination of fear and heat forced sweat to pour in constant rivulets from me. It mixed with dirt and dust thrown by the huge beasts pulverizing the earth.

Great clods of earth torn from the sod fell upon me. The fear came that I'd be buried alive, fear so strong I had to fight it off or I would stand and try to run. I would not have even reached my knees before being trampled to a pulp.

My God! Would this hell never end? Forever, it seemed, they passed over me. Then, like a thunder storm slacks off at its end, I sensed a thinning of the mass above.

I don't know how long I lay there. My first lucid thought was of shrieking, screaming quiet. I had never experienced a total lack of sound, and my ears hurt from it. Maybe I had gone deaf. That thought had hardly sunk in when my horse raised his head and snorted.

I came cautiously to my knees before drawing fully erect. Pulling my horse to his feet, I checked him for injury and found none. My next concern was for me. I hurt nowhere, but ran my hands over arms, legs, and body. Miraculously, I, too, was in one piece.

A glance told me how lucky we'd been. Blood, guts, hide, and mutilated bodies of several animals were stacked and trampled so they'd formed a ring partly surrounding where my horse and I had lain.

"Well, old horse, we've seen a lot together, but this is a first. We used up about ten lifetimes of luck today."

My brain wouldn't think, my throat wouldn't swallow, and my legs almost refused to hold me. I'd never had a thirst like the one that now parched me.

Reaching for my canteen hanging from the saddle horn, I saw it had been crushed. My horse had probably lain on it.

I mounted and turned back the way we'd come. Still wanting to hear something, even my own voice, I said, "This stampede was my first, but I hope never to go through anything like it again."

I wondered what had set off the stampede. The thought occurred to me that maybe Indians had been responsible. Sometimes, when hunting, they would stampede a herd. I hoped I was wrong. After the stampede, I didn't think I could cope with an Indian attack.

Back at the demolished roadbed, I saw that the thousands of hooves had churned it to a fine dust. I found a water hole and drank, watered my horse, and washed the filth off me and my clothes. Clean again, and feeling I had earned the rest of the day off, I set up an early camp. Sitting by my fire, notepad in hand, I made a notation to Casement to have the grading crew rebuild this part of the roadbed.

Drinking my coffee after supper, I watched sunset paint its masterpiece across the plains. Shadows shaded from beige to blue to purple. The crest of each ground swell, drinking in the last of the light, looked as though dipped in gold. Some of the higher hills were red, catching the fading rays of the setting sun. The scent of dried grass, dust, distance, and the sighing of the wind were my sole companions.

Times such as this brought my love for the mountains back on me. *If I can,* I thought, *I'm going to find a place against the base of some mountain where I can look out across a million miles of golden grass and then, by just turning around, see tall, tree-clad, majestic mountains. There'll be streams and grass tall as my knees.* I'd have it all. Betsy, Billy, and Adam made the picture complete.

Soon after sunup the next morning, a speck of dust appeared on the western horizon. Warily, I worked, keeping track of the dust plume as it grew larger, until I made it out as one man.

Still sketching the trestle I had been working on, I eased over and slid my Henry from its scabbard and leaned it against my leg.

When I finished with the drawing, I filed it in a saddlebag, picked up the Henry, and stood waiting for the rider. When he drew close enough, I saw he was a white man with shoulder-length hair and a flowing mustache. He held his hands wide of his guns, but being somewhat wary, I never took the bore of my rifle off his chest.

"That's far enough." My words stopped him about thirty feet from me. "Who are you, and what's your business here?"

"Careful sort, ain't you?" he said and smiled. "I'm James Butler Hickok. Some call me Wild Bill. I'm an Army scout right now. Who're you, and what are you doing here in the middle of nowhere?"

I lowered the muzzle of my rifle.

"Chance Tenery, UP engineer. I've heard of you, Mr. Hickok. Climb down. We'll have our nooning together."

Hickok's glance raked me from head to toe. "I've heard of you too, Tenery. Yeah, I'll stop awhile. The name's Bill."

Hickok threw his leg over the saddle horn and slid from his horse. "I'll gather the chips if you'll cook."

I grinned. "You've got a deal." His having heard of me caused me some worry. I didn't like the idea.

We had eaten and were drinking coffee when Bill looked

to the east, then over his shoulder at me. "What do you make o' that dust cloud over yonder?" He glanced at the trampled earth. "Long's it ain't 'nother stampede, I figure you an' me can take care o' anything else."

I hadn't seen the dust cloud and felt irritated. Hell, it wasn't his fault I'd been careless. I grimaced. "Not close enough to tell yet what it is."

"I don't figger it as Indians." Hickok still squinted into the distance. "I been watching it for some time now, and it ain't movin' very fast."

I looked back down the roadbed and saw what had drawn Hickok's attention. "Wagons, maybe?"

He nodded. "B'lieve you're right. Lotta dust and slow-movin'."

"At the rate they're traveling, it'll be midafternoon before they come on us. Make yourself at home. I'm going to finish this sketch I started."

Hickok walked over and sat on the slope. "I'll get some shut-eye while you work." He lay back, tilted his hat over his eyes and, as far as I could tell, went right to sleep.

My sketch finished, I watched twelve big Conestogas come nearer. Soon the squeak and grind of wheels were audible. Hickok sat up, grinned, and rolled to his feet. "Good rest. Didn't 'specially need it, but I'll take it whenever I can."

We stood there, shoulder to shoulder, and watched the wagons roll to a stop.

The wagon boss approached. "Any water close by?"

I nodded. "Yep. Good stream over yonder about a hundred yards. You figure to make camp here?"

"Long's they's water, might's well." He yelled in the direction of the lead wagon. "Circle up. We'll stay the night here."

A glance showed me the rest of the wagons. Randolph Donavan reined his horse from between a couple of wagons and rode toward us.

"I see Donavan managed to hook up with you."

"Yeah, he seemed right anxious to get to Cheyenne and

didn't want to try it alone." The wagon boss slanted me an inquiring glance. "Where'd you get to know 'im?"

"Back in Julesburg. He's a friend of a friend of mine."

"Dresses like a gambler but sure carries his load. Good man."

"What makes you think a gambling man won't carry his load?" Hickok said.

The wagon boss grinned. "No offense, Mr. Hickok. I seen a many who would and others who wouldn't."

A cold smile touched the corners of Hickok's mouth. "No offense taken, sir. Reckon I've seen the same."

Donavan rode up, dismounted, and extended his hand.

"Mr. Tenery, glad to see you. Thought maybe I would if the wagons stayed close to the roadbed."

I introduced him to Hickok, told him to call me Chance, and then asked how Lottie was doing.

"She's doing fine but wishes you were going to be in Cheyenne with me."

"I'll be there, and the way the UP's moving ahead, it won't be long."

That night, I ate cooking other than my own for the first time in over a week and was glad for the opportunity. We sat by the fire after supper and talked long into the night.

The next morning, the wagon train pulled out, Hickok with them. Before they left, I traded for another canteen. I stood alone again.

After studying the stack of drawings, I decided it was time to head back to my crew.

Again, no human being crossed my path until I raised the trestle crew late the afternoon of the fifth day. They had made good progress during my absence. I'd set it up with Casement before leaving end-of-track that I'd take whatever time I found necessary to give my plan a fair shot.

I believed now that I had enough accomplished and documented to convince Casement to go ahead with the plan. I'd see him in a couple of days and find out his reaction.

When I rode into the trestle site, I saw only half the men I expected there.

"Where the hell you been, boy? We were getting worried 'bout you," Mike greeted me.

"I've been all right," I said and looked around. "Where's the rest of the crew? I see only about half of you here."

"Yeah." I saw his face flush, his eyes narrow. "Had to send 'em back to the last trestle to rebuild it."

"What happened?"

His anger was close to choking him now. His words came out gravelly. "Them sonsuvbitches, them dirty sonsuvbitches."

"Who're you talking about?"

"They burned the trestle, that's what those red heathens done."

"Red heathens? You mean you've had Indian trouble?"

"Hell yes," Mike exploded. "You know any other red heathens around here?"

I walked away from him toward the fire, hoping he'd cool down a little. "Let's have a cup of coffee while you tell me about it."

We squatted, our steaming cups in hand. I waited for Mike to begin.

He sipped the hot liquid. I saw his face return to its normal ruddy color. "Well, boss, we wuz all workin' here, 'bout a week ago, when we seen smoke risin' out yonder in back of us." He made an angry, choppy motion with his right fist. "Hell, I knowed right off it wuz the trestle. I rode out yonder with a few men and, shore enough, they'd set 'er afire, built fires around each piling and burned 'er to the ground. They wan't nowhere to be seen. They'd done raised their hell and hightailed it."

I grasped his shoulder. "It's no fault of yours, Mike. I'm surprised we haven't had more of that sort of thing. Probably would have, except they don't usually make war against things that can't fight back. We can be thankful for that."

Mike eyed me a moment. "You ain't mad at me fer lettin' somethin' like that happen?"

I grinned at him. "If I'd been here, or if Jack Casement had been here, it would have happened. I just hope this isn't a sign of things to come."

Mike looked relieved. "Yeah, me, too, boss." He frowned. "You sure you don't hold it agin me for letting it happen?"

"Hell no, Mike. Like I told you, it would've happened regardless who was here."

He sighed. "Hot damn! That's a relief. I thought on it a good while, and I couldn't come up with any way I could've kept them from doing it. I worried 'bout how you'd take it."

My horse blew, and of a sudden I realized I hadn't loosened the cinches, let alone cared for him as I should have. "Don't worry about it, Mike. We'll just rebuild and go from there."

I walked to my horse, stripped my rig off him, and rubbed him down with a handful of grass.

Mike told me later that it was our turn again to go to Julesburg. I thought I might skip this trip and try to regain the time we'd lost due to the Indians.

"Casement ain't gonna let you do that, Chance. He believes in his men restin' up when they need it, and you need it." With a glance, he raked me from head to toe. "I figger you done lost a few pounds out there alone. Casement'll see that and make you go in with us."

His words were good to hear because I wanted to see Betsy and Billy. When a person takes on a job, he has to make up his mind to do what's right, regardless of his own feelings. However, if the boss told me to take time off, I'd just have to do it.

True to Mike's prediction, Jack looked me over and said that I would go in with the crew. "I'm not being entirely unselfish, Chance. With you in there, we haven't had a man killed or hurt. I want you with your men."

"If you let me go out ahead of them and make estimates of what we need to get through South Pass, it'll be a long time before I'm with them."

"Give me time to go over your reports tonight. I'll give you my answer in the morning before you leave for Julesburg."

The next morning, Casement walked with me to the railcar. "When you and the crew return, Chance, be outfitted to carry out your plan."

I smiled. "I'm thinking of taking Billy with me, Jack. I think it'll be good for him. He can learn to survive in this country."

Casement frowned, almost imperceptibly shook his head, then changed it to a nod. "As much as you think of that youngster, if you think you can keep the two of you alive out there, you have my blessings. I think it will be good for him, too. I don't know how Dodge will feel about it." He grinned. "But he's not here, is he?"

My eyes locked with his. "Thanks, Jack, I wouldn't take Billy with me if I didn't think we'd be all right." I boarded the car, and Casement signaled the engineer to move out.

chapter
eighteen

BETSY AND BILLY met me when the train pulled into Julesburg. I liked the feeling of having someone there. Betsy and I were alone during our walk that night when I brought up the subject of taking Billy with me.

Her chin tilted, and I read anger in her eyes. "You're not taking the child out in that Indian-infested country. You have no business going out there without an escort. The Sioux, Cheyenne, Crow, none of them are friendly. No, I'll . . ."

"Hold on a minute," I cut in. "The Indians you've mentioned will be going into winter camp. There'll be very little danger. Besides," I took out my pipe, filled it with tobacco, and started tamping it, "it would do him good to experience a little of the danger and learn how to cope with it. That's the purpose of taking him out."

"Oh, so you're going to look for trouble. You say you're going to teach him how to live out there. *I* think you're going to teach him how to die."

My face stiffened. I swallowed a couple of times to squelch my rising anger. "If we're to have a ranch, live in this country and thrive here, we're going to have—"

"If you take that little boy," she interrupted, "there will be no ran—"

"Don't," I interrupted. "Don't say a single word more.

Don't say anything we'll both be sorry for." My words fell between us, cold and inflexible. "I'm taking him with me. He needs to be trained in man-business, and *that's* my job to do. There'll be no further discussion on the matter."

She whirled, and walked, almost ran from me. We were only fifty yards or so from Dodge's car.

I felt empty, drained, sick to my stomach. So this was the end of a dream. My world had just fallen apart. These were the first bitter words we'd had, and probably the last words we'd ever have.

But I still intended to take Billy with me. A boy should learn to be a man, and no woman could teach him that. The walk back to town, although no more than a hundred yards, stretched a hundred miles.

The next morning, I bought Billy a sturdy little mustang, gentle enough that he'd have no trouble with it, but with enough spirit that he'd have to take the kinks out on cool mornings. I also bought a packhorse.

Buying things for Billy was supposed to be a time of happiness and laughter. Instead, I did it alone, with anger lying just under the surface.

A Winchester .44 carbine took my eye, and I bought it for Billy. Its magazine held thirteen cartridges, and would come in handy for game or defense against Indians.

A ground sheet, two blankets, sheepskin coat, shirts, Levi's, long johns, a new belt, saddle blanket, several boxes of cartridges, and saddle and bridle completed what he'd need while gone. We'd be in high elevations, and snow might catch us before we could steer clear of it.

Finished with shopping, I went by Dodge's car and tapped on the door. Tom opened it.

"Tom, please tell Miss Betsy I'll come by for Billy before the train leaves in the morning."

"Yes, suh." He hesitated. "But, suh, won't you come in and y'all talk over your troubles? I sure don't like to see you young folks act like this to each other."

I felt stiff, and knew I acted it. "Tom, I appreciate your concern, but it won't do any good. Miss Betsy's made up her mind, and I'm not changing mine, so I suppose there's nothing more to say. Please tell her."

"Yes, suh."

Tom looked as though he was the one who had lost his woman.

Sleep that night was long in coming. I crawled from my blankets several times and walked away from the tracks, out upon the prairie. Finally, the sky brightened, announcing the new day.

At my knock, Betsy and Billy stepped through the door; Betsy, stiff and cold, Billy puzzled, looking from one to the other of us.

"When, and if, you return, I would like to see Billy."

I nodded. "Of course, as often as you like." I shuffled my feet, wanting to say more, but pride stood between us.

I mumbled, "Betsy . . ." Quickly she leaned down, hugged Billy, kissed him on the cheek, whirled, went back in the car and closed the door.

My gut felt like I wanted to vomit. I had never hurt as bad in my life. My world stood behind that door. Anger pushed the hurt aside. I spun and called to Billy.

"C'mon, son, we've a lot of riding to do."

"But, Papa, why won't you let Miss Betsy come with us?"

"It isn't her place to come with us. This is man's work." My voice sounded harsh, unbending, even to my ears. "We'll go alone. All she has to do is understand why we're going."

Suddenly, I felt shame. What, I asked myself, was I doing getting angry with Billy? He was just a little boy caught in the middle.

I showed Billy his horse, rifle, and gear he'd be using for the next several months. Any other time he'd be ecstatic over them, but now he cast me glances, almost accusing, and stayed quiet.

I boosted him into his saddle, and we rode to load onto the train. When we dismounted, Billy tugged on my sleeve. "Papa, if Miss Betsy was supposed to understand, why did she cry all night long?" His eyes, wide, filled with tears.

"Papa, I heard her. She'd cry and then say, 'Chance, why, why are you doing this to us?'"

I blinked back tears and came within an inch of riding back to her. I shook the hurt out of my brain. This was something Billy and I had to do. If I got killed, he had to be prepared to handle life on his own.

It never occurred to me, then, that Betsy loved him enough to raise him, educate him, and see that he had a proper start in life. No, that thought never came to me until three months later when we were far beyond Fort Laramie. Even so, I knew I'd have done the same thing. He needed man-training.

With Laramie far behind us, we made a dry camp, cooked supper over a smokeless fire, and rolled into our blankets.

I stared at the stars. The hurt was still there in the pit of my stomach. It would be with me the rest of my life. It might dull a little, but not much. Billy, after about a week, snapped out of it. He would mention Betsy every once in a while and wouldn't talk much afterward.

I picked out a star and looked at it. I wondered if Betsy was looking at the same one, hoped she was, and maybe knew that I loved her more than life.

The next morning we rode on. We were climbing now, had been for several days. It wasn't a sharp ascent, but gradual. We would climb until we crossed South Pass. Then we'd have a gentle descent. I thought about that a moment and decided to turn back when we crossed the pass.

I had heard that telegraph wires ran past South Pass to Salt Lake City, and I felt comfortable with that because I never could predict when I might have to send a message. However, the Indians frequently tore the lines down and used the wire for bracelets and ornaments.

This was dry country; short grass stretched as far as the eye could see. There were no trees. The summers were hot, the winters fierce, and now, the cold nights told of short days and long nights not far away. I wanted to have Billy where we could find shelter in a hurry if snow began.

Autumn blizzards were not uncommon here in the high plains.

I looked at Billy. In the three months we'd been gone, he had filled out. He had good shoulders and a narrow waist. I thought he had grown a little taller, too, and carried himself with a pride and confidence I'd not seen in him before. This was good for him; it would make a man of him.

I had taught him to keep a constant vigil, never relax, never take it for granted that because the last time he had looked and seen nothing that there was not trouble close by.

In the distance I spotted four black specks and knew they were buffalo. I waited, wanting to see how long before Billy spotted them. He rode up alongside.

"Papa," he pointed with his rifle, "there's something out there. Don't rightly know what, though."

I smiled. It had taken him no longer to spot the beasts than it had me. "Good job, boy." Still peering into the distance, I said, "You ever shoot a buffalo?"

"No, sir."

"You won't be able to say that in about an hour. Those are buffalo."

We rode toward them and, when we were within about two hundred yards, I reined in. "Hold up, son. Let's get off our horses. Don't want a missed shot because of a skittish horse."

We climbed down. I studied the four. One old bull, head lowered, stood looking at us. "Billy, put your shot right behind the left shoulder. You pick out the one you want. Now, I'm not going to mess with you. You do it."

I watched him. He stared toward the humpbacked beasts. I could almost see him think, sorting out the one he wanted, picking the one that would give him the best shot. Finally, he raised his rifle, sighted, shook his head, knelt, and sighted again. Then, slowly, very slowly, I saw his trigger finger whiten as he squeezed.

When his gun fired, all four animals took off, running like a freight train.

Billy looked at me, his face tight. "I missed, Papa, I missed him clean."

I pulled him to me, hugged him, and smiled into his disappointed face. I shook my head. "No, son, you didn't miss. Look out there." I pointed to the spot where I'd seen a young cow stumble and fall.

His head swiveled as he followed my point. His face was like the sun coming from behind a thunderhead. "Gee, Papa, I got 'im. I really got 'im."

I felt as good about it as he did and hugged him to me again. "Let's go skin *your* buffalo, boy." I looked down at him. "You've got to remember, a large animal will seldom drop as soon as he's hit. Now, listen to me good, because this is important. Approach a buffalo, deer, or antelope with caution; their hooves can kill you." We rode toward Billy's kill.

"Son, a grizzly is different. They aren't afraid of anything. Don't ever figure one shot will do the job. When you pump a shot into one of them, keep on shooting until you see him go down. There's been many a man killed because he didn't. *They'll* keep coming at you."

"Yes, sir."

We led our horses to the downed beast while I wondered if my words sank in. Billy was so excited I wasn't sure he'd heard a word.

I did the skinning and butchering while explaining to Billy how and why each cut should be done the way I did it. This time, I knew he listened because he asked questions.

"We'll keep this hide and have a winter coat made of it." I smiled. "That coat will be yours, son."

He answered my smile with a big grin. I'd never seen as much pride in any man as Billy showed at that moment.

That night, we had buffalo steaks for supper. I didn't count the times Billy told me that *he'd* furnished the food for this meal, but he told me a significant number of times. I wasn't likely to forget.

Those nights by the fire with Billy were some of the most

fulfilling of my life. Betsy had packed four books for him, and I had him read awhile each night. Then we'd talk.

I told him about the places I'd been, the way life was in the big cities, how people dressed differently, talked differently, and even acted differently. What he'd learn out here, especially the ability to stand on his own two feet, would be useful in a city also, if he decided to live in one.

He told me Betsy had been teaching him proper table manners and that he wished he'd had a chance to learn more. His statement surprised me. "You want me to teach you good manners, etiquette?"

"Yes, sir, I surely do. I want to know how to do things right."

I nodded. "And so you should, Billy. We'll make a gentleman out of you."

Using sticks for flatware, I taught him the proper pieces to use for salads, desserts, entrées, soups, cocktails, and in what order he'd find them by his plate. He'd practice picking up the right one as I called out the imaginary course in front of him.

With me acting as the woman, we acted out seating her at a table, holding his arm for her when walking, that he should seat her first, to stand when a lady entered the room, and to offer his seat if all were taken. I taught him everything I knew about etiquette.

"Papa, I never knew there was so much to learn about being grown up."

"Ahhh, Billy, the things I'm teaching you are ones you should use any time, even as a small boy." I gathered up the sticks we'd been using and tossed them on the fire. "When I correct your grammar, or something you've done, I want you to understand that I'm not fussing at you. I simply want you to know the proper way things are done."

His face serious, he nodded. "Yes, sir, but there's an awful lot o' stuff you been teaching me. I reckon I ain't, uh, I'm not likely to remember it all."

"With practice you will, boy." I looked at the Big Dipper

and saw that it was nearly nine o'clock. "We'd better crawl in, son. It's getting late."

About midmorning the next day, I saw pony tracks. I dismounted and told Billy to stay where he was. I wanted to read them before they got stepped on.

The tracks were fresh. They'd been made since sunup. At first, I thought there had been four ponies but finally settled on three. I could tell nothing about the riders, but I could tell the horses were ridden.

When I'd finished, I called Billy off his horse and explained how I'd come to the conclusions I'd made. "They're traveling in the direction we are, but they might double back, so keep a sharp eye out."

"You think they'll try to hurt us, Papa?"

I shrugged. "Don't know, son. If they do, I think we can handle them. Remember, don't show fear. Look them right in the eyes and don't back off. I've found that all Indians look favorably on bravery. They look on a coward with contempt."

"I ain't afraid, Papa. Long's you're here, I reckon we can handle anything." He forgot to use good grammar, but this was no time to correct him.

My throat tightened. His absolute faith and trust in my ability to handle any situation filled me with humility and made me uncomfortable. Suppose the day came when I would fail him?

We rode with our rifles in hand. An Indian could rise right out of the ground to shoot at you. I didn't want any surprises.

"If we meet up with them, boy, just casually keep the bore of your rifle on them. Don't make a big thing out of it, but do it like it was the natural way."

Another couple of hours and the sun sank low on the horizon. They rode toward us out of the sun but were not riding as though to attack. They walked their horses.

"All right now, Billy, remember what I told you."

They sat erect, looking to be part of their horses. They were young warriors wearing only a breechclout, leggings, and moccasins. Their braided hair hung in front of their shoulders. One of them wore an eagle feather hanging from his braid. They all had medicine pouches hanging on a leather thong from their necks. Wild, handsome, dangerous men, they were self-assured, poised for whatever this meeting would bring.

When they drew rein, not ten feet away, I told them we came into their land in peace. I used sign language, not knowing their spoken one.

They returned my greeting, and I saw that they noticed our rifles never strayed.

They told me they were Hunkpapa Sioux and that they'd been hunting and had found no meat. I believed them, for I'd found game scarce as Billy and I trekked west.

I told them my son had shot a buffalo a couple of days back and that we had meat we'd share with them. They accepted my offer.

Throwing my leg over the saddle horn, I slid to the ground, keeping my eyes and my rifle on them. A glance at Billy showed him to be doing exactly as I'd instructed. He seemed more curious about them than anything else.

The slipknot I'd secured the meat with came loose easily. I separated a haunch from the remaining meat and tossed it to them. Their leader nodded only slightly, looked at Billy with approval, kneed his horse ahead, and led his small party away.

We watched until they were out of sight.

"They didn't seem to be bad men, Papa."

"No, son, they aren't bad men. They just have a different set of rules they live by. When I tell you not to trust them, I mean that they might kill you, and in their way it would prove they were brave, honorable warriors.

"If you are their friend or blood brother, then you can trust them. Never, under any other circumstances, figure you're going to have to do anything but fight them. And remember, they'll stack up with the fiercest enemies you'll ever meet."

That night I went through the mounting stack of drawings

and decided I'd better get them to Casement. To put them on a stage, I could ride up to South Pass or ride on to Jim Bridger's place. I decided on South Pass City, where I would also send a telegram asking for further instructions.

There were many who thought the UP would go through South Pass City, but the route chosen by General Dodge passed seventy or more miles south of there. If the gold mines petered out, there would be nothing to keep the town alive, and I anticipated anger from the residents. Hell, I'd had nothing to do with the decision.

Most thought of a pass through the mountains as a narrow trail, leading around the shoulders of steep peaks. In many cases, they'd be right, but South Pass crossed the continental divide on an open, high plain.

"Billy, you notice anything special about where the roadbed runs?"

"Yes, sir. It pretty well follows the wagon tracks. Must've been a lot o' wagons through here to cut ruts so deep."

"You're right, son. There have been hundreds, maybe thousands of big, heavy wagons through here since the midforties. People looking for a better way of life. They were going to the gold fields in California or to Oregon for good farm or ranch land."

"Were they poor people, Papa?"

I smiled. "No, son. For the most part, I imagine they were pretty well off. Those big Conestoga wagons and mules or oxen are expensive."

I hooked my leg over the saddle horn and took out my pipe. "I think most of those people just wanted more than what they had, and some of them were, no doubt, the victims of unscrupulous land promoters."

Billy frowned, looking puzzled. "Don't rightly know what un-unscru . . ."

"Unscrupulous?" I laughed.

"Yes, sir. Don't rightly know what that there word means, but I figure it's somethin' bad."

"You're right."

I reined my horse to the right, heading north.

"Where we goin', Papa?"

"South Pass City, son. We should be there by sundown tomorrow."

"Gonna be a lot of people there?"

"Don't know. Last time I was there it was small but pretty lively. They'd found gold, but it turned out to be spotty. No, I have no idea what we'll find there."

chapter

nineteen

WE PAUSED AT the top of the rise and looked down on the town. Ten buildings huddled there, unpainted, grayed by wind and rain, but still more town than we'd seen for quite a spell.

"You tired of listening to my voice, Billy? There are other people, other voices, down there."

He grinned at me. "You mean I'm gonna hear somebody say something to me without telling me the *right* way to do it?"

I laughed. "Has it been that bad, son?"

His eyes twinkling, he said, "Only when I messed up, Papa." He grimaced. "Sometimes, it seemed like I'd never learn everything you wanted me to." He kneed his horse ahead. "Reckon it was me that fussed at me more than you. I wanted to do it right all the time, and it seemed like I just couldn't do it."

"Billy, you've been a real joy. Most youngsters wouldn't have done nearly so well." I peered down the hill. "Let's go see what kind of town's down there."

We tied our horses to the rail in front of the hotel, a lean, narrow building I guessed to have no more than eight or ten rooms. The clerk looked up as we walked to the desk.

"You have any empty rooms?"

"Mister, all I got is empty rooms. You want one or two?"

"Depends on how much you're asking for them."

"Four bits."

"Give me two then."

After signing for our rooms, I told the clerk we'd like to take a bath. He said we'd have to go to the barber shop. He volunteered that the café was across the street. After stowing our gear in the rooms, Billy and I headed for the barber shop. Later, clean from the skin out, barbered, and smelling of lilac water, we went to the café.

I slanted a look at Billy. "Think you can stomach cooking that you or I didn't have our fingers in?"

Straight-faced, he frowned. "Well, Papa, I know it won't be as good as *I* can cook, but it'll sure as all get out be better'n yours. I reckon I'll chance it."

I took a swipe at him with my hat. "Get on with you, you little rascal."

Grinning, he dodged my blow and pulled the door open, then held it for me to enter.

I raised an eyebrow, but walked in ahead of him. He hurried to the table and pulled out my chair for me. I knew he played the game we'd practiced so often on the trail, so I went along with it.

"Thank you kind sir," I said, and took the proffered chair.

He bowed slightly, walked around the table and took his seat.

"Right mannerly youngster you got there." A thin woman, whose face looked like it had worn out two bodies, walked from the kitchen.

"Yes, ma'am. I'm very proud of Billy."

She glanced at him. "Billy, is it? Well now, that there's a right good name. What'll you have for supper, son?"

He grinned up at her. "Well, I reckon I'll eat whatever you got if it don't bite back."

She laughed, and when she did, I saw that some time, long ago, she had been a pretty woman. That laugh came right through the wrinkles and made her face light up.

"Son, that was the right answer. For an answer like that, I've got eggs, bear steak, biscuits, and I'll bet if I look *real* hard I can find an apple pie back yonder. I got some fresh cream you can pour over it."

She glanced around the café. "Now, don't you go tellin' nobody out yonder that I give you pie, or I'll be pestified by every miner in town. I ain't gonna go to cookin' pies every day for the likes o' them."

Wide-eyed, Billy looked at her and shook his head, then made a twisting motion with his fingers in front of his lips, like he'd locked them. "Ma'am, not one single word'll pass my lips."

While we ate, I glanced around at the people who'd come in since we had. I thought it would behoove me to listen to the good-natured jawing back and forth. I might get information I could use, so after supper I tarried over my coffee.

Several more people came in, and I had my ear cocked for what they might say. Most of the talk was of gold. They all seemed to think they would hit a rich pocket of it in the next hole they dug. From the looks of them, they all had hundreds of holes on their back trail, but, to the man, they still had faith that they'd one day strike it rich.

I hoped to hear talk of the Indians so I'd have some idea if there might be trouble. Chief Washakie and his Shoshones were close to the north, in the Wind River Country.

Most on the frontier knew that Washakie befriended the white man, carrying on the policy established by Chief Cameahwait, Sacajawea's brother. I knew this, but things can change, and I didn't want to take Billy into country that might get us killed, so I listened.

I heard nothing that refuted Washakie's friendship. I wanted to go see him and talk with him about settling close by. I wanted to make sure what lands he claimed as Shoshone. With his blessing, I wanted land close to him but not encroaching upon territory he claimed.

Washakie, now a little one side or the other of sixty years old, was considered by some of the young warriors as too old to lead them. They might be a source of trouble, and I wanted to avoid it if it came my way. I wanted friends, not enemies.

After listening for awhile, I thought that I'd not gain any worthwhile information, so I told Billy we'd walk about the town until bedtime.

"Sure does feel good to be able to just walk along without studying every inch of land for Indians or road agents, doesn't it, Papa?"

I smiled grimly. "It does that, son, enjoy it while you can, though, for we'll be leaving here in a couple of days."

"Seems like I'm still doing it through habit, Papa. I'll bet I could close my eyes and tell you where every building is, what it is, and where most of the people along the street are."

"Good habit to get into. It might come in very handy someday."

I wanted to meet the stage, but it was too soon to start looking for it. I'd heard it was due in about three days, give or take a day. In the meanwhile, I thought it would be nice to visit with the people and get to know them.

We went by the telegraph office and found that its services were available whenever we needed them. I wanted to draft a message to Casement.

The telegraph operator squinted at me from under his eyeshade. "Figger out what you want to say and bring it by. I'll be here. Fact is, I live here, so bring it when you're ready."

I stood there a moment, thinking what to say before I took a scrap of paper and wrote out my message.

The drawings would be on the stage leaving South Pass City about November thirtieth and I requested permission to look at the country to the north before returning to end-of-track.

A trip over into Utah Territory was unavoidable. The railroad would insist on it. I didn't know much about that land, and thought it would be a good idea to get Billy back to Betsy. It never occurred to me that she might refuse to take him.

The people here were friendly. Most of the men were rough enough that they wore out their clothes from the skin side, but they were friendly nonetheless.

Talking with them, I met a couple of prospectors who had been to the other side of Shoshone territory. In response to my question about what the country was like, they said that northwest of Washakie's territory looked like it might have good grass and water.

"You're lookin' fer cow country, ain't you, youngster?" The old-timer addressing me went by the name of Hardpan Joe.

I nodded. "Yep, you men can have the gold. All I want is a spread where I can raise cows and kids, if anybody'll ever marry me."

"I wuz married wunst. Married me a Nez Percé squaw. Give 'er back to her daddy, though. She got downright cantankerous. All the time wanting to tell me what to do. So I give 'er back. When I give six ponies fer that woman, her pappy give me twelve right back he wuz so glad to git rid o' her."

He bit off a chew that puffed his cheek out like he had a toothache. "Wuz awful fearful I wuz gonna have to fight him when I brung 'er back. Turned out he wanted to give me another twelve ponies to keep 'er. Well, sir, I skeedaddled out o' there in the middle o' the night. Ain't been closer'n two weeks ride o' that place since. Ain't never goin' closer, neither."

He squinted at me. "You wuz askin' 'bout that there country up toward Jackson Hole, I reckon. Well, the thing you got to worry 'bout up yonder ain't Indians. It's cow thieves."

I frowned. "Rustling? Out here? With the scarcity of ranches? This is Indian country; I wouldn't think stealing cows was very profitable. There's no market for them within driving distance."

"Naw, don't reckon it would be for most in that line o' work, but these here folks I'm talkin' about ain't the run o' the mill type folks. Them there folks up yonder are mostly runnin' from somethin'. Seems like they steal pretty much for their own eatin'."

I pinned him with a look meant to keep his attention. "You suppose if I went over there and talked with them I could make any sort of deal that would keep them off me?"

He leaned over the rail on the hotel porch and spat a stream of tobacco juice into the dust on the street below. "Wal now, I tell you, youngster, I wouldn't go amongst that bunch if'n I had ten arms with a gun growed to the end of each." He shook his head. "Nosiree-bob-tail, I ain't goin' nowhere near them."

We talked awhile longer. I found that he knew Chief Washakie and thought highly of him. They'd smoked the pipe together, and Hardpan had eaten at his fire. We talked on until I thought I'd learned about all the old-timer knew. It was getting late, so I told him good night.

"C'mon, Billy, bedtime."

After seeing Billy snug in his bed, I went to my room. Billy had gone to sleep almost as soon as he lay down on that bed, the first he'd slept on in a long time. I thought I'd drift off as quickly as Billy, but I didn't.

I kept thinking of Washakie and of what I'd been told of the bunch that hung out in Jackson Hole. Betsy's face kept getting in the way of my thoughts. Finally, a picture of the belt buckle and pistol my brother's killer had taken from him pushed all other thoughts aside. I had tried to rid myself of thoughts of revenge, thinking that if I ever met the man, I'd take care of him then. Bitterness welled in my throat.

I forced my thoughts back to the Jackson Hole outlaws. I didn't think they'd bother a youngster, but they might not take kindly to me coming in there. If anything should happen to me, Billy would be alone again, and in a worse place than Julesburg.

Some gunfighters were trying to develop a fast draw, and it seemed the idea would grow. I knew I got my gun out and in action faster than any other I'd seen. The important thing was that I took time to make sure I hit where I pointed it.

I'd never thought about it before. Could I stand up against the best? If Billy should go with me to Jackson Hole, I knew I had to be that good. I'd have to think on it a bit more. It was a new idea, and I wanted to be sure my motive in going was justified.

I gnawed every problem I could think of to a frazzle before I finally went to sleep.

Contrary to my thought that the people of South Pass would be belligerent about the UP passing them by, some were disappointed, but most seemed relieved that they wouldn't have to put up with a crowd every day.

South Pass City sat between the Sweetwater and Beaver creeks. I don't imagine anyone ever called it a pretty area, but it looked good to Billy and me. In the next three days, I believe we met everyone in town and some from the mines that surrounded it.

I kept an eye out for the stage. Depending on whether the driver figured he had a lot of time to make up, the stage might or might not stay overnight, and I had to get those drawings aboard.

I sat on the hotel porch most of each day. From there I could observe almost everything that went on in town.

The porch, although small, provided about the only shade for the spit and whittle club. I was a loafer, too, so I joined them. I sat there talking to whoever wanted to talk while I watched Billy and a boy he'd met knock a rock up and down the street with a couple of sticks.

Occasionally, I'd glance the length of the street to be sure I didn't miss out on anything. During one of these cursory glances, I saw the telegraph operator hurrying toward me waving a sheet of paper.

"Gosh-ding it, I figured you'd come by to see if you had an answer to your message, and here you sit rared back on the porch, doing nothin'. Had a terrible time finding you amongst all these here people." His quizzical look seemed to ask if I appreciated his attempt at humor. I played along with him.

"Well now, I started to come down there to see you 'bout an hour ago, but seein' as how I'd have to fight my way through all the people to get there, I figured to wait till they thinned out a little."

He grinned and handed me the message. It read:

"Permission granted for Wind River trip. After side trip, continue job to north of Pioche, Utah Territory, then return to base. Getting late to be in the mountains. Dodge mad as hell I let you take the boy with you."

I read it a couple of times, folded it, and stuffed it in my shirt pocket.

So Dodge let his temper flare up? Casement and I had thought he would raise enough hell to shake up the whole territory. I pulled the message from my pocket and reread it. His warning about it being late in the year to be in the mountains worried me.

That afternoon, the stage rolled in. I put my package in the hands of the driver and told him I'd give him an extra three dollars to give it to Jack Casement personally at the other end. He agreed after telling me that end-of-track had passed Cheyenne and that the first train in had been November thirteenth.

If trains were scheduled into Cheyenne, Dodge would have had his car moved. Betsy was closer to me, for all the good it did. I walked over to Billy.

"Son, we're leaving in the morning, going up to the Wind River Country. You'll see a whole lot of Indians up there and meet one of the great chiefs, Chief Washakie."

Billy squared his shoulders, threw his chest out, and said in a gruff voice, "Well now, Papa, reckon if we stayed here any longer, we'd get to be downright civilized. Ain't gonna stand fer that sort o' thing."

I laughed. He'd started to tease me with this grown-up, mountain-man talk more and more often. We had become fast friends.

Sunup found us several miles north of South Pass. For me, this was a new trail. To the northwest, there were several peaks I judged to be twelve thousand feet or more. They already had snow halfway down their shoulders.

"It's going to be mighty cold in a month or so, son." I peered at him closely. "If you'd rather, I'll take you back to town and let you stay with that nice old lady who runs the café. I'll be back in a few weeks."

Billy stared at me, his gaze never dropping. "Papa, cold, Indians, outlaws, even grizzlies, aren't going to keep me from going with you. If you don't want me along, say so and

I'll stay until you get back, but anything short of that, I'm going."

I tipped my hat to the back of my head, smiled, and scratched my ear. "You've learned a few things, boy. You just dumped the whole load on me in such a manner that I don't dare say you can't go. All right; stay with me. We'll see what that country up ahead holds for us."

The sky was so clean and blue it glistened, with not even a puff cloud, but the wind had shifted to the north and had an icy bite to it.

Worried, I glanced at the mountains, then toward Billy. "We're going to be in for some weather in the next day or two, son."

He looked at the sky, then toward the mountains. "How you figure that, Papa?"

I shook my head. "Don't know. It's just a feeling I have. This wind has turned mighty cold in the last few hours. I think it's blowing in off some snow fields somewhere."

By late afternoon, we were forced to stop and pull our sheepskins from our bedrolls. Billy shrugged into his coat and cast me a questioning look.

"What's worrying you, Billy?"

"Just thinking, Papa. I don't know how you do it, but I'll bet you're right about the weather."

As we rode, I'd been looking for a place that could be made to keep out snow, rain, or whatever came our way. I'd seen nothing that satisfied me here on the flats and had edged my horse closer to the hills on our left. There were trees there, and maybe a blowdown or hole we could crawl into. At least there was wood.

A little light still held when I found what I'd been seeking. It was a hollow in the side of the hill where a tall tree had been uprooted, but hardly enough to be called shelter.

"Billy, let's look for a blowdown. We'll need wood, and we can stack some branches over that hole. I'll cut saplings and lay them across the branches."

He helped me by pulling the saplings to our makeshift shelter. When I judged we had enough, with Billy's aid, I wove the saplings into the dead branches I'd leaned in front of the hollow. We soon had a shelter, but it was dark when we finished.

I dragged as much of the dead timber up close as I could find. With my ax, I lopped off all the firewood-sized limbs and dragged them inside with us. One log, about twelve inches through, I pulled in close to where we'd have our fire, and as I lifted and wrestled it closer, a few snowflakes settled on my shoulders. They didn't melt. It was getting colder.

"You start the fire, son. I'll see what might be good for supper. I'm glad now I had that storekeeper pack a haunch of elk, or we'd be on a bean diet for awhile."

After supper, we stretched out by the fire and talked. Our hole proved to be a lot more snug than I had thought it would. After a while, we slept.

I woke a couple of times during the night and threw on more firewood. About five o'clock, I woke for good but didn't get up.

It was so quiet that if a man lay still he could hear it. It was a hushed, tomblike stillness. I'd not heard it like this in a long time, but knew it for what it was. Snowfall had sealed our quarters in. I shrugged, thinking that a storm this early in the season wouldn't last long. I thought that by the next morning, the sun would come out and we could be on our way.

I removed a few branches and pushed snow from in front of the opening I'd left. There was over a foot of it on the flat. It still fell. Pulling the branches back in place, I crawled to the fire, threw wood on it, and pulled the end of the log onto the coals. Billy awakened.

"Might as well go back to sleep, son, we're not going anywhere today."

Instead, he scrambled from his blankets and looked outside. "Good gosh! Don't reckon I ever seen, uh, don't suppose I've ever seen so much snow." He looked back at me. "May I go out and build a snowman?"

I shook my head. "Better not. Way I judge it, the temperature is well below zero, and if you sweat under all those clothes, you could freeze to death pretty quick. Let's just take it easy until it warms up."

Despite my outward cheeriness, I worried. We didn't have enough rations to last out an extended cold spell, and I didn't want Billy subjected to weather like this. We might have to get out of our shelter and try to make it to Washakie's camp.

I had a pretty good idea where the Shoshone camp was from directions given me by Hardpan, but I hadn't considered that a fall cold snap would hang on for long.

chapter

twenty

I AWOKE SENSING something strange. We'd been huddled in our cavelike lean-to for three days and were running short of firewood and food. I'd left the shelter only to care for the horses. I lay still, very still, and then heard what had awakened me.

It was a sighing, and the steady splash of droplets from the branches I'd placed in front of our shelter. I smiled into the darkness, recognizing the sound for what it was.

A chinook wind was blowing, warming as it descended the mountain slopes. By noon there would be no snow left except in the hollows. The mountains would remain covered to their waists.

As it was not yet time to start the day, I lay staring at nothing, thinking. The hurt was as pointed and angry as it had been the day I took Billy from Betsy, but I had pretty much resigned myself to life without her. Her good-bye had been very final. My mind would not turn it loose, and I lay there gnawing at the problem, trying to find some way to make up with her.

I felt no remorse that I'd brought Billy with me. He needed the experience, the training to be self-sufficient in all circumstances. Every day he proved to me that he learned fast and retained it all.

Though young, he accepted responsibility. He thought of

things that had to be done and did them without a gripe. In this country, he might soon have to strike out on his own and now I knew he'd be ready.

I did not intend to keep him from Betsy and would take him back as soon as my schedule permitted. He needed the softness she'd build into him as much as he needed what I could give. I sighed, thinking how wonderful it would be if she and I could contribute to his growing up together, but it seemed that was not to be.

Billy stirred and sat up, pulling the covers from around him. He stopped and cocked his head to listen.

"Something's different, Papa. What is it?"

"It's the wind, boy. While we slept, a chinook blew in. We'll be leaving today."

He asked what a chinook was and I told him about the phenomenon, explaining that the downslope of the mountains warmed the descending winds.

He puzzled over my explanation. When he nodded, I knew he'd accepted it on faith, although there was a lot to it he didn't yet understand.

We prepared a meager breakfast, made up our bedrolls, picked up our saddles, and went to the horses.

The thawed mush made for hard riding. In the deeper drifts, our mounts struggled. We had to dismount and help them through, but by noon, just as I had expected, the flats were devoid of snow.

While we rode, I talked to Billy of the Shoshones, explaining how they came to befriend the white man; about Lewis and Clark, and Sacajawea, the wife of Toussaint Charbonneau who was the guide-interpreter Lewis and Clark recruited to lead them to the Pacific; how Sacajawea found her brother, lost to her for many years while she was captive of the Hidatsas.

I told him that her brother, the great Chief Cameahwait, befriended the exploration party, probably due to Sacajawea, and that the Shoshones had been our friends ever since.

"When did all that happen, Papa?"

I scratched my head, thinking, then it came to me.

"Sacajawea was reunited with her people on August 17, 1805, so you see they've been our friends for a long time."

"Even before you were born, Papa?"

I jerked around to look at him. He sat wide-eyed, staring at me, but a mischievous quirk trembled at the corners of his lips.

"Yes, you little devil, wa-a-a-y back before I was born, although I'm sure you think I came over here with the Pilgrims."

He snickered, then laughed, teary-eyed. "I almost got you then, didn't I, Papa?"

Grinning, I reached across the distance separating us and hugged him. "Yep, you almost got me then."

"Hey! Leggo, you'll pull me off my horse." He struggled free, and still laughing, kneed his horse ahead.

We rode closer to the swell of hills that folded themselves into the base of the mountains. I cautioned Billy that we'd better ride quiet. We needed game if we were to eat anything except hardtack.

With heavy snow on the slopes, I thought maybe the elk, deer, and other game might drift down here to the flats where there would be good forage. Our chances of getting a kill were better because of it.

Midafternoon saw us shuck our sheepskins. The chinook warmed so the air felt like early fall. Soon after tying our coats behind our saddles, I saw what we might have for supper.

A magnificent elk stood, his head held close to the ground in a fighting stance. He had not seen us. His attention was on more immediate danger. A tawny mountain lion crouched, his belly almost touching the ground, about ten feet in front of the elk.

I reached for Billy's arm and signaled him to stand fast. I slid my rifle from its scabbard. We'd not been noticed by either animal. Looking at them, I tried to decide which to shoot. There would be time for no more than one shot, so I had to make it count. If the cougar had not fed during the storm, he might stick around to argue about who the elk belonged to. Slowly, I raised my rifle, aimed, and fired.

The elk whirled so fast I hardly saw him go. He disappeared into the trees.

The mountain lion tried to gather his feet under him to spring but sprawled to the ground after the feeble effort. I urged my horse toward the beautiful animal, but reined in before getting close enough for a swipe of the claws to tear at my horse.

The cat lay there looking at me, his yellow eyes blinking, dripping hatred. I read in his hatred all the desire he'd ever need to attack, but life and strength weren't his to control. His sides swelled with a great breath and when he let it out, he died.

Admiration, tinged with sorrow, welled within me. I had never felt joy at killing a valiant foe, and I didn't now, but in order for some to survive, others had to die, and this had been his day for dying. I dismounted and slipped my knife from its sheath.

"We gonna eat a mountain lion, Papa?" Billy's question came from close behind me.

"Reckon we are, son. I've heard old-timers out here say they'd choose one of these big cats over anything else for just pure good eating. You and I are about to find out if they were right."

Skinning the animal, I took great care to keep the hide in one piece, thinking that maybe I could tan it and have something made for Betsy. Billy could give it to her even if I couldn't.

At supper that night, we found the old mountain men knew what they were talking about. That cat tasted as good as anything I'd eaten at Delmonico's in New York.

Billy sliced off another chunk from the haunch sizzling over the fire. This was his fourth helping. I cocked an eyebrow at him.

"I'm worried about you, son."

He looked at me, his face greasy all the way back to his ears. "Nothin' wrong with me, Papa. Why are you worried about me?"

Frowning, I replied, "Well, it's like this, one time I had a chance to observe a python. A python's a big snake," I explained. "This python, during the night, had crawled into a pigpen made of poles stuck in the ground close together, and when he got in there, he swallowed a small pig. When he tried to get out, that big lump of a pig in his stomach wouldn't go through the poles, so the python was a prisoner due to his own greed."

He grinned at me. "You saying I'm like that snake?"

"Yep." I nodded. "If you keep eating, you're not gonna be able to get to your blankets." I packed my pipe and lit it. "I suppose I'll just have to roll you to them, 'cause I sure as shooting won't be able to carry you."

"Aw, Papa, you're teasing me again."

My grin answered him. I dragged deeply on my pipe, blew the smoke out in a great cloud, then said, "Eat all you want, boy, there'll be times we won't have near enough."

He grimaced. "Yeah, like this morning." He reached for another slice. I shook my head in disbelief, thinking if he continued eating like this, he'd get skinny just trying to carry it around.

After supper, we crawled in our blankets early. With the thaw, the mosquitoes came out full force and our blankets were about the only defense we had against them.

I built a smudge fire, and we slept downwind so the smoke would give us some protection, but sleep was hard to come by, even then.

The next morning, we'd been in the saddle only a couple of hours when Billy said, "Somebody comin', Papa. I don't think he's an Indian."

"Yeah, I saw him awhile back. No, he's not an Indian." We reined in and waited for the man to ride to us. I noticed that Billy casually kept his rifle muzzle on the man.

"Howdy," the grizzled old-timer greeted. "Seen your fire last night. Figured to cross your path this morning."

A look at his gear told me he was prospecting. A shovel, pick, and gold pan were tied to his packhorse in plain sight.

"Howdy, stranger," I returned his greeting and nodded toward his gear. "Have any luck?"

"Naw." This was the answer I expected. If he'd found any color to amount to anything, he'd not tell anyone. "Been up to Virginia City in that Montana country. Panned enough to buy bacon, but that's about all."

He tugged at his beard and squinted at me. "They done got themselves a real people rush up there, maybe twenty-five thousand. Ain't no room fer a man to move around in, so figured I'd head fer the Green River, see if it held anything fer me. Besides," he grinned, "I won't have to elbow people out of the way jist to git a drink o' water, let alone wash my sand."

"You come through the mountains?" While talking, I saw Billy relax and let his rifle swing away from the stranger. The old man noticed it, too. A faint smile twitched the corners of his lips.

"Yep, and you can bet yore poke I ain't never gonna try that agin this late in the year. Danged snow's got them mountains choked up full. 'Most didn't git out."

He pulled a plug of tobacco from the front of his overalls and offered me a chew. After I declined, he bit off a sizable hunk and tucked it comfortably between his cheek and gum. He squinted questioningly at me. "Where ye headed?"

"Figured to go see old Chief Washakie, then head over into The Hole."

"You got friends in The Hole?" He'd become wary.

"Nope. Don't know a soul over there. Thought maybe if I talked right, they'd leave me alone if I went into ranching close by." He relaxed, but looked at me like I'd lost my mind.

"You goin' in The Hole, jest you an' this here kid?"

I nodded. "Figured to."

He scratched his head, all the while slanting me an "I don't believe it" look. "Mister, ain't no business o' mine, but they's some pizen mean critters in yonder. You'd have some terrible weather to fight this time o' year, too." He shook his head. "No sir, don't believe I'd do it even if I knowed the mother lode wuz in there."

"What makes those people in The Hole any different from others?" I asked.

He looked at me like I'd asked a dumb question. "If'n you don't know, reckon I'll jist have to tell ye. They's critters in yonder what's robbed stages, stole cows, an' murdered folks." He slapped his thigh. "Well, gosh-ding it, they done jest about all the mean kind o' things you ever heered of, and a whole lot you ain't never heered tell of."

He squinted a sidelong look at me. "Course, they's some in yonder what jest got caught in the wrong place at the wrong time. They had to run whether they done bad or not." He nodded. "Yep, they's some o' them, but them ones like that are in the mi-i-nority."

I laughed, packed my pipe, lit it, and said, "I appreciate what you've told me, and I'll think about it awhile. As a matter of fact, the weather worries me more than the people."

"Gosh-dinged good reason to, but I'd have to figger it an' them people 'bout a even swap."

We sat our horses and jawed awhile, then we bid him farewell and rode on. He was the second man to warn me away from The Hole. My doubts about going in there with Billy began to build some muscle.

Two more camps and I knew we were getting close to Shoshone headquarters. From first sun, I realized we were being watched. I felt no anxiety about that because those watching us made no secret of it. They rode in plain sight and didn't close in. About noon, I saw warriors on both sides turn their horses and ride directly toward us.

"Steady, Billy. These men are not intent on doing us harm. If they were, they could have long before now."

They lifted their hands in a sign of peace. I returned their greeting and noticed Billy did the same.

The tall, handsome warrior to my left nodded in greeting. I would have taken him for a Mandan had I not been so deep in Shoshone country. He was that handsome.

"You come to visit Snake people?" Snake was the name the Shoshones often called themselves. He spoke in evenly spaced English words, so I stopped wracking my brain to remember the sign language.

"Yes, I wish to meet with your great chief."

The other warrior said, "Chief Washakie is not in camp.

He's been gone four suns. You come sit at my fire. He'll come back soon."

I felt surprise that two warriors in the same band spoke English, but then I remembered the Shoshone had been friends of the white man for more than a half century. Perhaps I'd find many in camp who spoke my language.

Washakie's absence disappointed me. I wanted to see him, but I also wanted to make friends of the Shoshone. I looked at each of the warriors. "I thank you. My son and I will sit at your fire."

They escorted us to camp, riding ahead to show their trust. The camp we rode into was large. Tepees, a few log structures, and even a few soddies covered over a square mile on the north side of the Wind River. There were few trees, and those grew along the river's edge. This was the permanent winter camp of the Shoshone. I wondered where Washakie could be. With winter setting in, warriors usually stayed close to home.

The handsome warrior who met us on the trail took Billy and me to his lodge. His name was Mopeah, or Horn, because he wore his forelock like a horn sticking from his forehead. His wife, Woman Who Sings, brought us food and told us to bring our belongings into the tepee.

I gave her what we hadn't eaten of the cougar and asked if there was anyone in camp who would tan the hide for me. She took it, promising she'd have it done.

After eating, Mopeah and I went outside and sat on the sun side of his lodge. Billy wandered off with one of the boys in camp.

We sat quietly for awhile, letting our food settle. I gave Mopeah a couple of strips of rough-cut tobacco. We smoked and talked.

He told me that some of the young bucks had criticized Washakie's ability to continue leading them in war. Right after he overheard them, the great chief had disappeared.

He continued, "I see him slip from camp. He took his favorite horse, and he wore paint." Mapeah shook his head and smiled. "I think when he returns they'll know he can still lead."

"I hope his trip won't be long. I really wanted to see him."
I pointed the stem of my pipe toward Billy walking across
the area in front of us. "I wanted him to meet your chief
also. He'll tell his grandchildren about meeting the Great
Chief Washakie who is one of the greatest of all chiefs, a
warrior and statesman."

"No worry. Two suns and he'll sit again in his lodge."
Mopeah looked at me, his face solemn. "You talk well of
our chief. Your words are good. Shoshone feels big in here."
He pointed to his chest.

We ate again before bedding down in his tepee. The next
two days were much the same as the first: talk, eat, smoke,
and watch the boys play.

I expected to find a stoic, somber people when I rode into
the Shoshone camp. Instead, I found that they laughed,
played, cried, and loved. They were far from being the
savages our Eastern publications painted them.

In the late afternoon of the third day, warm from the sun,
and half asleep, I noticed a commotion at the end of camp
and looked at Mopeah. He puckered his lips and twitched
them toward the noise. "Washakie comes."

I had learned that, rather than point, a Shoshone puckered
his lips and twitched them in the direction he wanted you to
look.

We walked toward the man sitting proudly on his war
steed. By now, there must have been a thousand people
following him. He rode to the center of the encampment
where he stopped his horse and, still mounted, held aloft a
string of scalps.

"I have followed the warpath. The cowardly Crow,
droppings from a dog, think I, Washakie, am an old warrior.
They do not think with their heads now, only their spirits. I
alone took these scalps." He held up seven fingers. "No one
fought by my side."

His piercing gaze swept the throng around him. Then in
a roar he challenged every warrior present, "Let him who
can do greater than this claim my place." He held the scalps
aloft again. "Let him who would take my place count as

many scalps." No one stepped forward, and no one challenged his courage.

He threw his leg across his horse's mane and jumped to the ground. The spring in his step was not that of an old man. I had thought Mopeah one of the most handsome warriors I had ever seen, but that was before seeing Washakie. The term regal fitted him as none other.

That night, Mopeah took me to meet Washakie, who invited me to sit at his fire. Waiting for me to sit, Washakie took a pipe from the hands of Mopeah, lighted it, puffed on it a couple of times, then passed it to me.

I looked over the bowl at him and, following his example, also puffed a couple of times. We exchanged gifts then; mine a strip of tobacco, his a beautiful mink pelt.

After observing proper protocol, he looked straight at me and in a voice that rumbled up from his chest, said, "Speak, white man, I am here."

I nodded, and without preamble said, "I want to live in this great land of yours."

"You want my land?"

"No. This is why I come to talk with you. I want to make sure I don't encroach on land belonging to the Shoshones. I want to be friends with you and your people."

"I say no and you'll come anyway. That is the way of the white man."

I shook my head. "No, chief, I will not come anyway. I will be disappointed, but I want friends around me. I want to look you in the eyes and know you are my friend and that I've done nothing to anger you."

Washakie smiled slightly. "You're afraid of Washakie."

My eyes locked with his. "Do you think that?"

He laughed. "No. Talk would be over if my head tells me you're a warrior with no heart. You would be beaten from my camp."

I explained what I wanted to do. That my reason was not greed, but to have a home, a wife, children, and to raise them in the beauty of this land among friends. "And I will fight at your side against your enemies."

When I finished, he stood and said he'd think about the

things we'd talked of and would give me an answer in the morning.

In my bedroll I thought long about Chief Washakie. I liked him as a man and as a leader of men. He was wise, brave, human, and best of all, he had a sense of humor.

The next morning, I awoke to a sunny but cold day, ate, and had hardly finished before Washakie summoned me. He was sitting in front of his lodge smoothing a place in the dirt at his side. He motioned me to sit. I carefully avoided the two- or three-foot square area he'd been working on, but sat close enough to look at it.

Washakie picked up a twig and motioned to the spot he'd cleared.

"I asked the Great White Chief in Washington for a home for my people. The Wind River Valley is Shoshone. We live here, hunt food for our women and children, stand our tepees here, and fight our enemies here. We do this since those who came before. We do not fight the white man who is our friend. I asked the Great White Chief for this land."

All the while, he sketched in the area he'd smoothed. "Your leader has not spoken to me on the paper yet, but my heart tells me it will be so."

He pointed to the sketch. "This is land I ask for Shoshone." I saw that he'd sketched the area that surrounded where we sat. And he'd bounded it by rivers and mountains.

He tossed the stick to the middle of his sketch. "I told your chief more to write on the big paper; schools, cattle, seed for planting, teachers, and a fort built in the middle of this land to protect my people. These things I asked for.

"We will plant crops and herd cattle. My warriors will not like to do these things, but they will. I, Washakie, say it. We'll no longer be feared warriors. We'll lose the lust to war on the Crow, the Blackfoot, and the Sioux." He picked up the twig and touched the end of it to the northwest of the area he'd outlined. "This is your land."

I stared at it a moment, thinking it was land I'd thought he'd claim. I looked at the rough map a moment longer, then peered straight into his eyes. "I want you to sell me that land up there."

"No. It is not land I claim for Shoshone."

"Yes, I know. You and I know that, but the government doesn't know it. If I buy it from you, I believe they'll honor the sale as valid and still set aside your reservation as outlined here."

"You tell me to talk with forked tongue?" I saw that I'd offended him and quickly tried to make amends.

"No, I wouldn't ask such of you. Right now that *is* your land. It'll be yours until you and the government sign the big paper setting aside the land you will be satisfied with. The land I ask for and much more is now land that you claim as your hunting grounds."

I packed my pipe, studying Washakie while I did it, and saw that my words had mollified him. I wanted to stand and pace awhile but knew if I did, the talk would be over.

I sat still, lighted my pipe, and said, "The Wind River Valley belongs to the Shoshone. Your words to the great chief in Washington have been heard. You'll get all that you ask for within the next year."

My answer was the truth. I had heard it discussed, and knew that of all the treaties Washington had broken with the Indians, this treaty with Washakie would be made and kept because Washington knew the debt it owed the Shoshone.

Without help from the Shoshone, it is probable that Lewis and Clark would never have completed their assignment. Settling the West would have been delayed many years. I had even heard that it might be another fifty years, putting it in the early twentieth century before settlement could start, had it not been for the Shoshone.

He stared at the ground that had held our attention so long, then looked at me. "I believe you. Washakie never talks with two hearts. I give you the land."

"Chief, I want you to *sell* it to me, only in that way will the government let me keep it. They might not, even then, but I'll fight them right down to a nubbin if I know I have your approval."

He still wanted to give it to me, but I convinced him that

it would dishonor me to take it without giving something in return. I explained that he must demand that I teach his people how to raise cattle, till the soil, and build permanent houses, as well as have me furnish him with two hundred head of cattle, a hogshead of tobacco, and an unspecified amount of sugar. This would make the deal legal and permit me to retain my honor.

I explained that the white man thought anything like this had to be done with an exchange of gifts. He sat quietly, frowning, and I knew he gave my suggestion careful thought. Finally, he swung his head and pinned me with a penetrating gaze.

"Your words are good. It will be as you say."

"Chief, I have to finish the job I'm hired to do now, but as soon as it's finished, I'll bring you the things I've promised."

He nodded.

We talked awhile longer, and he advised that I swing south and go around the end of the Wind River Range, then cut north on the west side to get to Jackson Hole. He said I would never make it through Togwotee Pass this time of year.

To do as he recommended, I would have to backtrack almost to South Pass City, but it sounded like the best advice I'd get. He also warned me against going into The Hole, my third warning. My doubts grew as to whether I should go in there at all, especially with Billy. I shrugged, thinking I could make up my mind while we backtracked. I had to go that way anyway to get back to the rail bed.

We stayed a week with Washakie's people and made friends. Billy got to know boys who, I thought, would be his friends on into his adult life.

A slow, drizzly rain fell the morning we packed to leave. I looked worriedly at the sky, fearful it would snow. Mopeah apparently saw my concern and assured me that we'd see only rain out of this.

Woman Who Sings brought me the cougar hide, saying that it was a beautiful pelt, and that I could wear it with pride. I smiled and told her I intended to give it to my woman. She looked at her husband and told him I was a good man.

When we rode out, headed southwest, Mopeah rode with us.

"I ride with you to show you the trail at end of mountains. You might turn back too soon maybe, or maybe go too far." His smile was one of a friend.

Despite the rain, we made over thirty miles that first day. In the afternoon, after crossing the Popo Agie, Mopeah, who had scouted away, joined with us again. He carried four sage hens.

"We will eat good tonight," I said.

He shook his head. "No fire. I saw pony tracks, eight riders." He pointed to the east. "They may be Shoshone, but I do not think so."

Now I had two things to look for: enemies and a dry camp, which I wasn't likely to find unless we came upon a cave.

"I'm hungry enough to eat those hens raw, Papa."

"Pretty good raw," Mopeah said with a straight face.

"You two can have them, I'm going hunting Sioux." I kneed my horse to the left as I said it.

"We have time to find camp first, then hunt Sioux," Mopeah said and grinned at Billy. "Raw birds will be all right. I'll eat them with you later."

chapter

twenty-one

"WHAT DIRECTION WERE they heading, Mopeah?"

He pointed toward the south.

They might parallel our course and never see us, I thought. If they decide not to ford a creek or change course to go around a hill, they could come within plain sight of us. If they were not Shoshones, we would have more trouble than we could handle.

I didn't want to hunt trouble with Billy along. I thought about it awhile. It would be better for us to find them and fight on our own terms rather than be ambushed. Billy would stand a better chance, I believed, if we had them bring the fight to us. I looked at him.

"Son, keep your rifle covered and dry. Watch for any signal I might give."

"Yes, sir."

I glanced at Mopeah. "You think they heard your shots?"

He just held his bow out a little and smiled. "Did not use gun. Crow and Sioux come deep into our lands for buffalo. Herds are larger here. White man has killed many in their land and buffalo are few, so our enemies hunt here, and we kill them."

He said it so simply that it caused me to look at him again. Until now I had seen him only as my friend. Now, I saw before me a Shoshone warrior, proud of his fighting ability and as ruthless as any Sioux or Crow.

"Let's find a place we can defend and keep the horses safe. If we find the right place, we'll hunt them until they see us, then lead them to the ground *we* want to fight on."

Mopeah grinned, and I was surprised and pleased to see Billy join him. "I think we'll make a good fight. We'll find place to camp first, Iron Horse Man." He'd called me by that name since I told him I had a job with the railroad.

We'd been riding close to the trees, and I wanted to stay there if possible, so I looked for a place with tumbled boulders. There were many such places so it behooved me to find just the right one. It didn't take long.

The rock fortress we chose was more of an outcropping of granite slabs, where some ancient subterranean upheaval had pushed the earth's crust through the surface. The position would be hard to assault from any direction.

"Son, I want you to stay here. When we come back, we'll be hightailing it. Hold your fire until we get in here with you. We'll allow them to get as close as possible before we open up. We need as much edge as we can get. If we can knock three or four from their horses in the first volley, we'll have them at a disadvantage."

"Yes, sir, Papa."

Pride flooded me. My little boy never asked a question. He showed no fear, nor did he insist on going with us. He led his horse to the back of the rock slabs, staked him, dug in his saddlebags for more cartridges, then came back and settled into the boulders like he did this every day.

I tousled his hair, hugged him once, and turned my horse.

"Let's go, Shoshone warrior." I grinned at Mopeah and he returned it.

"Iron Horse Man, these may be my people. We'll not fight them."

"If it turns out that way, fine, but right now you think they are enemy?"

"Yes."

"Then let's go find them."

Before I could urge my horse away, Mopeah kneed his

alongside Billy. He held out his rifle. "Here, you take it. You'll need it to help collect scalps maybe." Billy reached out and took the rifle from Mopeah's hands and nodded somberly. Mopeah urged his horse into a trot.

The big Indian took the lead, always staying below the ridges. But mostly, the land flowed in gentle swells, and it would be hard to get very close to the eight riders without being seen. This afforded us as much protection from surprise as it did them.

The rain continued to fall. It was one of those rains that, given a day, would soak you. Anything short of that and you'd just stay damp and miserable.

We crossed the Little Popo Agie and traveled about two more miles when we cut their sign. Deep tracks showed where they had ridden. The sharp chops in the turf had very little water in them. There were horse droppings in the trail ahead of us.

Mopeah slid off his pony and toed one of them until it broke in two. It smoked with vapor when the warm, moist center opened to the chill air. The eight Indians were close, very close.

We rode slower now and searched the land about us with care. With luck, we could get in sight of them before they became aware we were trailing them.

I wanted to get close enough to attract them with a shot, but not close enough to hit them or to be hit by a stray shot of theirs. I wanted to fight this my way.

That thought had hardly settled in my brain when, yelling like the demons of hell, they poured around the bend of a slight knoll coming straight at us.

I reigned my horse hard about. Mopeah pulled even with me by the time my horse lined out, belly to the ground. A glance over my shoulder showed they had the angle and it was going to be close whether we made it back to Billy before they caught us.

Not expecting to hit anything holding my rifle pistol-fashion, I fired in their midst. No one went down, but my shot caused them to swerve and lose a little ground.

I urged my horse ahead with yells and spurs. He gave it

all he had, but those Indians continued to close on us. In the distance I saw where we'd forted up. I prayed that Billy would stay out of sight, and if we didn't make it to him before the Sioux caught us, that he'd stay hidden.

We were still a hundred yards out when Mopeah's horse stumbled and fell. I reined toward him. He stood by the side of his dead pony, calmly loosing arrows at our attackers. On the run I held out my arm. He saw my intent, grabbed hold of it, and swung up behind.

They were almost on top of us now and I pulled my handgun. I couldn't see him but felt Mopeah behind me working to get his bow in action.

I fired at a warrior coming up on my left and saw him clutch his gut and grab his horse's mane. Another rode into my sight pulling at an arrow sticking from the center of his chest. I heard rifle fire from in front and knew that Billy had disobeyed me.

A glance at the rocks showed him standing in clear sight, calmly firing at the attackers. Then we rode among the rocks and slipped from my horse. The warriors were scant feet behind.

Reaching out, I grabbed a handful of Billy's shirt and pulled him down beside me. Two Sioux dived from their horses straight at us.

I fired the last two rounds in my handgun, missed with both shots, rolled under the feet of the one who landed closest to me, and knocked him down. He twisted clear and started to rise when I stuck the barrel of my rifle at him like a bayonet. It caught him in the throat. He went down again and I pulled my bowie knife, swung it and took off half his skull.

I spun quickly toward where I'd seen Mopeah go to ground. He grappled with the second warrior against a slab of upright rock. Billy had two rifles and sat calmly loading one. He tossed it to me and started loading the other.

I caught the Henry, twisted, and fired right into the wild-eyed face of a warrior hung out like fresh laundry as he jumped from the top of a rock. His face blew apart in an explosion of bone, brains, and blood. That made four that I knew of who wouldn't eat supper that night.

I twisted toward Mopeah in time to see him squeezing and twisting his antagonist's head. A sharp wrench and the Sioux's head twisted all the way around. Mopeah tossed me a satanic grin, grabbed his bow, and mounted the slab in front of him. Five down, three to go.

At that moment, I heard Billy's rifle talking, looked to see what he fired at, and saw a warrior atop a splendid horse swerve to miss ploughing headlong into our position. He held onto his horse's mane. Billy had hit him.

"Papa! Behind you."

I ducked and whirled.

The cause of Billy's warning sailed over my back, swinging his club in a desperate effort to crush my skull. I put the brakes on my spin and threw myself atop him. He spun, throwing me off to the side, but he lost his club at the same time. He rushed to grapple with me.

My fist slammed into his gut. He bent, his breath whooshing between thin-drawn lips. I clubbed him with both hands behind his neck, bringing my knee into his face at the same time. The force of my knee lift twisted me to the side.

A rifle barked at that instant, and he went down. I could have put both fists in the hole in his chest where Billy's bullet exited. It splattered me with blood and flesh. Billy had been calm enough to hold his fire until just the right moment. Mopeah had one of them engaged in a knife fight, with Billy now dancing from side to side trying to get in a shot without hitting the wrong man.

"Leave him be," I shouted. "He'll handle it." A glance showed the last of the Sioux war party, the one Billy had wounded, running his horse in the direction he'd come from. I turned back to watch Mopeah's fight. I didn't intervene. It would have been an insult. They had drawn their knives and were silently moving for advantage.

Warily they circled, each looking for an unguarded moment. A quick slice, a parry, then again moving apart. Mopeah stepped toward the Sioux, swung, missed, and got a slice across his chest for his effort. It welled, then streamed blood in a slowly increasing rivulet down his side.

His expression never changed, but I saw respect for his adversary grow in his eyes.

The Sioux got careless. He stepped in toward Mopeah and thrust at his gut. Mopeah twisted to the side and sliced at the arm extended toward him. I saw his blade cut to the depth of its full width across the muscle in the Sioux's upper arm.

The knife dropped from nerveless fingers, but the Sioux grabbed it in midair with his other hand and spun away, causing the next swing at his gut to miss. The Sioux's arm bled in great spurts. They circled.

The Sioux weaved and stumbled. Then, in a desperate lunge, he swung at Mopeah's throat, but by now his weakness made him miss slices that he'd have scored with only moments before.

Finally, he stood straight, his arms at his side. He made an effort to raise his knife hand but could only bring it to his waist. His arm and neck muscles bulged with the effort, but his hand fell slowly to his side. It would not obey his will.

I saw Mopeah's eyes lock with those of the Sioux, then he walked up to him, touched him with his left hand and shoved his knife to the hilt in the Sioux's gut. He held him erect for a moment, spitted on his blade, then with a jerk, withdrew it. The valiant warrior fell at his feet.

"He fought well, it is an honor to kill such as he," Mopeah said and wiped his blade on the Sioux's breech-clout.

I nodded. "Yes, he was a worthy foe." I looked at Billy. "Come here, son."

He walked to me, and I gathered him in my arms. "I'm proud of you, boy. You fought as well as any man."

His eyes searched my face. "Thank you, Papa. You're not mad at me for disobeying you."

"No. You did what needed doing, when it was needed. That's the important thing."

"You became a warrior today, little one," Mopeah interrupted. "You killed an enemy and wounded at least one other. I give you a Shoshone name today. In the lodge of the Shoshone, you're now Coyote Man. Someday you'll go alone on your vision quest and get another name. Maybe, though, you'll decide to keep the name I give."

I knew Mopeah had honored Billy with a most sacred name. The Shoshone believed they had come from the coyote before they became men.

Billy stood a little straighter. "Thank you, Mopeah," and then he surprised me. He said, "It is an honor to receive my new name from a warrior as brave as you."

Mopeah cast me a glance that said I now had a man for a son. I allowed a slight smile to show I agreed with his assessment.

Late the next afternoon, we crossed the Sweetwater and turned west. Soon after changing directions, the Shoshone guided us to a copse of mountain pine and dismounted. "Tonight, we'll camp here. I leave you at first sun." He motioned to the Wind River Range. "Keep those mountains on your right, and you'll get to the place you call Jackson Hole."

"Thank you, Mopeah. You're a good friend. I'll hate to say good-bye."

"We'll meet again in a few moons. You and Coyote Man will come back soon."

I nodded. "That we will, Mopeah."

We set up camp by a small stream that would eventually wend its way to the Big Sandy River.

After supper, sitting by the fire, Mopeah busily fashioned a small bag from a piece of hide. When he finished with it, he called Billy over.

"Coyote Man, I have a gift for you. Look what I place in this bag." He took a small blue stone from a pocket in the side of his leggings and held it for Billy to see. "This is big medicine to Shoshone. It'll keep you safe."

Then he reached into the top of his right legging and pulled out a coil of coarse black hair. "This hair is from the Sioux warrior you killed. It'll always make you brave." After placing it in the bag, he pulled a hammered silver ring from his finger and held it for Billy to look at. He smiled.

"This is my gift to you. It will bring you luck." He carefully placed them all in the bag, pulled the drawstring, and handed the bag to Coyote Man.

"Wear it around your neck. It's big medicine."

Billy didn't even look to see if I approved. He solemnly took it from Mopeah's hands and pulled the thong over his head. "Thank you, great warrior of the Shoshone. I will always wear it and feel good because you gave it to me."

Billy stood, reached in his pocket, and pulled out his most prized possession, the jackknife I'd given him in Julesburg.

"Mopeah, great warrior of the Shoshone, I, too, have a gift. I prize it highly because it is the first thing my father gave to me, but I want you to have it now."

Mopeah took it from Billy's hand, looked at it, then at Billy, and swallowed hard. My son had touched his heart. "Little warrior, son of the Coyote, I take it from you as great gift. Thank you." Mopeah looked from Billy to me, and his eyes said this was now part of his heart.

I walked to the fire and poured each of us a cup of coffee. I didn't usually let Billy have strong drink like this, but the night air crawled under our coats and chilled with a bite.

When I handed Mopeah his cup, he nodded his thanks and again leaned against the tree he'd been using to prop himself up. "I'll tell you now about the Shoshone." He tasted his coffee. "Good," he grunted, then continued, "The Coyote made all Shoshones from clay. Coyote was a man then, and he looks after us up to halfway when we die.

"At halfway, Wolf, Coyote's brother, looks after a Shoshone spirit, the *mugua,* and the ghost, *tsoap.* Wolf washes the *mugua* and *tsoap* of all dead Shoshone warriors. After Wolf washes them, the warriors again become alive.

"Buhagant, the medicine man, is the only one who can see the spirit and ghost until Wolf washes them and makes them live again. Buhagant gets power from Apo, the sun." He looked at Billy and smiled. "You know now, Coyote Man, you have a strong name, big medicine."

Mopeah told us more stories of Shoshone belief, and I knew that, once started, a story had to be told to the end or it was bad luck for the teller. When he finished and before he could start another, I walked to my blankets.

"We better let Coyote Man get some sleep, Mopeah, or he'll sleep in the saddle all day tomorrow."

He smiled, eased down the tree trunk to the ground, and said nothing more, just went to sleep.

After breakfast the next morning, I cut the hind quarter off a deer I'd killed the day before and gave it to my friend for his trip home. We said good-bye, and it was a hard thing to do. I could tell that Mopeah felt the same, but we'd meet again. Billy and I turned our horses to travel up the west side of the Wind River Range.

About midmorning, we passed another prospector heading south who said he wouldn't spend the winter in this "gosh-danged" country for all the gold in it. He said he was going to find a place where it was warm and stay there forever. He'd wintered in Virginia City for three years and said that never during any summer had he thawed out before everything froze up again.

chapter

twenty-two

WE RODE ANOTHER seven or eight miles before stopping for our nooning. I built a fire while Billy went to a small stream for coffee water. Our meal of venison, coffee, and biscuits was about done when Billy looked at me. "Papa, you hear horses?"

I cocked an ear toward where Billy pointed. Yes, I thought, it sounded like two horses.

A gruff voice hailed, "Hello the camp."

"Billy, drift back into those trees and keep your rifle ready. I'll see what these people are about." He did as I directed.

"Come on in," I yelled, "but keep your hands where I can see them." I thumbed the thong off my .44.

"You won't need that, stranger. We just want to set a spell and drink some of your coffee if we're asked." The words came from a thick stand of saplings to my right. He'd seen me slip the thong. They rode in, hands crossed on their saddle horns.

"Climb down and sit, coffee's about ready."

"No need in your youngster settin' out yonder in the cold, less'n you'd jest plain feel better with a ace in the hole. We ain't lookin' to hurt nobody."

I grinned, looked over my shoulder, and said, "C'mon in, Billy. No need to sit out there as hungry as I know you are."

The two men who walked their horses to our fire would not breed trust in any man. They were rough looking, bearded, but appeared clean, which gave them at least one thing in their favor. Also, if they had meant us harm, they would have already caused it.

"You'll have to use your own cups, 'less you want to wait until we get through." I knew that didn't sound very hospitable, but looking at them, I just plain didn't care.

"Naw, we got our own." They dug in their bedrolls and pulled out granite cups.

The talker, who looked larger than a grizzly, cocked an eyebrow and asked, "What ya'll figger to do in The Hole?"

"What makes you think we're heading for The Hole?" As soon as I asked the question, I knew how dumb it sounded.

"Hell, you know anywhere else you could be goin' up this way?"

Chagrined, I smiled, feeling my face flush. "No, I suppose that was a dumb question."

For the first time, the other spoke. He must have stood six feet five, and he spread out sideways almost as much as he did up. He was square-built, rawboned, and tough looking. His words were those of an educated man, and sounded British or Scot. I settled on Scot because I thought I detected a slight burr to his words.

"Don't be harsh on yourself, laddie. I've asked many a question no smarter than yours." He held out his hand. "I'm Harry Longden, and not too far in my past I'm from Scotland." Then, with a hint of reverence, he added, "I'm an American now."

A Scotsman proud to be an American didn't surprise me. The West had many from diverse nationalities and backgrounds. Some had found themselves on the wrong side politically in their country and had fled, while others came in search of adventure, and still others scraped for gold.

I picked Harry Longden as one of those seeking adventure. After introductions, I invited them to share our food.

While they helped themselves, they talked of Jackson Hole, correctly assuming I knew little about it.

It seemed The Hole had been named after a mountain

man, David Jackson. And The Hole being off the beaten path, it had no law but that in a man's holster. As a result, those avoiding prosecution migrated to its lonely protection.

There were many such places. Until settlers came in and set up their own government and enforced their laws, the brigands would remain safe.

We talked long into the afternoon. I glanced at my timepiece and found that 4:30 had crept upon us.

I said, "If you men are in no hurry to make an afternoon business meeting, we might as well set up camp here for the night." Peter took me seriously.

"What the hell you talkin' 'bout? Ain't nobody in these here woods we got to see. Got no business to tend to, noway."

"Oh hell, Peter," Harry said, laughing, "Chance just made a joke."

Peter's face flushed, and he squirmed deeper into the pine straw. He looked at us a moment, then laughed. "Reckon sometimes I'm a mite slow. Yeah, let's take it easy the rest of the day. Can't remember when we last done such."

"That's it then," Harry said. "I'll rustle up the firewood. It'll be bloody cold in these mountains before daylight. I've heard this end of the valley's a little over six thousand feet and slopes up to over seven thousand at the north end."

We each carved out chores for ourselves and went about setting up camp. Billy didn't hang back when the others worked. He brought more coffee water and picketed the horses after we'd off-loaded saddles and bedrolls.

I hung enough venison over the fire to last past supper. We settled in to swap lies.

It turned out that Harry and Peter met in Nevada City, Montana Territory, and decided to partner up and take a look at the mountains down Colorado way.

Harry had Billy goggle-eyed with tales of the English cities and countryside, and of Paris, Rome, and other European places.

Peter was one of the last of the mountain men. He knew Jim Bridger, Sublette, and others. He took his turn out-lying Harry, then I took my turn but felt I fell short.

During a lull in the conversation, Harry dug in his possibles bag and pulled from it a beautiful leather-bound book. Holding it so we could see, he said, "This may be my most treasured possession. It is volume one of the second edition of William Wordsworth's *Lyrical Ballads*. I have volume two in my bag yonder. I'd like to read a poem or two from it, if I may."

I urged him to do so. Peter only grunted, obviously having listened to Harry read many times.

Harry moved closer to the fire and held the book facing it so he could see. The first poem he read had long been one of my favorites. He read:

Lines Written in Early Spring

I heard a thousand blended notes,
While in a grove I sate reclined,
In that sweet mood when pleasant thoughts
Bring sad thoughts to the mind.

To her fair works did Nature link
The human soul that through me ran;
And much it grieved my heart to think
What man has made of man . . .

Harry finished reading the poem and read a few more of Wordsworth's short poems, among them, "A Slumber Did My Spirit Seal," "I Travelled Among Unknown Men," and a longer one, "Lucy Gray, or Solitude."

I noticed that Billy hung on every word, and during the reading of "Lucy Gray," his eyes misted. Harry noticed it, too, and began to read "Michael," a poem of when a boy leaves home. *My* eyes misted this time. It would be such a short time until Billy would want to go out on his own, and rightly so.

Harry closed the cover, walked to his possibles bag, and stowed the book in it. He looked at Billy and smiled. "You like listening to Wordsworth, boy?"

"Yes, sir, I don't know that I ever heard anything as

pretty. I think when we get back where they have books to sell, I'll see if I can find a copy like yours."

Harry silently studied Billy but said nothing.

Peter stretched, and sober-faced, said, "Reckon I might's well turn in. Got some 'portant business to shove at them there folks what's running all my companies fer me. I'll tend to it first thing in the mawnin'." He walked to his blankets, crawled between them, and soon jarred the camp with earth-shaking snores.

Billy went to his blankets, looked at Peter a moment, then asked Harry, "Mr. Harry, how many miles from him do you bed down at night?" He shook his head. "I don't believe anybody could sleep with all that rucktion going on."

Harry laughed. "Well, you see, son, I sleep all the sounder when he's in camp because of it. He scares away mountain cats, snakes, Indians, everything. They think he's an earthquake trying to happen, so they leave for distant parts."

Billy stared at Harry a moment, then smiled. "Aw, Mr. Harry, you're kidding me like Papa does." The smile slipped from his face and he nodded. "Yep, I reckon I can see how it could be true." He crawled between his blankets, and Peter might as well have been in the next territory. Billy slept with a smile to keep him company.

Harry said, "The fact is, I don't think even a snake could slither into our camp at night without waking Peter."

We packed our pipes, poured another cup of coffee, lighted our smokes, and sat there staring into the fire. When we'd finished and knocked the dottle from the bowls, we, too, went to sleep, but not before I heard Harry mutter, ". . . one of the finest lads I ever met. The world's safe with youngsters like him." I knew he referred to Billy, and I choked with pride, although I thought I could take little credit for Billy being as he was.

Night still clung to this side of the mountains when we ate, packed, and made ready to get on the trail the next morning.

We said our farewells and were ready to ride out when Harry rode up to Billy's side and held two books out to him.

"Son, I've carried these with me a long time. They're my

favorites. I'd like you to take them and read them when you have a yearning for good literature." He handed Billy the two leather-bound volumes of Wordsworth's *Lyrical Ballads*.

Billy looked at me, questioning whether he should accept a gift of such value. I nodded.

"Sir, I thank you, and yes, sir, I'll surely read them, every line of them."

"If you'll look in the front, son, you'll see that the author signed them for me." He held out his hand. "Here, if you'll hand them back a moment, I'll sign them over to you."

I noticed when he had the books back in his huge, work-hardened hands, they tenderly caressed the fine leather of the books' covers while he wrote something to Billy on the inside.

When I shook Harry's hand in farewell, my throat swelled until I had difficulty saying, "Harry, that was the most generous, unselfish thing I've ever seen a man do."

"I turned them over to a very worthy custodian. Take good care of him, Chance."

"That I will, Harry. Take care of yourself."

Long after they disappeared on our back trail, Billy rode holding his books where he could look at them, and he read the inscription Harry wrote to him over and over again.

"Papa, you know what Mr. Harry wrote to me?"

I shook my head. "No, but I'd like to hear it."

"He said, 'Billy Tenery, you're a young man in a young land. You have it in you to become great as your country becomes great. But whatever you become, always feel that you can look any man in the eyes, ashamed of nothing you've ever done. One more thing, son; whatever you attempt in life, do your very best, and I'll assure you it will give you great satisfaction to know you could do no better.'" Billy looked up at me, his eyes big, his face sober. "Papa, he signed it, 'A friend met on the trail who thought a lot of you, Lord Harry Longden.'"

The title didn't surprise me; to the contrary, I think I suspected it from his speech, his courtly manners, and his bearing.

"Billy, if I talked myself blue in the face, I couldn't give you better advice. Now, I want you to understand one thing, all advice is not necessarily good. Look at the person giving it and assess whether they're worthy of giving it. If not, shun it.

"To my way of thinking, Harry Longden is a man whose advice you could follow and never go wrong. It makes me very proud that you made such a good impression on a man of his caliber."

Although we'd only shared a night's camp with Harry Longden, he'd left his mark upon us. We'd never forget him.

I looked toward the north and sighed. I had no right to take Billy into what promised to be a very dangerous experience. I wished now that he sat safely in Betsy's drawing room.

"Son," I looked at him a moment until I had his full attention. "If anything happens to me while I'm in here, don't let any man influence you to do the things they do."

"What might happen to you, Papa?"

"I don't know that anything will, Billy, but just in case. I think you are now as good a frontiersman as most. I don't think you'd have too much trouble getting back to Miss Betsy if you had to. You just always do the things you know are right and you'll grow to be the kind of man Lord Harry thought you to be."

I think, in the back of my brain, I'd been mulling the danger of taking Billy with me, for suddenly I drew rein.

Billy looked questioningly at me. "What's the matter, Papa?"

"I'm taking you back to South Pass City, son. I'll not subject you to the danger that might be waiting for us. You'll stay with the lady who runs the café, and if I'm not back in five days, I want you to head for end-of-track and find Miss Betsy."

"You might need me to cover your back, Papa. I'd surely be better off with you."

I shook my head. "No, son. We're going to do it my way." Seeing his crestfallen expression, I continued. "Billy, there are some things we can't help each other with. This is one of them. When a man is in an extremely difficult situation, it is often best that he tackle it alone. He can give the problem his undivided attention if he has nothing else to worry him." Billy stared at me a moment, squeezed his eyes tightly shut, and nodded. "Yes, sir. I suppose I just hate to be away from you any time at all."

I cleared my throat. "Son, you know I feel the same way, but now we *must* be apart. As soon as I can make it so, we'll be together again."

Billy nodded. HIs eyes were swimming in tears now.

"Son, if you cry, I don't think I can leave."

He tried a smile that didn't work. "Papa, if I thought crying would keep you here, I reckon I'd just cloud up and cry all over you."

I knew he was dying inside and here he was trying to make a joke so I'd feel better. I almost canceled the whole idea, but knew if I did, I would always wonder if Vance's killer had been just beyond the reach of my gun. "Now, you promise, if I'm not back in five days, you head for Miss Betsy."

"Yes, sir."

The trip back didn't take as long as coming out, but it seemed longer. Billy kept casting me glances, glances that seemed to try to pull me into himself. I knew the thought of being separated tore him apart, as it did me, but his safety was all that mattered. I should have left him after parting from Mopeah.

The old lady seemed glad when I brought Billy in. She promised to take good care of him and see that he ate well.

He walked out to my horse with me, holding my hand tightly just as he'd done that first day in Julesburg, which seemed so long ago. It was all I could do to keep going, but I managed it somehow. He pulled on my hand and looked up at me. "Papa, you *will* come back to me, won't you?"

"Son, there is nothing in this world that will keep me from coming back to you." I leaned and looked straight into his eyes. "I'm a grown man, but I want you to know that without you, I'm nothing. You are all I have in this world, and I love you very much." I nodded. "Yes, Billy, I'll be back."

In the middle of South Pass City's only street, I pulled him to me. I hugged him, kissed him, and had him promise once again to find Betsy. He clung to me as though afraid to let me go. Finally, I pulled his arms from my neck and held him so I could again look into his eyes which were heavily misted. "Billy, please don't cry. I don't think I could leave if you do, and I must."

He swallowed a couple of times, blinked the tears from his eyes, and smiled at me. "Papa, I'll not make it any harder than it is. You go ahead. I'll see you in about five days."

I hugged him again until his arms around my neck relaxed. I pressed my cheek to his and turned him loose. I mounted and rode off, not daring to look back.

Leaving South Pass City, I headed northwest. I'd heard the valley, or The Hole, as most called it, was about six miles wide and forty-eight miles long from north to south. I crossed Big Sandy Creek and the Green River and tracked toward the Snake, which rose out of Jackson Lake. I rode in Shoshone country but also flirted with the chance of coming on white men who didn't want me there. And they were the ones I wanted to see.

Only a few of the men known as outlaws killed without reason, but the fact remained, those few needed no reason. They seemed to enjoy it. There had always been those who seemed to enjoy killing. I hoped to avoid their kind, except for the one who had killed my brother.

Looking at the high, jagged peaks, snow-covered and majestic, and the grass- and tree-covered plain between the mountain ranges, dotted with lakes and streams, I thought there was no more beautiful place on earth. Wapiti, or elk, sometimes by the hundreds, grazing without fear, raised in me a feeling that my body was too small for my soul. I felt godlike to be part of this, and at the same time, a feeling of insignificance bludgeoned me back to mortality.

I wished Billy could be here to see it with me.

Breathing deeply, I savored the scent of pine, spruce, and mountain air. Inhaling seemed like drinking pure, cold water. I couldn't believe that heaven could improve on this country but must be much like it.

Riding close to an upthrust of granite slabs, I heard a marmot whistle, piercingly, to warn me away. A little farther along, a pica sounded his diminutive bark. The sounds of nature were all about.

The middle of the second day after leaving Billy, my horse carrying me at a steady walk toward the Snake, I became aware that the only sounds were those that I made.

I felt edgy. A hard, cold knot formed between my shoulder blades. Someone stared at me. I felt eyes on me as if the sensation were physical. I reached for my rifle and then drew back my arm.

chapter

twenty-three

"SMART MOVE," a voice said from behind a tree. "Now, just keep your hands clear of leather, and I'll come out. We'll palaver a bit."

I folded my hands over the saddle horn.

A rotund man, bearded, but with a cherubic, jovial-looking face, stepped from behind the tree. "Welcome to Sherwood Forest. I'm Friar Tuck, as you probably could guess. I'm one of Robin Hood's band." He might have been joking, but the snout of the big Sharps he pointed directly at my brisket was no joke.

"Yeah," I smirked sarcastically, "and I'm Kris Kringle. Seriously, Mister Tuck, I'm Chance Tenery. I came here to talk to Robin Hood."

The humor left his eyes. They became hard as agate. "Put a name to Robin Hood, stranger. If you got business with one o' us, say his name."

I looked him square in his eyes, trying not to show my fear. "Mister, I'll tell you honest. I don't know the name of a single person who lives here, much less the name of your leader. I thought, though, that most groups have leaders, and if you do, I'd like to talk with him. If you don't, maybe I could talk with the bunch of you."

Even as I said it, I knew my real reason for coming here was the chance that I'd find my brother's killer. I had tried to bury my desire for revenge since Billy and Betsy came into my life. I had convinced myself that I was through looking for those who had done it. Now I realized that part of my life would never be over until Vance's killer lay dead at my feet.

Tuck studied me a moment. "You on the run?"

I shook my head. "No. I work for the railroad, but I intend to start a ranch across the mountains yonder when the tracks are stretched as far as we can run them. That's what I want to talk to you men about." I realized what a weak excuse it was, but I said it anyway.

"Hell, we ain't got nothin' to do with that land over yonder. You'd have to talk to old Chief Washakie 'bout bein' on his land."

I nodded. "You're right. I've already done that. Before I do anything else, I want to talk with you men. In the summer, it's just a short haul over the mountains to where I'll be ranching, and I want those of you in here to leave me alone. If you're hurting for food, I would probably spare a beef or two."

He grinned satanically. "And if we don't?"

"Then I'll kill as many of you as I can before you get me."

My response surprised him. He settled his gaze on me. He seemed to be trying to figure out what kind of damned fool I was. Then he surprised me. He laughed and slipped his rifle into its saddle scabbard.

"Ride on to the Snake. Make camp on this side of it. I'll bring someone to you for a talk. Was I in your shoes, I'd be mighty fearful." He winked. "That ain't a bunch of panty-waists you say you'll kill."

I felt my face become stiff and hard. "Mister, I don't make threats, I make promises."

"Now, don't get your hackles up." He squinted slyly at me. "How good are you with that hogleg you're packin'?"

"There's only one way to find out, and I'm sure you don't want to push your luck that far, yet."

With an amused look, he nodded. "Didn't think you was a pilgrim." He melted back into the trees.

Riding toward the Snake, I watched the sun top out on the Tetons to the west and send purple shadows down their sides. A glance at the Wind River Range showed crests still aflame with sunset.

The shadows turned black, edging their way from under trees and crevices. Before last light, I drew rein on the bank of the Snake River. "We're here, old horse. I hope it turns out well."

Friar Tuck, who had given me no other name, had said to wait here. He had not said for how long. So, I prepared camp for comfort in case I had to stay two or three days.

If I'd tried to slip in, a fire would have been out of the question. But I thought by now every man in The Hole probably knew I was here and who I was. I built a nice fire and had a hot supper.

I wondered if they would let me keep my guns when I got to their hideout. That was a problem I'd have to face later.

I spent three days loafing, fishing, and scouting the area. I didn't stray very far from camp, however. At midmorning on the fourth day, Friar Tuck rode in, whistling as he came.

"Got any coffee brewing?"

I nodded. "Climb down and have a cup."

"Don't mind if I do," he said, and despite his bulk, slipped lightly from the saddle.

I handed him my cup, and he poured the coffee. He sat on a large stone, sipping it and studying me.

I said nothing, just sat smoking my pipe, thinking that when he was ready, he'd have his say. Finished, he tossed the dregs to the ground, walked to the fire, and pointed questioningly to a trout still warming over the fire.

I smiled, amused that he'd ask. I was in his territory. I was the one asking favors. "Help yourself. It came out of your river, Tuck."

"Everyone's river," he said around a succulent bite. "Forgot that I didn't tell you my name, but Tuck's as good as any." He slurped and smacked as he ate. "These fish are good, but wait till you sink your teeth in them cutthroat trout what comes outta the lake up yonder. You know 'em by the red-colored slash along their throat. I hear tell this area is the only place in the world they're found." He slurped and smacked again.

When Tuck had devoured the remainder of the fish, he motioned to my horse. "Saddle up. Robin Hood says to bring you to him." He glanced at my bedroll. "You might as well pack, he says you can stay at his place tonight."

I didn't know what to expect. Was there a town where Tuck would lead me? Were there cabins, caves, soddies, tents? How many men were there, and what kind of men were they? I knew most were probably outlaws, but thought only few would be considered ruthless. I hoped there would be damned few of that kind where Tuck led me.

It came to me with a jolt that the only smart thing I'd done lately was to leave Billy behind. It was one thing to put my fool neck in a noose, but to bring my son into it would have been pure stupidity. For the first time, I admitted Betsy might have been right. Billy might have gotten the training I'd given him in some safer way.

I made my bedroll, saddled, and followed Tuck from camp.

Although we rode the prettiest country in the world, I barely saw it. I knew only vaguely when we forded the Snake. My mind toyed with what to say, how to say it, and what kind of man I would be talking with. Finally, I squared my shoulders and quit borrowing trouble. I'd have to take things one at a time. A man couldn't eat a buffalo with one bite.

We rode into late afternoon and still saw no one. The sun slid from view and shadows engulfed the valley when Tuck turned sharp right. We rode around a cluster of aspens, and a small town sat snugly in front of us.

Cabins clustered near the lakeside, and a crooked street meandered past them. Across the street from the cabins, a large building, flanked by two others almost as large, sat with the golden glow of lamplight painting the windows. I recognized the largest of the buildings as a saloon. The other two I guessed were a general store and maybe a feed store.

Tuck led me to a cabin of peeled logs at the end of the

street. Larger than the other cabins, it looked to have five or six rooms. This, I surmised, housed the leader.

How could a cluster of buildings, a town such as this, as small as it was, not be known ten miles away? I didn't have to wonder long. Any strangers would be unlikely to find it, and if they came too close, they'd be encouraged to take another route.

When settlers of significant numbers came to the valley, these men would simply pull stakes, move on, and history would never record them as having been there.

In front of the house, Tuck reined to a halt and hailed the occupant. In only a moment, a tall, spare man opened the door, stepped outside, and looked us over. "Climb down and rest your saddle." When I stood by my horse, he stepped toward me and held out his hand. "Tuck tells me you know me as Robin Hood. That will do for the time being."

I shook his hand and told him I was Chance Tenery.

"Come in. Tuck"—he smiled when he said it—"will care for your horse."

Robin spoke in a well-modulated voice. It was obvious he'd seen the inside of some pretty good schools. He handled himself like a gentleman.

I reached toward my rifle to take it inside with me. "Leave it there; it'll be safe." His words now had the ring of steel in them. They didn't suggest, they ordered. He reverted to the suave, polished gentleman, and ushered me into a living area with a large fireplace located along one of the outside walls. The furniture, although rustic, was well-made and built for comfort.

To my surprise, a rather formal dining area adjoined it. A massive table sat in its middle, surrounded by chairs enough for twelve people.

Despite his demeanor, I knew now I dealt with a very dangerous man. A man who could control a situation with such icy calm would bear all the respect I could give him.

"Have a seat. May I get you a drink?"

"Whiskey, straight," I answered. Although astonished that civilization existed in this remote area, I was damned if I'd show it.

While Robin poured drinks, I studied him. He stood close to my height, had thinning yellow hair, and a sensitive face. His body gave the impression of spring steel. I thought he might be about forty years old.

Robin brought my whiskey. He cupped a glass of brandy in his hand to warm it. "Please, make yourself at home. Tonight we visit. In the morning we take up your business."

He waved the brandy glass under his nose to catch the bouquet before he put the glass to his lips.

"Tell me about yourself." I felt his request fell between us more as a command than just idle curiosity.

I told him about my job, Billy, Adam. I had nothing to hide, so I told him, but I left Betsy out of it.

My story finished, I stared at him a moment. "I would ask about you. Somehow you don't fit the mold of what I expected." I shook my head. "No, I can't say that, because I formed no opinions as to what and who I'd find in here." I smiled crookedly. "Somehow, I think it would be futile to ask about you."

He shook his head. "Not at all. I'll tell you about me." He sipped his brandy. "Have you ever heard the name Carston Blade?"

I knew probably everyone, Union or Confederate, had heard of Carston Blade who had stolen a half-million-dollar gold shipment from Virginia City, Montana Territory.

Henry Plummer, the sheriff, and his gang of cutthroats had organized the holdup with the help of a Major Blade, Army of the Confederate States of America.

After successfully pulling off the stage holdup, Blade disappeared with all the gold. As a result, he was hunted by the Union *and* Confederate armies, as well as Plummer's gang, but to no avail. He got away clean and had not been heard of since.

"Yes," I answered Robin's question, praying to God that he wouldn't tell me he and Blade were one and the same, but I knew that was exactly what he was going to do. "I imagine everyone, North and South alike, has heard of Major Blade."

He smiled a thin, cold smile. "Then you have guessed by

now that I am Carston Blade. But I'll tell you, here and now, I didn't keep the gold. I turned it over to the Confederacy."

I let an expressionless mask slide over my face. Blade was lying. I had ranked high enough in the Confederate military to receive secret dispatches. Blade had never turned one cent over to the South. He was wanted there as much as in the North. If I let him see that I doubted his word, I would never leave here alive.

He went on to tell me his version of what happened on that cold, lonely trail out of Virginia City, where five men had died. Their frozen bodies were found the next day. He justified his part in the robbery by saying it was simply an act of war.

I nodded, as if agreeing with him. He seemed pleased, and even more so when I said I'd been a captain in the South's army. I dared not tell him I'd been a colonel or he might have wondered how much information I'd been privy to.

"What made you think you'd find anything or anyone here?"

I shrugged. "Rumors, whisperings." I spread my hands as though at a loss to define my reason for believing them. "You know how those things get started, and there's usually more than a little truth in them."

Musing, as though to himself, Blade sighed and said, "We will soon have to abandon this place and move on." He smiled sadly at me. "It's a helluva life, Chance."

I wanted to tell him that he'd made his bed and had to lie in it. Instead, I said, "Carston, places like you have here will be scarce in ten, maybe twenty years. The West is filling up. Settlers will take up all the space."

When dinner was announced, I went to the back stoop to wash my face and hands. While drying, I studied the area. Blade's house backed up to a stand of tall, stately pines. There was very little underbrush, nowhere to hide if a person wanted to leave in that direction. I hung the towel on the peg and returned inside.

An Indian woman served dinner. There were many of our nation's best hotels that would have been envious had they seen the food on this table. Venison, elk, trout, vegetables that were canned due to the late season, and a berry pie made up our meal.

Carston kept glancing at me, and I knew he tried to gauge whether I was surprised by the quality of the meal.

I pushed my chair back and took my pipe from my pocket, looking questioningly at Blade. He nodded. "I'll join you."

Our pipes lighted, I smiled at him. "Yes, to answer your questioning looks. I'm very surprised to find quality living this far from civilization."

He laughed. "I didn't know I was that transparent, but yeah, I did wonder what you thought."

After our smoke, I joined him in a brandy. Soon after, he showed me to the room I'd have for the night. It didn't surprise me to find luxurious appointments. The bedrooms matched the rest of the furnishings.

"Sleep as late as you wish. I'll probably run down to the store for a while in the morning, but I'll join you for breakfast."

I nodded. He had not offered a way to take a bath, and I didn't ask. I turned in. The mattress, stuffed with corn shucks, offered more comfort than I'd had in some while.

Over breakfast the next morning, I explained to Blade what I wanted of him and his men. I didn't mention that I looked for my brother's killer. Finished, I waited for his reply.

He'd stared at his plate during the last part of my explanation. When he looked up, a sad smile crooked the corners of his lips.

"Chance," he shook his head, "some of the men in here are really desperate. They've killed, stolen, raped. You name it and they've done it. For that matter, there are three here who know you and have an itch to kill you."

He said it as though informing me the time of day and went on explaining the town's existence. He motioned to indicate the settlement. "This is the only sanctuary they have. I provide it to them for a fee, and they abide by my rules or they get buried."

He sat back and looked at me. "What I offer them is safety. What I have here is a well-guarded fort. If I let you go out of here, intentionally or not, you'd soon let it slip how many of us are in here. The law, or the Army, would bring in enough force to defeat us." He shook his head. "If that happened, there would be no more sanctuary.

"If you try escaping, you won't get to the river." He again shook his head. His voice hardened. "You're my guest for awhile."

His statement hit me in the gut like a sledgehammer. He had not only sentenced me to his prison, he'd pronounced a death sentence on me.

chapter

twenty-four

I STARED AT Blade. He'd just told me three of the men here wanted me dead and, in so many words, I was his prisoner, and worse yet, that I wouldn't leave here alive.

"I'll have to ask you to give me your weapons," Blade said and held out his hand.

"Major, you already have my rifle. You just told me three men here want to kill me. How shall I defend myself? Will you permit them to shoot me down in cold blood?"

"No, there will be none of that. I've put the word out you're to be left alone. If they touch you, I'll have them hanged."

"A hell of a lot of good that'll do me."

"They won't bother you. You have my word for it."

I thought of going for my gun but knew it would be futile. I'd never get out of town alive. I thanked God Billy was safe.

Unbuckling my gun belt, I wrapped it around the holster and handed it to Blade. This was not the time to make a try at escaping. *So, I have your word for it,* I thought. I'd found the worth of his word when he told me he hadn't kept the gold stolen from Virginia City.

"Where do I stay? I'm sure you will not keep me here in your house. After all, I'm your prisoner. Where do you intend to lock me up?"

Blade's face hardened. "I hoped you wouldn't take this attitude. I don't intend to lock you up. You'll be my guest, here in my house, until I figure out what to do with you."

The man's crazy, I thought.

He walked to his desk, took a key from his pocket, unlocked the bottom drawer, shoved my gun in, and relocked it. He turned back to me. "You will have full freedom to walk about the town." That icy smile again twisted his lips. "I don't think I have to warn you that any attempt to leave and you'll be shot down, no questions asked. If you're hungry, thirsty, whatever you want, short of a weapon, help yourself. I'll continue to conduct my business as usual. I'm going to the store now. Would you like to accompany me?"

I thought it a good idea to let the men about town see me with Blade. "Yeah, I'll tag along. I would like to see what kind of setup you have here."

While we walked, Blade talked of the town. He pointed out the livery stable, hotel, and saloon. As I'd guessed, the two buildings flanking the saloon were the general store and a feed store. Cabins housed the more permanent residents; the rest stayed in the hotel.

Everything about Carston Blade was a contradiction. On one hand, he was the polished gentleman, but only a thin veneer hid the savage, ruthless killer I knew him to be.

I noticed as we walked that I drew quite a bit of attention. Invariably, those we passed scanned me from head to toe, eyes lingering on the place along my right leg where my Levi's had not faded from the sun. They knew I'd worn a gun, and they didn't have to guess that Blade was the cause of its absence.

They respectfully—or fearfully—stepped from Blade's path. I suspected the latter because, thinly veiled under his polished surface, I'd detected steel and a volcanic temper. Nobody in his town wished to cross him.

We walked into the dark coolness of the store. The complete stock it carried surprised me. The clerk, a woman, walked to Blade. "Yes, Mr. Blade, is there anything I can show your guest this morning?"

So the word had already been passed that Blade detained me. Otherwise, I thought, she would have asked *me*.

Blade smiled. "No, I don't think so, Nita, but let my guest have anything he wants—short of weapons."

She looked at me, and I thought I saw a flicker of pity in her glance. "Is there anything you'd like now?" I could see she'd known some hard living, but she might have a soft spot. I'd have to keep her in mind.

"No, if I think of anything I'll come back." I laughed. "It's not like I'll take my business elsewhere."

We walked about the store. Like most shoppers do, I felt the goods, looked at some, and passed by others. I made note of the stock of Hudson's Bay blankets and thought I'd like one each for Billy and me.

A good assortment of knives took my eye. They had Barlows as well as Green Rivers. I thought to buy Billy a Barlow to replace the knife he'd given to Mopeah. A Barlow would be best because the blade folded into the handle, whereas the other didn't. I knew better than to ask for it now with Carston along. Perhaps later.

Nita might not consider a pocket knife a weapon. Here on the frontier, knives were usually considered a tool. But I knew damned well my host would know how they could be used.

Next, we walked to the saloon and found it busy for this early in the morning. In addition to liquor, there were several dance hall girls. Blade had seen to it that the men who used his facility had all the necessities. I supposed the town's citizenry had little else to do when they weren't planning mischief.

We walked to the bar. A space opened for us immediately. If Blade had not been along, I'd have had to elbow my way to it.

I asked for a cup of coffee. Carston Blade had a whiskey, which the bartender poured from a bottle under the bar.

My eyes were accustomed to the reduced light by now.

I glanced around to make note of the people as well as the location of the furnishings. I'd taught Billy to do this, too.

A person never knew when he might have use for such knowledge.

A voice from behind drawled. "Well, well, look what the cat drug in."

The saloon did not boast a mirror behind the bar, but I didn't need one to know who stood behind me, nor would I have to guess who it was in this settlement that wanted me dead. If I ever wished Carston Blade to be true to his word, it was now. I had a cold knot in the pit of my stomach.

I turned slowly. Snake Thompson, Shorty, and Rip Tate, Thompson's hatchet-faced friend, stood not five feet away.

"Well, Snake, I see nobody's killed you yet, so you must still be shooting them from behind."

He sprang toward me, and I backhanded him, opening a cut under his left eye.

He stumbled to the side, grabbing for his gun. He was fast, very fast. My stomach muscles tightened as though to stop the bullet.

A shot rang out, deafening in the confines of the room. I felt nothing, no pain, no numbness, nothing, and I wondered where he'd hit me. Through the stinking black smoke of gunpowder, I saw Snake's life pumping out of the hole in his throat.

A glance at his two friends showed them standing frozen, staring past me. Turning, I saw Carston Blade holding a small, snub-nosed pistol in his slim hand. Smoke poured lazily from one of its barrels. It was a two-shot, Remington .41, over-and-under–style pistol. I had not even known he carried it. Snake had been fast, awful fast—but not fast enough.

"I told you," Blade said, speaking to all in the room, his voice hardly above a whisper, "that Tenery is not to be bothered while he is my guest. When, and if, I cut him loose, he'll be carrying. Then you can blow him to hell for all I care."

Snake Thompson was no longer a problem, but I'd rather face two of him than one Carston Blade.

I expelled the breath I'd held, thankful for Blade's twisted sense of honor, but I knew it wasn't only honor that made him do what he'd done. He had just set an example of what would happen to anyone disobeying his orders—any orders.

I looked at Blade, raised my eyebrows, and smiled crookedly. "Thanks."

"I didn't do that for you. Let's go back to the house."

Again, I realized he didn't suggest, he ordered.

I followed him toward the door.

That night we repeated the same format we'd observed the night before: drinks, dinner, smoke, and conversation. We observed this ritual every day of the week that followed.

We talked about books, places we'd been, and people we'd known. He seemed hungry for knowledge of what went on out in the world from which he'd isolated himself.

It occurred to me that a good part of the reason Carston protected me was that he hungered for company, an educated person he could talk to, one who'd seen and done things that those surrounding him never imagined existed. *Think, Chance, what will happen when he gets bored?*

After we went to bed, I thought long into the night, trying to plan my escape. I would no more than fashion a method before I'd cast it aside. There was no way I'd be able to shoot my way out.

Oh, I would get a gun somehow, but that was the least of my worries. There were a lot of guns here, and they would all be turned my way. I must, absolutely must, devise a scheme that would get me out with a minimum of gunfire. When sleep finally came, the solution was still just as far away.

The next morning, I had a leisurely breakfast served by the Indian woman. I didn't know whether she had the freedom to leave if she desired or not, but I decided to cultivate her friendship. When the time came to leave, any friends I might make would be that many less I'd have to worry about at my back.

She poured me a cup of coffee. I glanced up at her. "What is your name?"

"Morning Star Woman." Her voice came out flat, devoid

of expression. It didn't encourage further conversation, but I tried anyway.

"I have a good friend among the Shoshone; he is called Mopeah." I watched her eyes to see if I got through to her and thought I saw a glimmer of interest.

"I'm Shoshone. Crow warriors took me from the people many moons ago. I will return to the people someday."

That answered my question. I could not count her as an ally, but maybe I could cultivate her friendship. I would have to plan carefully and not hurry. When I made my try, it would have to be good. There would be no second chance.

My mind went back to Blade. I didn't think he'd harm me as long as I afforded him the company for which he was so hungry, but the day our conversation became commonplace, he'd let his men take care of me.

I smiled thinly, thinking how often greed became a man's prison. Blade had stolen that gold, and I was certain he had it hidden somewhere close by. He didn't dare try to move it because the very men he harbored would kill him for it.

If he managed to get it back East, he'd immediately become suspect. Even though there were many producing mines in the West, gold in large amounts was not a commodity that could be peddled easily east of the Mississippi.

There was no doubt he wanted to return to, as he'd put it, the civilized world, and he hung onto my company as a fragile thread to the world.

So, my dangerous friend had tied himself to an anchor that would someday get him killed or keep him imprisoned.

It wasn't his nature to trust any man, much less ask for help. I cast aside the thought that I might try to persuade him to let me assist in moving the gold. I couldn't try to escape in that manner. Besides, he didn't admit to having kept it after the robbery.

He would wait for the right time, but the longer he waited, the less likely he was to succeed. The country became more populous every day. The more people who saw his heavily laden wagon, the more probable he'd be discovered. A commotion in front of the cabin broke into my thoughts.

When I opened the door, the first thing I saw was Billy. A man had him by the scruff of the neck, pushing him up the street. Billy kicked and squirmed to break the man's grasp every step of the way.

How I reached them so fast I didn't know, but in less time than it takes to tell about it I was at their side. I swung at the side of the man's head. I don't think he had any idea I was there. He went to his knees and tried to stand. I kicked him on the knee. His feet went from under him. A right I brought up from my waist caught him in the mouth. A left to his gut, and another right to his mouth put him down. This time he stayed down. I turned to Billy.

"What the *hell* are you doing here? You're supposed to be on your way to end-of-track."

He looked me straight in my eyes. Standing straight as a raw plebe at West Point, he said, "Papa, you made me think something bad might happen to you. I figured I would as soon be dead as not be with you, so I came lookin' for you."

My anger melted. How could I stay angry with my son when his only wish was to be with me? By now a few men had left the saloon and were coming toward us. I had no intention of explaining to them what happened. I took Billy by the arm. "Come, let's get in the house."

We had been in the cabin only a short time when Carston came through the door. His eyes were blue slits of ice, his face pale. "Why did you attack my man?" Each word he spat at me was like a bullet.

"Mister, you or your men can take your best shot at me, but I'll tell you right-damn-now no one, *no one* lays a hand on my son. Leave Billy alone." Some of the anger drained from Blade's face.

"Your son? What's he doing here?"

I explained that Billy had been left in South Pass City, and was to head for end-of-track if I didn't show up in a given time. "He disobeyed me, Carston, pure and simple. He disobeyed me."

Carston shifted his gaze from me to Billy. "Well, it looks like I have two guests, doesn't it?"

If he'd ranted and raved, I would have felt better. The cool way he seemed to adjust to every situation worried me. I had already decided that he was crazy. That decision left me to wonder what he would do next.

Looking at Billy, I asked if he had eaten, and discovering that he hadn't, I asked Morning Star Woman to fix him something.

Afterward, Billy and I walked to the store, leaving Blade to pore over his accounts. Again, I looked longingly at the Hudson's Bay blankets, and Billy stood over the case of knives, staring at them. Only then did I realize how much he'd prized the one he'd given Mopeah.

I wanted to ask Nita to let him have one but kept my patience. Let her get used to seeing us first.

"Hello, Chance, who you got there? What y'all doin', shoppin'?" I looked over my shoulder and saw Tuck grinning at us.

"Hi, Tuck, how you doin'? Let me introduce my son, Billy. He followed me, despite strict orders to go to the railroad."

"Doin' pretty good, Chance." He glanced at Billy. "Hi, son, glad to know you." He shuffled his feet a couple of times. "Reckon y'all might as well know. My real name's Yancy Tetlow, from down Tennessee by way of Kansas."

I grinned at him, and tongue in cheek, said, "Somehow, don't know what gave me the idea, but I didn't think you were Friar Tuck."

He laughed. "No, reckon you wouldn't." He sobered. "How you gettin' along with Mr. Blade?"

I shrugged. "About as good as could be expected." The fact Yancy had called Blade "mister" said a lot for how close this bunch was.

I indicated the knives Billy still looked at. "Billy has drooled over those knives ever since we came in here. He gave his to an Indian warrior."

Yancy glanced at them, then at Billy. "Yep, a boy needs

a knife; shouldn't be without one, for that matter. What made you give yours away?"

Billy told him about the fight we'd had with the Sioux, and about Mopeah giving him a present. "I suppose you know it would have been bad manners for me not to give him something; besides, he's my friend."

Yancy studied Billy a moment, then nodded. "You make some good friends, boy. Good goin'."

We talked a little longer. I bought us each a blanket and ground sheets to go with them.

After leaving the store, we walked briskly around the compound to get our breathing going good. If we sat in that house all the time, we'd get soft. We might need the stamina to run from this town.

I wanted to see how hard it might be to slip into the livery and take a couple of horses, so we went to the stable next. Those blankets weren't heavy, but they were bulky, so I didn't want to spend much time away from our room.

A stringy old gent sat in the door on a straight-legged chair, the chair leaning back on two legs. He whittled a piece of pine wood.

"What you carving?" I asked. Not that I really wanted to know, but it seemed a good way to start a conversation.

He tongued a cud of tobacco into a more comfortable place in his cheek, slanted me a glance, and looked back at his stick. "Now I woulda thunk anybody could see I'm carvin' me a little boy like you got there. Always wanted me a boy, an' looks like this is the only kind I'll ever get less'n o' course, you'll give me that one."

I hid a smile. "Nah, he ain't much good fer nothin', but I reckon I'll keep 'im. Why just the other day I turned down a chance to trade 'im fer a hog."

He cocked his head and glanced at me again. "Don't say? Well, cain't say as I blame yuh much. Even a no-good kid's sometimes hard to come by." He nodded jerkily. "Yep, better keep 'im, somebody might give ye a horse fer 'im, but I sort o' doubt it. People put right smart store by their horses."

Billy danced from one foot to the other. "Aw, Papa, I kinda liked that man with the hog, and wanted to go with him somethin' awful. I tried to get him to give you that hog and one o' them little piglets, but he wouldn't go that high for me."

I laughed and tousled his hair. "You little devil, keep that up and I'll sure enough trade you in on something."

The getting-acquainted talk over, the old man asked me what I wanted.

"Just tired of being cooped up in that house and thought we'd take a walk and look at the town. We've seen everything but your stable. Care if we look it over?"

"A stable's a stable, but go ahead." He picked up his rifle. "Don't reckon you mind if I come along?" he said dryly.

I smiled enough to feel my eyes crinkle at the corners. The old boy was cagey. He wasn't taking a chance that we'd latch onto a couple of horses and try to race them out of there.

I saw the stalls that held our horses and many other beautiful ones in stalls of their own. These outlaws kept the best. And why not? Their lives more often than not depended upon a good horse.

I saw all I wanted. Stealing a couple horses from here would be next to impossible. The old man was friendly but no fool. Well, I'd had to see for myself.

On the way back to the house, we stopped at the store again. I wanted a book if they had one.

Nita laughed when I asked. "The only books you'll find here are in Carston Blade's house. Most of these men here find their entertainment at the saloon. If they aren't drinking, they're upstairs bedding some woman. Ask Blade. He might let you read something of his, although he's right selfish about sharing."

I gathered Nita didn't like Blade very much, but that didn't mean she'd cross him. I would have bet my life's savings she feared him worse than a rattler.

Not finding anything to read, we walked back to the house. Blade, sitting in his favorite chair, looked up when we entered. "Enjoy your scouting expedition?" he asked, smiling coldly.

"Yeah, but didn't see any ready way to make a run for it."

That cold smile didn't slip a bit. "I'm a very thorough man, Tenery. The longer you stay here, the more convinced you'll be."

"Oh, I would never doubt that." I started to add that I never underestimated an opponent but didn't want to reveal that much.

"By the way, I notice you have a pretty extensive library. May I read some of your books?"

"By all means. I suppose I've read most of them at least twice, and many others three of four times." He nodded to the shelves. "Help yourself."

Under different circumstances, Carston Blade would be a very likable person, as long as no one opposed him. Already, I knew him too well. Everything we were was at odds with the other.

After supper, I read a couple of Mark Twain's short stories, "The Celebrated Jumping Frog of Caleveras County" and "The Stolen White Elephant," both published in 1865. I had not read them before.

When I finished with them, I noticed Blade had already crawled into his brandy bottle, so I asked if he and Billy would like to take a walk. He declined, as I hoped he would. I noticed he didn't get drunk, just more cautious.

We hadn't gone far when I heard steps behind and turned to see who followed. Yancy hurried to catch up.

"Y'all mindful of me taggin' along? I sort o' like a walk this time o' day."

As cold as the weather had turned, I had to wonder if he'd been assigned to guard us.

"No, come along. We walk briskly, though."

He glanced at Billy and saw that I held his hand while we walked. His hand dipped into his pocket and came out again. "Mind if I hold your other hand, little one? Ain't had a chance to walk with a little boy in a long time."

Billy's head jerked up to look at Yancy when he took his

hand. His mouth opened to say something, but Yancy cut him off. "Don't say nothin' or act like anythin's happened, son. Jest keep on holdin' to my hand. When I leave you down by the last cabin, put it in your pocket."

We slowed our pace a bit, and Yancy smiled sadly. "Taken a likin' to your youngster, Chance. It might get me killed, but I'm gonna help you if I can."

Narrow-lidded, I stared at him, not daring to trust what I heard. "Why would you do this for us, Yancy?"

He looked at the ground a moment while we walked. "Well, I'll tell you," he said finally. "I ain't never done nothin' real bad. Stole a few cows, tried to hold up a stage but messed it up. Didn't even shoot or kill nobody. I got to thinkin', if you're really gonna go to ranchin' over yonder across them mountains away from everything, well, I wondered if maybe you'd give me a job?"

Our footsteps were the only sounds for a few seconds, then he said, "Aw, it wuz only a idee I had. Don't blame you if you don't want the likes of me around. I got to thinkin' though that it might be my only chance to ride the straight trail. Just thought I'd try."

"No, Yancy, it's not that at all. I was just struck dumb that you'd help us. I'd be mighty proud to have you come with us."

"Aw-aw, well, for Pete's sake. You really mean it? You really want me with you?"

"Yancy, you know your neck'll be stuck way out. I want to make sure you know what you're getting into."

He nodded. "Yeah, I know, but this might be my last chance to do something good and get outta here at the same time."

"All right. When I come up with something I think will work, I'll let you know what to do."

Yancy glanced at the cabin we came up on. "This is my place. I'll try to talk with you every time I see y'all are alone. Okay?"

I nodded and turned back toward Blade's house, feeling for the first time that maybe we had a chance to get out of here alive.

I had a nagging doubt about Yancy. Was he Blade's spy? I finally decided not to look a gift horse in the mouth. Yancy, so far, was the only hope we had.

chapter

twenty-five

THE HEAT OF the house felt good. Maybe some warmth came from the knowledge that Billy and I were not alone.

When Blade killed Thompson, he'd cut my troubles considerably, but not enough to make getting away seem any easier. There was still the short outlaw and his buddy, Rip Tate. They were the back-shooting kind.

They'd hold both Blade and me responsible for Snake's death and would try to even the score. But my big worry remained the kingpin of this hideout.

"Wintry out?" Blade asked as soon as we'd shucked our coats.

I nodded. "Getting close to zero, I'd guess."

"We'll get snow soon. When we do, we'll be in here till spring thaw."

I frowned. This was something I hadn't counted on. "You get that much in here? I thought perhaps these mountains might shelter The Hole somewhat."

"Oh, on the flats it'll be all right, but you can be riding along, and all of a sudden you and your horse will be in a drift over your head. Makes for pretty hard traveling."

He looked innocently at me, a slight smile crooking the corners of his lips, but I knew he gloated over giving me another worry.

I picked up a book and sat across the room from him. Billy asked if he might go to bed, saying he was tired. "Sure, son, go ahead. I'll have a cup of coffee and be in shortly." I pulled him to me and gave him a hug. I knew he couldn't wait to look at his new Barlow. That had to be what Yancy had placed in his hand.

"Night, Papa, Mr. Blade."

"Good night, boy," Blade responded, and at the same time called Morning Star Woman. "Get Mister Tenery a cup of coffee, Star. Get me one, too."

Silently, on moccasined feet, she brought our coffee and left just as quietly.

"That woman's almost spooky, the way she moves around without making a noise."

"How did you come by her?"

"Traded a new Spencer rifle for her. Thought at the time that Crow buck got the better of me in that trade, but she's been a good servant. She thought I wanted her to spread her legs for me, but I don't want a damned squaw stinking up my pallet."

I wanted to tell him Indians were cleaner than most whites, but left it alone. After his remark about Star, he studied me. I waited.

"You any good with that Colt you carried?"

I shrugged. "About as good as the army made me be. I suppose after I get it out of the damned holster, if I take time to aim, I can hit what I want to." I grinned. "But no, I don't think there's a man here would call me good."

I thought I detected a slight disappointment in his face and wondered if he'd counted on a shoot-out with me. If it ever came to that, it helped knowing about the hideout he carried. I'd been looking at Snake when Blade shot him, but I saw how fast Snake was, and Blade beat him.

When I went in to bed, I saw that Billy feigned sleep. After I crawled into my cold side of the bed, I turned to him. "I'll bet you brought it to bed with you."

I couldn't see his face, but he turned toward me. "Papa," he whispered, "it's such a pretty thing I just had to look at it. And Mr. Yancy honed a good edge on it for me."

"Yeah, I know, son, and it may help us get out of here, so keep it out of sight."

"Yes, sir."

One day slid into another, and Billy and I walked, spent time in the store, and visited the corral, mostly to visit with the old man who kept it. He was a salty old devil, but I liked him.

It got colder with each passing day. Again, during our evening walk, Yancy fell in with us.

"Cold enough to freeze hell a mile," he said, and took Billy's hand. He seemed to like walking like that. I noticed Billy did, too.

"Chance, I bought two packhorses, at least that's what I told that old geezer down at the livery they were for. They're good sound ponies. Not as good as most around here, but you won't be ashamed to ride 'em."

He slipped and righted himself. "When you tell me the day you're gonna make a try for it, I'll leave a day ahead. I'll talk around like I'm headin' out for better weather. I'll wait for you where I first seen you down yonder at the Snake. Like to stay here and help, but then we might not make it at all. Too many of us will jest make things harder."

I agreed and told him I wasn't ready yet. The fact he'd gotten horses gave my morale a boost. Thus far, all my planning had been built around having to walk or run out of here.

We'd still be afoot in the early going, but that, too, might work to our advantage. A man can hide easier without his horse under him.

"You mind if I lead us outta here? I know where the snow's less likely to cause us trouble. Agin the south wall it'll be a lot better ridin'."

"Once we meet up with you, you're the boss, Yancy."

"Nah, I ain't wantin' nothin' like that, but I'll get us outta here."

"That's all I could ask." I knew as I said it that I had gotten rid of any doubts I had about Yancy.

We split up, Yancy going to his place and Billy and I to ours.

When Blade was out of the house, Star had gotten so she'd talk rather freely. Billy told her about how we'd fought Sioux and that Mopeah had named him a warrior.

She smiled and pointed to his medicine pouch. "Good medicine. I don't know Mopeah, but he must be a good man."

"Star, when we leave here, do you want to go with us?" Billy's question both surprised and irritated me. A woman along would make getting out all the harder.

"I think about leaving here a lot, but I haven't seen a way to do it."

"Star, we'll be afoot, and it'll be very hard. Do you think you could stand the pace?" I asked, hoping to discourage her.

Stoically, she gazed at me. "You don't want me to come, I'll not come."

I felt like I'd just pulled a breast from a hungry baby's mouth and held it dangling, tauntingly, in front of his puckered lips.

"No, Star, it's just that it's going to be very dangerous. You might get killed."

"That would be better than staying here. You and Billy are captives, but you have more freedom than I."

I nodded. "Then it's settled. When we go, you go." I frowned. "We'll have to find another horse."

"You have horses?"

"Yes."

"I'll get a horse."

"We'll ride double if we have to, but you're coming with us." Thoughtfully, I looked at her. "Try to get a horse without raising suspicions."

She smiled. "I'm Shoshone. I can steal your horse while you sit on it."

I chuckled and nodded. "So be it."

More days passed. More snow fell, and fell again. Each

time Blade came inside, his shoulders thick with flakes, he'd grin sardonically at me.

I never let on that he angered me, because it would have given him pleasure. I always returned his grin with an amused smile. That would worry him.

Despite my demeanor, the snow did worry me for two reasons: it would make travel harder, and it would make tracking us easier. But come snow, fire, rain, or blood, we were going out of here.

Billy's knife now entered into my plans. I must use it to get a better weapon. I could see no other way. Every move Carston Blade made, I gauged his strength, his quickness, his awareness. The knife would be chancy, but it was all I had.

Lying next to Billy, feeling his warmth curled up close to me, I stared at the dark ceiling. I had done this every night, planning and discarding, but tonight all the lost sleep paid off. I knew how I might do it. There would never be a cinch way to protect Billy, but this seemed the most foolproof of all.

During our walk the next night, when Yancy fell in beside us, I told him to ride out the next day and to expect us when he saw us. "I'm going to take us out of here in broad daylight. I won't take time to tell you how, but I think it'll work. The way I've got it planned, I want as many people in town to see me as possible."

Yancy slanted me a look that said he thought I'd lost my mind. He grimaced. "I hope you know what the hell you're doin', Chance."

"So do I, Yancy. So do I."

Cautioning Billy, I told him to act as he'd always acted, and that it might be a good idea for him to go to bed early tonight to lessen the odds that he'd say or do something to alert Blade.

After we'd had our usual talk that night, I went in the kitchen for a dipper of water. I stopped to tell Star to be ready early the day after tomorrow. Blade came in while we talked.

Always suspicious, he glanced from one to the other of us. His eyes slitted. "What are you talking about?"

I shrugged. "You didn't seem to cotton to sleeping with her, and I haven't had a woman in a good while. Thought maybe she'd be pretty good in bed."

Star, bless her soul, understood what I was doing immediately and butted in, heatedly, "He said he'd pay me to sleep with him. I told him I'm your woman, and that I don't sleep with white men, not even you."

His eyes raked each of us. "Why don't you go ahead, Star. Give him what he wants. You know damned well I don't care."

"No, I'm your woman."

He shrugged, raised his eyebrows, and turned away. I winked at her, grinned, and drank my water.

Back in the sitting room, Carston looked at me. "Why don't you go down to the saloon? There are women down there, any one of whom would give their eyeteeth for a big devil like you to crawl between their thighs."

I shook my head. "Not in a month of Sundays, Carston. No telling what else they'd give me besides their body." I shook my head. "No thank you. I'll do without."

He laughed. "Women never bothered me much. As long as I have the good things in life, I'm happy."

Yeah, I thought, and for the first time I wondered at his lack of interest in women.

The next day, I made certain Billy and I did everything exactly as we'd always done. About midmorning, I watched Yancy ride out leading two packhorses. Things were beginning to fall into place.

That night, I asked Billy for his knife before he went to sleep.

The next morning, I watched Blade take his usual walk to the store and stationed Star in the kitchen door. Blade never stayed gone long. I hoped she'd attract his attention when he walked through the doorway. I had Billy sit reading in front of the fireplace. Where I stood, the door would hide me when it opened. Finally, all was ready. We had not long to wait.

I heard Blade's footsteps crunch the snow, melted and freshly frozen, on the stoop. I held the opened knife in my right hand. The door swung toward me, and I stepped toward Blade's back, wrapped my arm around his head, and pushed the point of the knife into his throat enough to start blood flowing but not enough to kill him.

"Don't even wriggle, Blade, or I'll shove this in all the way." I turned him toward the wall, leaned him against it, and kicked his legs apart so he couldn't move without losing his balance. Releasing my hold on his head, I reached in the pocket I'd seen him put his keys in every time he used them. They were there.

I tossed them to Billy. "Get my pistol, and then give Star the keys."

Next, I felt for a gun. The little hideout was all I found. I pushed it inside my shirt and turned him around.

His face was screwed into a mask of fury, his eyes wild and red like a grizzly's I'd once seen caught in a trap, and his mouth worked to push words between his foaming lips. "You-you dumb sonuvabitch. You think you can get away with this? You're trapped in here. Even if you kill me, you won't leave the front door alive."

Holding the knife at his throat, I told Star to take the keys Billy handed her and to take two rifles from the gun case.

She did as she was told, checking the chambers to make sure they were loaded.

"Can you kill a man, Star? If you can't, Billy can."

"I can kill." She nodded toward Blade. "I can kill him. It would be better if I could kill him like a Shoshone kills."

"Good! Now I want you and Billy to stand there and keep your guns on Blade. Don't shoot him unless you have to."

When they had guns trained on him, Billy with my .44 and Star with a rifle, I pulled the knife from Blade's throat, picked up the first rifle Star had taken from the case, and saw it was a Henry.

Knowing it held a load in its chamber, I walked toward the kitchen. "Keep him right where he is until I get back," I ordered.

It didn't take long to find a ball of twine and return to the sitting room. I took my holster, belt, and gun from Billy and buckled them on.

I pulled the Henry's hammer back, keeping it under my thumb while I pulled the trigger back to the fired position. I then let the hammer down easy. Still holding the trigger back, I wrapped twine about it and the trigger guard. Now, once the hammer was pulled back, it would fire the rifle without having to pull the trigger.

Satisfied it would do the job, I walked to Blade and stuck the end of the barrel up under his throat, then pulled the hammer back, holding it there with my thumb.

"Now, you suave sonuvabitch, if anything happens to me, or if I even stumble, you're coyote meat." I nodded to Star. "You can relax now, but if anything happens out there, run for where Yancy has the horses. Billy knows where they are, Star."

I was forgetting something. Then it came to me: the blankets.

"Billy, go in the room and make our bedrolls. Be sure to put the ground sheets in."

"Yes, sir."

"And Star, you go in Blade's room, take the best blanket he has, and make yourself a packet that'll keep you comfortable on the trail. You'd better take another rifle. We may need it."

The success of my plan hinged on the men Blade catered to here in his private little hellhole. They'd be so terrified of him they'd not do anything to get him killed. There might even be some of them who were loyal and wouldn't want to see him die. Either way, we were walking a tightrope. Then there was Shorty and Hatchet-Face. They hated Blade *and* me. They wouldn't give a damn if we killed each other.

"When I open this door, Blade, I want you to step out on the porch and call every man you see to muster around.

Then I'll tell them what I want them to know. This rifle stays under your chin all the way to Rock Springs if need be."

I reached for the door and pulled it toward me.

chapter

twenty-six

CAREFUL TO NOT slip on the slick, ice-coated stoop, Carston Blade and I stepped out where all could see, but there were only two men out in this subzero cold.

"Call them to you," I ordered.

"Hey, Benny, Slick, come here." Blade's voice fell flat from his lips. He showed no emotion. Whatever else he might be, he was no coward.

The two walked cautiously to the foot of the steps. They didn't have to ask questions. My rifle pushed up under Blade's chin told them all they needed to know.

"You want the men to come down here?" Blade asked me.

"Yes. I want them to be able to gauge how much chance you'll have if any of them try to free you."

Blade held his head high, not from any degree of pride, but to keep my rifle muzzle from hurting. I had it pushed under his chin that hard. He cocked his eyes down to look at the two men.

"Go to the saloon and bring every man there back here—on the double. I can't stand here like this all day."

After watching them head toward the saloon, I looked at Blade and grinned, even though my stomach felt tight and in knots.

"You'd better hope you can, or you'll be a dead bastard."

Grumbling, the men trickled from the saloon. Seeing me

standing there with Blade's head near spitted on the end of my rifle, they quit grumbling and hurried closer.

My eyes flicked from one to another, constantly shifting, side to side and around the periphery, hoping no one would try slipping up on me.

My back was well covered with Billy and Star standing in the door. I strained to hear any sound that might indicate movement I couldn't see. My edge was a thin one at best. Not seeing or hearing a threat, I looked at those gathered by the porch.

Their eyes took in the tied-down trigger and the eared-back hammer under my thumb. They were all gun smart. I didn't have to say a word. Any questionable move on their part and the top of Blade's head would disappear.

My eyes locked on those of each man before moving to the next. "I see you've got the idea. One shot, at me or the two people going out of here with me, is all it'll take. Don't follow us or I'll get nervous."

I stepped carefully toward the edge of the porch. "Now, you men get in out of the cold. I wouldn't want you catching pneumonia on my account. That would be a terrible thing to have on my conscience." I hoped my words and demeanor indicated a coolness that I certainly didn't feel.

"Billy, you and Star get our bedrolls. Time to leave."

They came out just as the last of Blade's men disappeared into the saloon. I knew that, once in the saloon, they would have a few drinks while they talked things over.

It would take them a while to decide what to do. Many of them would do nothing. Those who didn't like Blade would eventually decide they didn't give a damn whether I killed him or not, so they'd come after us. *They* were the ones I feared.

It wouldn't take long to figure out that, without a landlord, they'd have a free ride. They'd not stop to think that *he* was the one who knew how to get supplies without rousing suspicion. The first thing they would think of would be that without Blade or us, they'd be riding high.

We struck out at a jog. I tried to stay in the tracks left by Yancy's horses. That wouldn't fool anyone, but the going would be easier. Every time one of my feet hit the ground, it jarred me, and I took a firmer grip on the hammer. I didn't want Blade dead—yet.

A glance at Star showed her striding with us easily. "If you get tired, let me know."

"I won't slow you down. Everything I did in this town, I ran to do it. Blade thought I did it for him, but I've been thinking of this day since he brought me here. I can run as long as any man."

Even with the seriousness of the situation, I couldn't help smiling at how embarrassed I'd be if I let a woman outlast me.

Had it not been for the trail Yancy left, we'd have been exhausted in the first couple of hundred yards, but even with that, the going was slow and tedious.

I frequently called a halt for a short breather. During the second one, I pulled the rifle from under Blade's chin and rested the muzzle against his spine. "The only thing that's changed, Blade, is that you'll be a cripple the rest of your life if my thumb slips. Get going."

"Come on, Tenery, I haven't a weapon, so take that damned rig off me. I won't try to run, I give you my word."

His statement was so ridiculous it seemed funny. I laughed, and his eyes shot poison.

I looked behind. They're on their second drink by now, I thought, and still arguing—I hope.

"We'll walk awhile," I told them, the words coming in gasps. "We'll have to keep a hard pace. Either of you too tired?" They pulled hard at the thin air. Blade was gasping.

At their head shake, I said, "Okay, let's go."

"What about me, Tenery? I can't keep this pace up." Carston's voice came out reedy and thin.

I looked at him and felt my face harden, but he couldn't see it, muffled as I was. "Blade, you'd better damn well stay with us until your legs drop off and your lungs explode, or I'll break your back with a .44 slug."

"I treated you well, why treat me like this?"

I didn't answer him. "Let's go."

Every few paces, I glanced behind. My faith in this

method of escape dwindled. That bunch behind us had no sense of loyalty. They wouldn't give a damn if I killed Blade. Their only concern would be to stop our escape. They wanted no one telling those in the outside world about their hideout.

By my guess, we had four or five miles behind us when I saw riders hanging behind just out of rifle range.

"We have company," I told Billy and Star.

"Want me to shoot at them, Papa?"

I shook my head. "No, son, you'd be wasting ammunition. Hang on for another couple of miles. We'll be close to Yancy then. Don't shoot at anything unless you think you can hit it."

Blade's head snapped around when I mentioned Yancy.

"Careful, my thumb's getting pretty tired."

His eyes narrowed and he smiled. "I don't think so, Tenery. You need me more than I need you. You have the boy and the woman to think about. I have only me, and besides, if you kill me, your ace in the hole will be gone. There will be nothing to keep them from attacking."

"You'd better hope it doesn't come to that."

"You rotten sunuv—"

"Tch, tch, there's a little boy and a lady present, Blade. That kind of language is not nice."

A shot rang out—from ahead, and it cut a furrow through the sleeve of my coat. "Get in the brush." I didn't raise my voice, but Billy and Star acted almost as I spoke.

With the shot, I was surprised that I'd had the presence of mind to keep pressure on the rifle hammer. I pushed the barrel hard against Blade's back and pushed him flat among the bushes.

That shot had come from in front. Had Yancy double-crossed us? No. I didn't think so. I'd never been that wrong about a man.

The outlaws were mounted, so any one of them could have circled and waited for us.

We lay there in the cold, and I feared the perspiration we'd worked up would freeze. If it did, we would not last long. "Let's go."

"I'm not moving." Blade's voice rasped.

"The hell you're not. Get moving."

"Whoever that was that fired at you will do it again."

"Then he'll just have to take his best shot. Either way, you die."

Reluctantly, Blade wriggled from under the brush. I never let the rifle barrel waver.

With every step, I expected to feel a slug tear through me. My muscles tensed and strained against the expected impact, but we had to keep moving.

We'd gone perhaps another hundred yards, and no shot. Was the rifleman toying with me? I didn't think so. Maybe one of Blade's friends had restrained him.

"Papa, I think I saw an Indian. Just a shadow over there in those bushes, but I believe I saw one."

"I doubt it, son. Probably one of Blade's men." Another shot. Blade grunted and stumbled. My thumb slipped a little. I clamped harder against the hammer.

A raw, vinegary taste flowed under the back of my tongue. Someone out there tried to take away my edge. As thin as it was, having Blade under my hammer was better than nothing, and now one of those rotten bastards had figured that out.

"You hurt bad, Blade?"

"Don't know. Numb. My right side."

"Hold on. I'll look at you when we stop."

"Goddammit, I might bleed to death by then." There was fear in his voice.

"That's too damned bad." I jabbed him with the rifle. "Move out. I'll support you as much as I can."

I shifted my grip on the slim part of the stock to my other hand and gripped the hammer with that thumb. Then I slid my free arm across his body and hooked my hand under his far arm. He slumped against me. I had to let the rifle dangle at my side.

"Don't push your luck, Blade. Put all you have into walking, or I'll leave you right here in the middle of the trail—dead."

He glowered at me. "I took you for a gentleman, but-but you're just—"

"I never made that mistake about you," I cut in, "so shut the hell up."

Another shot. My glance flicked to each of my party. They were all right. The shot had not come close. Maybe it had been Yancy.

A volley of shots sounded nearby, but not close enough to be of danger to us. Who could be shooting? The bullets had not come near enough for me to hear them. Maybe Yancy had circled to protect our rear. I kept plowing toward the meeting place.

Blade was almost a dead weight hanging on my arm now. I glanced at his face. He struggled to keep on his feet. The man had guts. Had he taken a different trail, he wouldn't be in this trouble.

Another rifle cracked off to the right. With its sound, I felt a red hot streak across my shoulders. Creased me. I felt the warmth of blood flow down my back. At the same time I felt the blood start, I thought I heard a moan.

"You hear somebody groan, Papa?"

I nodded. "Yes, I heard it. Maybe someone hit their shin on a log or something. See anything?"

"No, sir."

"White man fell in that stand of aspen off to the side there," Star gasped, no doubt in her voice. She pointed in the direction of the shot that had creased me.

Someone's helping, I thought, and wondered if it was Yancy. Could he kill without a sound? Maybe Billy *had* seen an Indian.

Before I could voice that opinion, there was another din of shots.

"Get into those trees and take cover."

Billy and Star went ahead of me. I went in, dragging Blade as gently as I could. He was badly wounded and suffering. I could not mistreat him more than was absolutely necessary.

Making him as easy as I could under the conditions, I saw

he'd passed out. With no time to look at his wound, I turned my attention to our surroundings.

Looking down the trail we'd traveled, I saw no sign of another human. Slowly I looked from one tree to another, clumps of brush to stark white drifted banks. We might as well have been alone. I saw no one.

I thought I detected a slight smell of smoke. If so, we were almost upon Yancy's camp.

A whisper passed close by my head, and a sharp thump sounded behind me. I whirled in that direction and fired. The short puncher who traveled with Snake Thompson stood not ten feet away, eyes bulging, mouth working furiously, trying to suck air into lungs that would never hold air again. He grasped an arrow buried half the shaft's length in his chest. My shot had made no difference.

I spun in the direction from which the arrow came and saw only snow and trees.

What the hell, I thought, Billy *did* see an Indian. Was that arrow meant for me?

I sensed that a fight to the death was taking place all around, and I wasn't playing much of a part in it. We were the pawns.

Two shots, close together, came from my side. Billy and Star looked down smoking gun barrels. In front of them a man stood, stumbled toward us, and fell. Another appeared where he'd stood. I slipped my thumb from the hammer and fired. The slug knocked him backward, his head lolling to the side where my bullet cut half his throat away.

Then they came. I dropped the rifle and drew my .44, thumbed off a shot, and saw a hole appear through the Durham tag hanging out of my target's pocket. He fell at my feet.

Billy and Star were sending shots out in front of us.

I thumbed off another shot. Half the head of another disappeared. He kept running on rubbery legs. His momentum carried him past me, and he fell in a heap at the base of a tree. I eared back on the hammer again. There was no target. Silence drenched the forest like a summer rain.

The total action had lasted only a few seconds but seemed

an eternity. Then I saw that three other bodies lay a few yards from where we'd forted up. They were Billy's and Star's contribution. I had gotten two. Billy and Star had counted three.

The silence broke. Another bunch came at us from the side.

I was in the middle of reloading, but slammed the gate shut and swung my pistol to fire. My shot blasted just as the last of them fell.

Seven were on the ground and all had arrows protruding from them. Some looked like porcupines they had so many.

"That should be all of them," a voice with a slight burr in it yelled.

"Mistuh Chance, don't shoot, we're comin' in."

Adam? And Harry? What the hell were they doing here? I had to be wrong.

chapter

twenty-seven

"ADAM? IS THAT you?"

"Yes, suh, Mistuh Chance, it's me sure enough."

"What the hell are you doing here? You're supposed to be working. And I thought I told you to quit calling me mister." The relief from the tension did something to my tongue. I couldn't stop talking.

First a deep-chested laugh, then his beautiful black face emerged from a thicket to my right. "'Tween us, I reckon we'll answer all your questions."

"Us? Who's us?"

I was so relieved, the questions kept coming. The switch from death staring us down to being among friends happened too quickly. I still felt that I should be looking for something to shoot. Nervous energy quickly evaporated, and I slumped against a tree, tired as I'd ever been.

Feeling like I should say something, I grinned tiredly and said, "To hell with the mister, Adam. I've never been so glad to see anyone in my life."

While Adam and I almost pummeled each other to a pulp, it seemed that half the Shoshone nation stepped into sight, led by Mopeah. At his side walked Harry Longdon and Peter.

"We make good fight this time, too, Iron Horse Warrior."

I noticed he'd changed the Iron Horse Man to Warrior. That seemed all the time we had for words.

I thought my back would be sore for a month from all the pounding I took. And Billy was up in Harry's arms being, to his embarrassment, kissed on both cheeks.

I glanced around me and saw Star standing to the side, not engaged in any of the revelry.

"Hold it a moment," I yelled.

When all had quieted, I took Star's hand and led her into the circle of men. "Mopeah, you have great warriors in your band, but none better than this one. Morning Star Woman helped us when we needed it and fought at our side. *She* is a Shoshone."

A tall, well-built warrior stepped forward, peered intently at Morning Star Woman, then took her face between his hands. "You have been gone many moons, little sister. Our lodge has been empty without you."

"Eagle Wing?" Star asked in a hushed voice. He nodded.

I don't know where she found it so fast, but she draped a blanket over both their heads, and from underneath it joyful sounds echoed. Star had found her brother.

We rigged a travois and took Blade to camp.

That night, by the fire, I pieced together the story of how they came to be here.

"Well, Mistuh Chance, when you'd been gone so long without Mistuh Casement hearing from you, Miss Betsy just got madder and madder and worrieder and worrieder. When she came to me, she was strainin' her boiler.

"She told me to get my black self outta there and go find Billy. She didn't care what happened to you, but she wanted me to find Billy. Besides, I don't reckon she's got much need for you with that New York man hanging around." His words tore my heart to shreds. If I'd had any hope of patching things up between Betsy and me, Adam's words destroyed them.

"When she told me that, Mistuh Casement had a connip-tion fit. Said he needed me right where I wuz.

"Well, I thought I'd seen things blow up during the war, but I knew pretty quick *that* war wuz just a maypole dance compared to the way Miss Betsy exploded all over *him*. She was all fangs and claws. Reckon I left end-of-track faster'n anybody ever did."

I went to check on Blade. He slept, but moaned while I looked down at him. I hated to see him die. Despite his being what he was, I liked him. I glanced over my shoulder at Adam.

"How did you know where to find me?"

"Your letter to Mistuh Casement said you were going to see Chief Washakie, so that's where I headed, not knowing if I wuz gonna get my scalp lifted any minute. But then, I figured whatever the Sioux, Crow, or any Indians did to me would be a whole lot better than what that little white lady threatened me with. So I lit out. When I—"

"I'll tell this," Mopeah cut in. He took his time about getting started. He packed his pipe with *my* tobacco, and grinned as he did so. I knew he still had most of that I'd given him at the winter camp. At this rate, it would last a long time.

He went to the fire, picked up a twig from its edge, and stuck the glowing end in his pipe bowl. When he had the tobacco burning good, he glanced at Adam. Somehow I knew from that look that Adam had found another friend.

"A scout came to camp in big snow and tells of big, big, big man out in the cold. He thought big man would die because he was so cold he'd already turned black." Mopeah sucked on his pipe a couple of times and looked at me.

"I didn't tell my warriors," he continued, "but I remembered stories told at our council fires. Some of them were of a big black man who'd been in Chief Red Hair's party when Sacajawea led them to the great waters of the setting sun. I thought this black man might be from the same tribe, so I took a few of my band with me, and we found him, not frozen—but still black."

Adam slapped his knee and laughed. "Mistuh Chance, when all those Indians came down on me, I was scared to death, but I figured I didn't have a chance in a fight, so I just stood there."

Mopeah nodded. "See how smart your friend is, Iron

Horse Warrior, our arrows were already nocked. We could have put twenty arrows in him if he'd raised his gun.

"At my fire that night, he told of a tall, white warrior he looked for. I knew it had to be you, Iron Horse Warrior. I told him we'd take him to you."

Mopeah glanced around at his band. "I had big trouble. All my warriors wanted to come with me, but Chief Washakie let only these come." Then he bragged a little. "We could have made a good fight of it if I'd had only half as many."

Adam poured coffee for himself, Harry, and Peter. He'd obviously found out that most Indians didn't like the bitter taste of it, and had not found out yet that Mopeah liked coffee. He sipped and grinned at Mopeah.

"Mistuh Chance, you should've seen those Indians. They came up to me and rubbed on my skin and looked at their hands to see if my black had come off. Lordy, I told them there had been times I wished it would, but it was there to stay. They just couldn' believe it. I was something special."

"You have always been something special, Adam," I said, "and being black has nothing to do with it. You're *very* special to Billy and me."

My words embarrassed him, but they were true.

Before I could say more, Mopeah looked at Adam and broke the serious vein of our conversation. "I noticed one of the young women in our band looking at Thunder Cloud Warrior. I gave him the Shoshone name because of his color." He grinned. "Seemed like that woman wasn't afraid his color would come off, she wanted to share her blankets with him."

Adam stared at him a moment. "When we get back to the Wind River camp, I think I might come courtin' her."

"Bring many horses if you want *her*. Other warriors want her, too, but have not interested her. *You* did."

"Seems like you're going to have to shop for some horses, Adam."

"Well, reckon that's about the first thing I'm gonna take care of when we get back." His glance showed me he meant every word of it.

I withheld my smile. Mopeah had given Adam a Shoshone name, and it was far from describing a man that gentle. And Adam, it seemed, was serious about bringing a wife to the ranch.

Obviously to shift the center of attention from himself, Adam picked up the conversation.

"Soon after we crossed the Green River, we come up on Mistuh Harry and Peter. They allowed as how they would come along, too, not having had any excitement in a few days, and—"

"Now that's not quite right," Harry interrupted. "I thought we were about to have more excitement than we could handle when I saw all these redskins coming out of the brush at us, with two big men in the lead, one black and the other red.

"I was ready to fire when Adam yelled they were friendly. After we sorted it out and they'd explained what they were about, we joined forces and set out to find you."

Peter took up the story then. "We run on to Yancy there, and he told us you'd be comin' out soon, and that we could do you a lot of good by hidin' out along the trail and keepin' those outlaws from gettin' you. Well, Chance, we did like he said, and you did like he said, and here we are."

I walked over to the pallet we'd fixed for Blade. He was in bad shape. He'd taken a bullet under his rib cage and it had gone all the way through, tearing a good-sized hole where it came out. That, with his loss of blood, meant he probably wouldn't last the night.

Stooping by his side, I asked if he wanted anything.

"No, well, if there's a drink in that crowd, I'd like a few sips."

"Anybody got a jug?" I asked.

Harry dug in his possibles bag, found one, and held it out to me along with a granite cup.

I poured it half full of whiskey, knelt by Blade's side, and held his head for him to drink.

He sipped, coughed, and sipped again.

"You'd better not take too much of that, Carston. It'll

burn like fire, maybe even kill you when it gets to your insides."

He favored me with a wan smile. "Makes no difference, Chance, and you know it." He studied my face a moment. "I won't last until morning, will I?"

I shook my head. "I doubt that you will. You're hit bad."

"Thanks for telling me straight. Chance, I said back down the trail a ways that you were not a gentleman, but you are, you know. Oh, you're a hard man, one of the hardest I've ever known, but you *are* a gentleman."

"Thanks, Blade. I think probably you were, also, back in the past somewhere."

He gasped, grimaced, and held his breath a second. Then, even more pale than before, he stared at me. "I'm from a good family, Tenery, but I'm the black sheep. Don't let them know how I died or what I became."

I clasped his hand. He wouldn't last much longer.

Oddly, he seemed to gain a little strength. Maybe it was the whiskey. He looked at me with some of the old mocking glint in his eyes. "You knew all along I kept the gold, didn't you, Tenery?" He closed his eyes and seemed to struggle to open them again.

"It, the wagon and all, is up where the Snake rises out of the lake. I caved the lip of an undercut over it. It's covered, so you'll have to dig, but it's there on the west side about twenty yards from the stream bank." He squeezed my hand tightly. "Hold my hand tight, Chance. Don't want to ride this trail alone."

Those were his last words. His head lolled to the side. He rode alone now. We buried him there beside the Snake where it bends to the west to cross the Teton Range.

Before we broke camp the next morning, I told Mopeah about the town and the goods there that would be useful.

I said nothing about the women, for I knew they'd be taken as slaves. It was the Indian way, and I could do nothing about it. Nor did I mention the saloon where there would be whiskey. If they found it, I was just happy that I'd not be there to see the drunken orgy.

When Mopeah and his warriors got through, there would

not be enough of Blade's town left to indicate that it had ever been. The town would die, and maybe some of the talk of Carston Blade would die with it.

I watched Morning Star Woman lead them in the direction of the town. We had not said good-bye because Billy, Yancy, and I would see them in a few months.

The rest of us headed for end-of-track. There was still a lot of railroad to build. I wanted to do the job I'd agreed to. I would not try to see Betsy. She had made it perfectly clear to Adam that she didn't want to see me, and I didn't trust myself not to kill the man trying to court her.

chapter

twenty-eight

THE FIVE OF us rode wearily into Rock Springs four days later. We had taken our time, but the bitter cold sapped us. Yancy, being rather timid about showing his face in a populated area, had turned off at South Pass City. He'd stay at the Shoshone winter encampment until we showed up.

Rock Springs, a stop for the Overland Stage, had a saloon, livery, general store, and blacksmith shop. I hoped it also had overnight accommodations. To my eyes, it was a metropolis.

I slanted my companions a grin. "Anyone here who wants to keep eatin' Peter's cookin', or will you join me for a meal at the stage stop?"

"Papa, *I'm* about ready to start cookin' before I eat another bite of Mr. Peter's grub."

Peter cast Billy a sour glance. "Young 'un, you ate more than any full-sized man in the bunch—at every meal. Feedin' you was a chore for any cook."

"Hey, let's go see if they have any apple pie or bear sign," Harry said. "If they have bear sign, you gentlemen can start after I partake of the first batch."

"Like hell," Peter grunted.

Adam just grinned and said nothing. I knew he'd be there with the rest of us when our hands reached for the delicacy.

After we'd eaten and were drinking coffee—with that

fried sweet bread called bear sign, we discussed our next move.

Harry and Peter decided to catch the stage to Salt Lake City. End-of-track was only a few miles east of us, so I told Adam and Billy I'd ride that far with them, check in with Casement, and head back west.

"Aren't you takin' me with you again, Papa?"

I looked long at him before answering. He was a man now in a boy's body. There was something in his eyes that told one he'd seen it all and measured up in every case. I knew he wanted to go with me, and I wanted him to, but he needed a woman's influence.

"Son, Miss Betsy can do things for you that I can't. She needs you, Billy. You see, there are things that you can give her, too. She needs your love, son. I wish she wanted me there, but I'm afraid that's not to be. She doesn't want it that way."

"You could talk to her, Papa."

"No, I'm afraid not. Adam will see that you reach her safely. I have to finish this job. After that, Adam and I will go back to the Wind River country."

I wanted to take him in my arms. He bit his lower lip and tears flooded his eyes, but he didn't cry. "Yes, sir." I saw his Adam's apple bob as he swallowed hard.

"May I come to see you at the ranch when you get your cabin built?"

"You bet you can come. If you don't, I'll come get you. Just let me know when you're ready, and I'll meet you here at Rock Springs. The rails will be laid by then, and you can ride the train this far. Send me a letter in care of the café at South Pass City. The lady will make sure I get it."

I saw Billy slide his hand across and grasp Adam's, almost as though he shifted love and loyalty with the gesture. I found it hard to swallow, and couldn't see very well for the moisture in my eyes, but this was for his own good. I must not weaken.

We slept in beds that night for the first time in several days. I wish I could say that I slept well, but I didn't. Being closed in with walls and the softness of the bed kept me awake. Thoughts of Betsy and parting from Billy had a lot to do with my restlessness. I supposed that someday the hurt would fade, but in the here-and-now, I wanted Betsy so bad I ached.

After breakfast the next morning, we told Harry and Peter good-bye again, after they promised to stop by the ranch whenever they were in the area. Adam, Billy, and I rode toward end-of-track, thinking to reach it in time for our nooning.

My estimate was good. The sun showed high noon when I spotted the gandy dancers hauling rails and dropping them in place. We nudged our horses into a trot and rode up to Casement's car, which stood only a couple of hundred yards from the work crews.

The three of us climbed the steps to the door and I knocked.

"C'mon in," Casement's voice yelled.

He looked up from a pile of papers in front of him as we stopped at his desk. He didn't move, just stared at me a few moments.

"Have a good vacation, Tenery?" His voice dripped sarcasm. "I see you were kind enough to bring back my office force." He glanced at Adam. "Sit down and get to work. Not a damned thing's been done right since you let that slip of a girl bully you into leaving. Everything I touched turned to crap, so straighten it out."

I turned to Billy. "When the next supply train heads east, you can ride it as far as General Dodge's car. Miss Betsy will be there for you."

Casement frowned. "Aren't you going to take him? I'm sure Betsy will miss seeing you." He pointed his thumb down the tracks. "Dodge's car is only about ten miles from here."

I looked at him a moment, knowing he had no idea how I felt about her, and wondered that the whole world would not notice.

"No, sir, I think I'd better get out to the crew. Billy will have no trouble finding her."

"But he's just a little boy."

Billy spoke up. "I'll have no trouble, sir."

"Jack, you'd better take a closer look at Billy. He was a little boy when we left, but a hell of a lot happened since then. Billy's one to ride the trail with now."

Jack looked across his desk and studied Billy a moment. "I see what you mean, Tenery. As much change as I see in him, there must be quite a story behind it. When we have time, I'd like you to tell me about it."

He walked around the desk and held out his hand. "Welcome back, Tenery. Sit and have a cup of coffee with me first, then don't waste any more time. Get the provisions you need and head out. You can start your estimates one foot in front of the trestle crew. They've been doing the estimating when they come up on a job."

He walked to the stove and poured me a cup of coffee. "You can get your own, Adam, but don't drink too much of it. I hear it'll turn you black if you do."

This was the first indication we had that he was glad to see us. But, even with his little joke, I knew things had not been going smoothly. Jack Casement was a hard man but usually far more cordial.

"Adam can fill you in on what happened while we were gone. Right now I think I'd better get to work." I hesitated. My investments in the Credit Mobilier had bothered me for some time. I knew nothing about high finance, but what they were doing didn't seem quite honest. So, whether or not I'd made much out of the money I'd put into it, I wanted to get out.

"Jack, when you see General Dodge, ask him to sell my stock in the Credit Mobilier and to give the money to you. I'll collect it when we finish this job."

"Why not leave it in awhile longer then?"

I shook my head. "No. Pull me out of it."

"All right. I'll have it when I see you next."

I picked up my hat, shook his hand, hugged Billy, slapped Adam on the back, and left. I could not have endured it if I'd stayed to tell Billy a real good-bye.

About two hours after sundown, I rode into Rock Springs and decided to stay the night there. I checked the stage station to see if Harry and Peter had left on the last stage out. They had.

The clerk gave me the same room I'd slept in the night before. I wondered if they'd bothered to change the sheets but didn't care. I was tired and ready for sleep.

When I awoke, I had to light the lantern in order to see, although I'd slept late. A glance out the window showed it to be snowing. It would be a cold ride today.

I hurried through breakfast, saddled, and hit the trail. I came up on the trestle crew by noon. They worked despite cold and snow.

Every mile counted now, and they were beginning to feel the push to beat the Central Pacific's crews. The CP's chief engineer, Strobridge, along with his construction boss, General Crocker, were gifted at getting the best from their Chinese.

The falling snow was so thick I rode into the construction site before the lookouts spotted me. Mike Mulroon and Red Brady walked up as I loosened the cinches. I would not unsaddle, as I expected to be here only a short time.

"Well for hell sakes, look what the cat drug in," Mike bellowed, shoving his hand out. Red pummeled me on the back while I shook Mike's hand.

"C'mon in the tent. Coffee's on," Red said, dragging at my arm. "Good excuse to get out of this weather."

I noticed there were several tents and knew the men were as comfortable as they could be, under the conditions.

Later, sipping a second cup of the gut-warming liquid, I glanced at Mike. "Any Indian trouble since you cleared the Cheyenne and Sioux stomping grounds?"

Mike spoke over the rim of his cup. "Naw, I don't know whether to credit the weather, or maybe they're all in winter camp. I reckon it's mostly the latter."

I nodded. "Yes, I think so, too. You're pretty well into Ute country now. They can be every bit as bad as the Sioux, so be careful."

One of the men stuck his head past the tent flap. "Mike, we gotta get some hay in here soon, or them horses gonna starve." He glanced at me. "Hi, Chance, you jest git in?"

At my nod he asked, "See any sign of supply wagons on the way?"

I shook my head. "None."

"I bet the bastards are holed up outta this weather."

I grinned. "Wouldn't you be if you could?"

Chagrined, he admitted that he would.

Mike filled our cups again and invited the trestle hand to have coffee with us and warm up a bit.

Handing me a mug, Mike asked, "What now, Chance? You gonna keep on out in front of us, estimatin' our needs?"

"Yep. That's what Casement wants. He seems to think I do a lot of good."

"Hell, I reckon so. We've built two trestles and one bridge without knowing from one day to the next what we'd need. *That* ain't no way to run a railroad."

I finished my coffee. "Better get going. I want to be at least three or four sites ahead of you by the time you finish this trestle."

Red scratched his chin and squinted up at me. "I hear the country gets a lot rougher from here on. With more mountains, cliffs, and a few streams, the lay of the land's not what we been used to."

I nodded. "I've been over this country before. It *is* rough. We're going to get a taste of what the Central Pacific bunch has been fighting almost from the beginning. We'll be able to blast and grade around some of those mountains, but we're sure as hell gonna have to tunnel some, too. I figure the Wasatch Range is going to give us the most trouble. As soon as I finish the job I'm on, I'll get back with you for the tunneling."

Mike sighed. "Glad to hear you say that, Chance. I can handle bridges and trestles, but don't think I'd know what to do in a long tunnel."

I smiled. "Then I'll make it a point to be back in time to help. If I'm going to do that, I better start moving. See you in a few weeks."

The snow let up, but it was bitter cold and stayed that way. The farther west I worked, the more rugged the country became. The Wasatch Range was all I'd expected it to be.

I found where we'd need to punch through four bores. Three of them we could handle, but the one at the head of Echo Canyon would be a long one. I estimated we'd have to dig and blast at least eight hundred feet to get through, and it would have to be shored up to prevent caving.

The more I studied that damned pile of rock, the more I was convinced we had to do something besides go through it, or the Central Pacific would gain miles on us. Even feet were money. The UP was already scraping the bottom of the barrel for dollars to pay the crews.

Dodge would have to make the decision, but I wanted to take him an alternative. So I camped on that mountain in the cold for over a week. I rode around it, over it, everything but through it, making sketches with near-frozen fingers.

Finally, huddled close to my fire, with smoke in my eyes and burning my nostrils, I peered one more time at what I took to be a solution. We'd build a temporary looping bypass. We could come back and finish the tunnel after hooking up with the CP.

I pondered continuing on west with my estimating but decided to get back to Casement, explain my ideas to him, and let him fight Dodge for the decision.

Another thing prompted me to get back to Casement. While trying to ferret out a solution, I'd come on Central Pacific grading crews almost at the foot of Echo Summit.

The competition for miles of track promised to get nasty. Jack would want to know about the CP crews for I'd heard our grading crews were moving dirt and rocks well over a hundred miles west of Ogden. That being true, both the UP and CP were wasting manpower. Casement might want to use our crews to lay track.

The UP and CP had an overlap of a couple of hundred miles and were ignoring it. Neither Congress, nor money, would permit this sort of waste.

The rights of way, running almost parallel, were often so close that blasting charges dumped rock and dirt on the opposing crew. Neither one found it expedient to warn the other. I didn't give a damn who built what as long as we had a railroad across the continent. I headed back to end-of-track.

When I walked into Casement's car, I was so cold I put my gloved hands right against the potbellied stove momentarily, so they'd thaw and not be so stiff. When I smelled leather burning, I pulled them away and removed my gloves.

I didn't wait for Jack to offer me coffee. I walked to the pot and poured a steaming cup, put it to my mouth, and sipped, before recognizing that he just sat there staring at me, a slight smile crooking his mouth.

"You cold?"

I didn't answer right away. I swallowed a full mouthful and felt it burn down my throat, catch my chest on fire, and settle warmly in the pit of my stomach. Only then did I look at him and answer. "Hell no. I'm not cold. I'm frozen clear to the bone."

He reached into his bottom drawer, pulled a bottle of bourbon from it, and held it toward me. "Here. Lace that coffee with a couple of ounces of this. It'll do you good."

My hands shaking, I placed the cup on the table and took the bottle in both hands, afraid I'd drop it otherwise. After pulling the cork with my teeth, I dumped a healthy amount into the hot coffee, then sat down and began a yeomanlike job on my drink.

"What the hell did you ride back here in this weather for?"

The warmth of the coffee and liquor were thawing me and, at the same time, making me realize how tired I was. If I'd not had so much to talk about, I think I might have gone to sleep as the heat soaked in.

I stirred and looked across the room at him. "Jack, we've got trouble, big trouble, but I think I know a way around it." I knew he liked solutions, not problems.

He leaned back in his chair, a grim expression clouding his face. "Tenery, we've had trouble on this road since the first tie. What is it this time?"

I explained about the tunneling and gave my opinion that

only one of them would cause a delay that we couldn't abide. I told him about my plan for the looping bypass.

"Why not just go ahead with the tunnel now?"

I nodded. "I think we should, but we can't let it hold us up. The bypass will just be a temporary affair until the tunnel is finished." I leaned toward him. "Jack, the CP grading crews are at the base of Echo Summit now, and our grading crews are well west of there. We've got to lay track on our grade or we'll lose miles of construction to them."

"You make drawings of your plan?"

"Yes, sir. I have them and the material estimates here." I unbuttoned my sheepskin and withdrew a rolled packet of drawings. I spread them on his desk.

We went over them in detail. When we finished, Casement poured himself a drink and freshened my coffee with one. "Chance, you've done a good job. I agree. We should bypass the Echo Summit tunnel. I'll take it from here. You go in the spare room and get some sleep. I'll see Dodge."

When I awoke, it was dark. I hated to move. My muscles, even my bones ached, and this was the first time I'd been warm in so long I couldn't remember the last time. Finally, I groaned and threw the covers off. I washed up, dressed, and went in to see if Jack had returned from seeing Dodge.

He was sitting at his desk when I entered his office. I wondered when he took time to relax.

"Pour yourself a cup of coffee and sit."

I did as he bid. He studied the papers I'd brought back with me. He'd get around to telling me what he'd found out when he'd made up his mind how he intended carrying out Dodge's orders. The general told you *what* to do, not *how* to do it, and we respected him for that.

Half my coffee was gone before he looked up. "Dodge wants you to take charge of the tunneling. I agree with him."

I crooked my mouth into a thin smile. "I've already told Mike I'd be there for that. I'll leave in the morning."

Casement nodded. "Good, but I want you to finish estimating for perhaps another hundred miles, then come back to your crew. I don't think they'll get as far as the Wasatch by then."

"All right. Now," I asked, "what do you think of the materials I asked for to get the tunnels bored?"

He jerked his head in a perfunctory nod. "I go along with what you ask, Tenery. Do you feel comfortable with your estimates?"

"Jack, when I made the estimates, I expected to be the one to do the job." I nodded. "You bet I'm comfortable with them."

He laughed. "I suspected as much. Now, get back to bed. I'll see you in the morning."

"No, I'll be long gone by the time you crawl out of your nice warm blankets. See you the other side of the Wasatch."

chapter

twenty-nine

Spring had come and would soon move into summer. We finished the tunnels, except for the eight-hundred-foot monster, which we bypassed, and were past Ogden with the bridges and trestles. The grading crew was a couple of hundred miles ahead of us.

Leaving Mike with the trestles, I rode down to Salt Lake City. I wanted to buy a Conestoga wagon and supplies for the ranch. When the rails met, I didn't want to waste any time. I couldn't, if I would have my cabin built before winter.

On the way in, I rode by Camp Douglas, about three miles northeast of the city. It looked big enough to quarter about fifteen hundred troops, and both cannon were mounted so as to command Brigham Young's house. I had to smile, wondering how it felt to live under the sights of two cannon.

I found quarters in the Salt Lake House, the most noted hostelry in town. My bed was hard, but no harder than the ground I was used to. The room was warm, a condition I had *not* known recently.

After my noon meal, I wandered out into what had been a town the last time I saw it. It was now a thriving city. I shot a game of billiards with a gambler, and he took me for three dollars before I smartened up and wandered down to the livery.

The collection of wagons amazed me. The liveryman said that he'd gotten most of them from immigrants who'd decided this was the end of the trail for them. They'd settled down and sold all of the trail gear they didn't need for town living.

I made a deal for the largest of the Conestogas and six mules to pull it. The liveryman pointed out a store he thought might have most of my other needs, including a large cast-iron stove and the duct pipes to go with it.

He was right. I bought almost all I'd need to set up housekeeping: bed, linens, a couple of bolts of turkey red cloth for curtains, cast-iron cooking pots and pans, and the iron hooks to hold them over the fire. A pretty set of dishes caught my eye, and I bought it, wishing Betsy would be there to help me use them. I felt sure I'd forgotten something. I might need to buy additional items in South Pass City.

After studying on the problem of my brother's killer, I decided that if I ran into him, I'd kill him, but if I continued to hunt him and never found him, I would be wasting my life as well. Reluctantly, I shoved revenge to the back of my mind.

I bought a newspaper, the *Deseret News*, and a book by Sir Edward Lytton, *What Will He Do with It*.

Stopping for a cup of coffee, I saw on the front page of the paper that the Commission of Civil Engineers, under the orders of Secretary of the Interior Orville H. Browning, had decided the rails of the UP and CP would be joined at Promontory Summit, only fifty-six miles west of Ogden.

That meant the grading crews had finished, and my trestle crew had little more to do before they, too, could head home, although I was certain they'd stay to see the end.

According to the paper, neither of the companies involved took the decision lying down. There had been threats, back-room dealing, grumbling, and cajolery, but the decision stood.

Finished with my coffee, I walked about the town, noting that there was a fine theater named after it. Standing near its front, I would have sworn I'd seen it before. Of course, that was impossible. I would have remembered it. I walked another block before it came to me that it was built exactly like the Drury Lane Theater in London. My father had taken Vance and me to England before we entered the military academy. I wished I could tarry to see a play.

I sighed. I'd done what I'd come here to do and had best be getting back to my crew.

Retracing my steps to the hotel, I heard my name called and looked to see who knew me here. Charlotte McKinsey hurried to catch up.

"Lottie! What in the world are you doing here?"

She threw herself into my arms. "Oh, Chance, it's so good to see you. I have a small café. You'll have dinner with us tonight, won't you?"

I knew I had to get back to the rails, but I could start in the morning just as easily.

I nodded, holding her close. "Of course, but *you'll* have dinner with *me.*"

"No. I have a surprise. Come."

I followed her into a cozy, neat café and saw Randolph Donavan standing behind the counter.

Over dinner, they explained that, as planned, they'd built an elegant brothel in Cheyenne, sold it for a handsome profit, and decided they could now resume the life they'd had before the war. They were married and living a respectable life.

I told them how happy I was for them, and that I would be ranching in the Wind River country. I invited them to come see me when they had time. I left them feeling happy for the way things had worked out for them.

I spent another hour or so looking for a gift for Betsy. I found a cameo brooch I thought she'd like. She might not see me, but Billy could give it to her.

The next day, I drove my wagon to Ogden and left it in the care of the liveryman. I exacted a promise from him to keep a careful eye on my goods. I saddled my gelding and headed for the railroad.

We erected the last trestle east of Promontory with gandy

dancers puffing at our heels. Word had come down that the tracks were to be joined on May 8.

Plans were made for a great celebration, with dignitaries coming from both the East and West coasts; among them would be railroad officials, newspapermen, special guests and, of course, the ever-present politicians who could not pass up the chance to have their pictures and names in the papers.

May 8 came and went. The last section of track lay along the right-of-way, waiting to be placed and spiked down.

The Central Pacific's Leland Stanford arrived first, but Dr. Durant of the UP didn't show. He wired that he'd been held up due to a washout at Devil's Gate Bridge in Wyoming.

This was true, but rumor had it that the real reason he was late was because he'd been kidnapped by his own tie-cutters to force him to pay them wages overdue since January. When he'd raised enough money to pay them, they let him go. He arrived at Promontory on the tenth.

I stood back from the crowd, watching drunks, prostitutes, gamblers, crooks, and gunmen rush in from the hovels alongside the track to mix with the dignitaries.

The gandy dancers dropped the last rail in place. A polished laurel tie was then slipped under the last joint. And, contrary to common belief, not one, but four spikes were used to commemorate the occasion; two gold, one silver, and one a composite of silver, iron, and gold were dropped into specially drilled holes.

An iron spike, partway driven into a tie and wired to the telegraph system would be struck by a hammer also wired to the system. It would signal the nation that the last spike was in place.

I stood off to the side, wanting to see the ceremony, but hurting for just a glimpse of Betsy and Billy.

Searching the crowd, I finally saw them standing in a cluster of dignitaries. My heart ached. It was all I could do to stand fast and not rush to them. I decided right then that as soon as the festivities were over, I'd ride to Casement and get the rest of my money. Then I'd go to Betsy and ask for a fresh start.

I shifted my gaze to the CP's Leland Stanford, standing ready to hit the spike on signal. He raised the sledge, swung—and missed. A roar of laughter went up from the crowd. Durant took the sledge, swung, and also missed. I thought he did it in deference to Stanford.

General Dodge stepped forward, took the hammer, and drove the spike home. I found out later that the telegraph operator sent the message to the nation as soon as Stanford swung. The United States of America now had a transcontinental railroad, and it had cost a life for every mile.

I walked slowly through the crowd to see Jack Casement.

He tried to talk me into staying with him. There were other railroads to build. But I assured him I wanted only to ranch. He gave me the money I'd made from the Credit Mobilier investments and my back wages. It came to quite a pile of cash.

"There's more than forty thousand dollars there, Chance. Be careful."

I thanked him for all he'd done and went to find Adam.

I found him sitting on the rails under Casement's car. He looked lost and at the end of his tether. The driven spike ended his job.

I bent and told him to come on out where we could talk. The first thing he told me was that Jack had tried to talk him into staying with him, but he'd declined.

"Oh, come on Adam, if you want to stay with him, I'll understand. I'll feel lost without you, but I *will* understand."

He shook his head. "No, suh. I want to be with you, and besides, how you gonna get the wagon to the Wind River if I don't go?"

I gripped his shoulders. "All right, *partner,* let's get to work. If we're to get our cabin built by first snow, we'd better get moving. The way I figure it, we have four months. That way, if we get snow in October, and we could in that high country, we'll be in our own home."

I told him where to find the wagon and to head for Rock Springs. "I might catch you before you get that far, but if not, I'll meet you there. I'm going to wait until this crowd clears out before I try to see Dodge. There are a few things I have to talk to him about."

I took out my pipe and tamped tobacco in its bowl, lit it, and reached into my money belt. "Adam, I'd like you to buy a few gifts for Mopeah and his band. Get them tobacco, sugar, and the other things they can't get for themselves. Use your own judgment." I peeled off a thick sheaf of bills and held them toward him. I had already bought the gifts I'd promised Chief Washakie.

He stood there, grinning, not reaching to take the money. "We're partners? Well, I got money, too. *I'll* buy the gifts."

Somehow, I knew this was important to him, so I didn't insist.

Still grinning, he looked at me a moment longer before his gaze slid off to the side. "General Dodge won't be in his car until late, with all the doin's goin' on. I got some packin' to do, but I'll get goin' as soon as I can. I'll see you in about two days?"

I nodded. "Think I'll go over to one of the saloons and have a drink. By the time I finish it, I'll see how the crowd looks."

Puzzled, I watched Adam breathe deeply, obviously relieved about something. "Anything wrong, Adam?"

"No, suh." He shook his head. "Nothin's wrong. Reckon I'm just anxious to get goin'. Waitin' gives me the heebie-jeebies."

I shrugged and turned toward the cluster of shacks no longer an end-of-track town.

The saloon was crowded with men standing shoulder to shoulder, all drinking and talking at once. I didn't know how long I could stand the stink of unwashed bodies. The noise beat mercilessly on my ears, but for one of the few times in my life, I really *needed* a drink.

Elbowing to the bar, I asked for bourbon, knowing I'd get grain alcohol with tobacco juice for coloring, but I didn't give a damn. I had to bolster my courage to face Betsy.

The bartender handed me my whiskey, and I turned my back to the bar. When I looked down at my drink, I saw the thing I'd tried hard to forget, a CSA belt buckle. When my eyes slid to the gun hanging in the holster, I saw it was a Navy Colt with my initials cut in the grip. The belt was buckled below the enormous gut of the man directly in front of me.

It was the gun I'd given my brother before he left home, and although he'd fought for the North, he'd been proud of the Confederate belt buckle I'd given him.

I felt two years of carefully nurtured hate turn brassy in my throat. I restrained the impulse to draw and kill the son of a bitch. Instead, I put my drink carefully on the bar and walked to him. He was big, burly, bearded, and filthy.

"You have something of mine," I said, looking him squarely in the eye.

He looked down at me, a thing not many men could do. "What you mean? I ain't got nothin' o' yours. Ain't never seen you before."

I felt my face harden. "That's right. You've never seen me before, but you took that gun and belt buckle off my brother's body."

His eyes closed to slits. He studied me a moment. "Yeah, you do look like him." He threw back his head and laughed. "He wasn't much man. I beat hell outta him 'fore I plugged 'im." He balled his fists and stepped toward me. "Now I'm gonna fix you the same way."

In that instant, the packed crowd found more room, pushing and cursing to get away from us.

I hit him coming in, a right I brought up from my side. His breath exploded from his lungs with my fist sunk to the wrist in his gut. My left followed close behind and caught his fat-encased rib cage.

He staggered, planted his feet, and swung. It caught me a glancing blow on my cheek. The big bastard could hit. Lights danced behind my eyes, and I stepped back beyond his reach.

My sight cleared a little, and I went inside his wildly swinging fists. Two more hard body punches and I again stepped back, but caught a right with my forearm. He followed his swing with his foot, swinging it behind my leg to trip me.

My back hit the floor, and breath pushed from me in a rush. He spread his arms and dropped. I saw his intent and rolled, but even then he half fell on me.

With my free right hand, I grabbed his beard and pulled sharp to the side. His head twisted, giving me a needed split second to push him off and come to my feet.

He rolled and pushed to his knees. I swung my right foot, and caught him under his chin with the pointed toe of my boot. Following through with the kick, the heel caught his chin. He fell back to the floor.

This time he was much slower getting to his feet. I stood back and waited. I knew I had him now. The kick had done it. My hate had cooled to an icy knot in the pit of my stomach. I intended to send him to hell, but I was going to do it my way. I had waited too long for this.

He stumbled toward me. I let loose a right that damned near tore his head off. His nose flattened. I swing a left that caught him above his right eye and dropped his eyebrow over his lid, blood pouring from the cut.

Most men in my situation would have let him have another right and ended it, but I wasn't through.

Deliberately, I cut him to pieces. I knocked out several teeth with two more swings. Now, I took great care that I didn't knock him out. I wanted him conscious when I ended it.

He carried cuts above each eye, so I chopped him below them and saw the skin open to spill more blood down his face and onto his filthy shirt, what was left of it.

I walked up close and swung my left foot behind his knee, dropping him to his back. I drew back my right foot and let him have my boot toe in his ribs and heard them crack.

Panting, I stood over him, aware for the first time of the crowd yelling. A voice from among them said, "My God, man, you done near beat 'im to death. Let 'im go."

I raked them with my gaze. "He killed my brother—from behind. He'll get no better treatment. The first man who interferes will die with him. Now, stand back."

I looked down at the sodden hulk at my feet. He gasped with pain, drawing ragged breaths between shredded lips, eyes gazing fearfully up at me. I knew he was lucid and would know exactly what was coming.

Slowly, very slowly, I eased my brother's Navy from its holster, and holding his gaze with the big maw of the barrel, pointed it between his eyes.

"Don't—don't do this, mister. Please." The words pushed past his tooth stumps.

I eased the hammer back, seeing his eyes widen when he knew he looked into the jaws of hell. My thumb slipped off the hammer. The sharp explosion fell into complete silence. Smoke from the black powder mixed with the skull, brains, and matted hair that had once been his head. I stooped and unbuckled my brother's belt and wrapped it around the gun.

Then, as though explaining my action to the bastard, I said, "This was a family matter, a matter of honor." I spat on him and walked toward the door, hearing the silence broken by the mournful whistle of a departing train. My brother could rest in peace.

The door swung shut behind me, and a roar rose from the crowd as if at a signal.

My thoughts were on Betsy and Billy. Angry with me she might be, but she was my woman, and Billy was the little boy I loved as much as though he were my own son. I wanted us to be a family. I had to try.

The crew's water barrel stood at the side of the rails. I walked to it and washed blood from my face. He'd hit me a few times. My face and ribs were sore, but they'd get well soon enough. When I'd tidied up as much as possible, I walked toward Dodge's car. Now I would see Betsy.

At my knock, Tom answered the door and announced me to the general.

"Come in, boy." Dodge stopped short, his hand extended, and stared at my face. "You've had trouble."

I shook my head while shaking his hand. "No, just settled an old debt."

I still carried the gun and gun belt. I held it so he could see. "I found my brother's killer."

He looked over his shoulder and said to Tom, "Bring us a drink, please. I think Mr. Chance needs one."

I nodded, and thought of the drink I'd left on the bar, untouched.

"General, I'd like to speak to Betsy, if I may."

He had lifted his drink to his lips, but pulled it down at my words. I noticed he had a guarded look about him. "Chance, Betsy's gone. She took Billy and left." He looked at his watch. "They've been gone about twenty minutes. She said she was going to get married. She didn't ask my permission or anything, just packed and left. I suppose that fellow from New York finally convinced her. It's not the way I wanted it, but I didn't feel I should interfere."

He pulled his drink back to his lips, sipped, and gave me a sympathetic look. "She said she was taking Billy and, if the man she's to marry objected, she'd take care of that problem when it arose. In her exact words she said, 'Come hell or high water I'm getting married, and Billy's going to have a mother *and* father.'" He nodded. "Yep, that's exactly what she said."

With each of his words, I died a little. When he'd finished, there was nothing inside me but a big, festering batch of pain.

The train whistle I'd heard when I left the saloon must have taken them from me. If I had known, revenge would have taken a backseat. I didn't even know the name of the man I'd killed, but name or no name, he was just as dead.

All of the hurt I thought I'd learned to live with came back. I had convinced myself that I could make things right between Betsy and me. Now I'd missed my chance, if I'd ever had one.

Holding myself under tight control to prevent him from seeing how badly I hurt, I shook hands, thanked him, and left.

Tightening the cinches on my horse, I thought to chase the train, but that would be futile. I'd only end up killing my horse. A train traveled as fast as thirty-five miles an hour. My shoulders slumped. I mounted and rode aimlessly toward the west.

Camp that night was lonely, and that was the way I wanted it. I neither built a fire nor ate. I spread my bedroll and lay staring at the sky.

I wondered that I had it in me to kill brutally and cold-bloodedly as I had this afternoon. The revenge tasted bitter in my throat. It had left me empty inside, unsatisfied. And while I did it, I lost the two people who meant most to me in the world.

Through the many lonely nights I'd spent after our quarrel, I had refused to admit she wasn't mine, but now I was forced to face the truth. I had lost her.

My first thoughts were to saddle in the morning and ride on—anywhere. I couldn't do that, though. There was Adam, and he was my friend. Somehow we'd make a life out there with the Shoshone.

The sun shouldered its way above the Wasatch Range in the east. I saddled, mounted, and reined toward the sun. I didn't feel better, but decided I had to live with it. I had to catch Adam.

Feeling dead inside, I passed Promontory, Ogden, and rode toward Rock Springs.

The gelding picked his own pace, allowing me to get my thoughts straight. By the time I saw buildings on the horizon, I had shoved Betsy and Billy into a private corner of my mind, a corner where I could be with them in my most private moments. A tightening of my thighs on the horse's barrel urged him to a canter.

When I paused in front of the stage station, I saw our wagon pulled up at the livery. Adam saw me at the same time, waved his arm, and clucked the team ahead. His horse trailed behind, tied to the tailgate.

He was a hundred yards out of town before I caught him. The look he cast me was a smug know-it-all one, causing me to wonder what the hell he had on his mind.

"Mistuh Chance, you reckon you'd mind drivin' these stubborn, hard-headed animals for awhile? I just about had my bait of them 'tween here and Ogden. I'll ride my horse."

"Of course not, Adam," I answered, thinking that must have been what caused his smug look. He figured to saddle me with driving the team. "Climb down and I'll take over."

I cast him a crooked grin. "You anxious to get on and see your Shoshone maid? You know all you have to do to get married the Shoshone way is for both to say you want to, and *boom*, you're married."

"Aw, Mistuh Chance, quit funnin' me." If he hadn't been so black, I know I would have seen his face turn red. "You might as well know, Adam, I stopped by Dodge's car to tell Billy good-bye—and, and, to try to get Miss Betsy to forgive me. Although I still think I did the right thing, I sure handled it wrong. Ruined everything."

I shrugged and shook my head. "Didn't do any good, though. Dodge told me they'd left about twenty minutes before I came to him. I suppose she caught the train that left about then. Can you believe it? She's going to marry some damned body that I'll bet isn't near good enough for her. She wasn't even sure her man would want Billy.

"The thing that I'll have to live with is that I caused the whole thing."

Adam looked away, I supposed so I wouldn't see the pity in his eyes. "You sure do love that girl and little boy, don't you, Mistuh Chance?"

"You're the only person in the world who knows how much, Adam, but let's don't talk about them anymore right now. Maybe after awhile, but not now."

I climbed up into the box and took the reins. I waited until Adam untied his horse and rode alongside.

Then, as I was about to get the wagon in motion again, four arms almost strangled me from behind.

"Oh, Papa, I love you."

"Chance Tenery, don't you say a word, just drive on if we're to get to our new home."

"Bu-but, I thought you were going to marry your man from New York!"

"Chance Tenery, there has never been any man I'd marry but you. Now, drive on."

Betsy might as well have been talking to the wind. I stopped the wagon and pulled them into my arms, kissing each as fast as I could, afraid they'd disappear before I could get enough. I glanced over Betsy's shoulder and saw Adam grinning like an idiot. I'd been set up. Dodge had been in on it, too.

"We'll get married in South Pass City."

"No," Betsy said emphatically. "We'll get married the Shoshone way."

I hoped she knew what she said, because if she did, she had just put us in double harness.